# CELINE L.A. SIMPSON

First edition

ISBN: 978-1-7635659-0-6

Editing by Joeli Woodrow
Illustration by Ashley Quick
Cover art by Murphy Rae

This book was professionally typeset on Reedsy.
Find out more at reedsy.com

*For my brothers, Clarke and Kirk.*
*I wouldn't be me if I didn't have you.*

*If you've ever been scared to reach out with both hands for the things that you want, if you've ever been scared to jump for those things that are just out of reach, this is for you.*

# 1

## January 5th

### Poppy

I'd never been to this bar.

Actually, frequenting any kind of bar was so far down on my list of things to do it wasn't even on the page. I was only out due to equal parts support of my best friend, celebrating her random and unexpected though not at all unwelcome visit, and out of fear for the safety of my goldfish, Natalie, who'd been threatened with waterly harm if I didn't agree to join her on this expedition (an incredibly below-the-belt maneuver in my opinion).

"Aren't you having *so* much fun?!" Leah projected her voice with startling hardiness. It not only made her dance partner jump, but an older gentleman who I'm pretty sure was dozing with his fingers *in* his beer jolted awake and sloshed his beverage on his wife? Sister? Cousin? *Mother?*

"Uh-huh!" I lifted up both thumbs in front of me while bopping from foot to foot. My shoes were sticking to the ground. *Sticking.* If my feet weren't heavily laced into them I was positive I'd have already lost one.

I just really wanted to go home to the caramel popcorn recipe I'd been hyping myself up to make and my half typed out post for Natalie's instagram account, *@queen.nat.the.first.*

That wasn't something I shared with too many people, but Nat was a star. With over two hundred and fifty thousand followers online, it was probably more respectful to call her what she really was: an icon.

"I think it's getting late!" I called back, my voice at a much more suitable level.

"It's only 10:30!" Leah's voice was filled with what I could only assume was happiness due to the fact that she thought, with great amounts of delusion, that it was still early in the evening.

"I have work tomorrow?" I tried again.

"Tomorrow's Saturday." Leah stopped dancing. With hands on hips she stared at me like she was hoping that I could feel the mental wedgie I knew she was delivering.

Her complete lack of movement made me realize I was still bopping from foot to foot with my hands *still* raised in front of me…*still* giving her the thumbs up. I dropped them to my sides immediately, rubbing my palms down the front of my jeans.

"Stock take?" I wasn't even sure what that would entail in a job like mine. The way my voice heightened in pitch did nothing for my case.

"Poppy, I leave tomorrow, and plus, you *promised.*"

"No– *no,* I never actually–"

She was giving me her puppy dog face. It looked more like she was trying to get spinach out of her back molars while attempting to scratch her nose without using her hands.

"Uh, fine. *Fine.* But I'm going to the bathroom."

"Perfect! Yes, good." She was smiling in a way that was so severe I felt my own face begin to morph into a less-than-ideal picture of concern, "Nothing like emptying your bladder to increase your comfort levels. You'll be lighter. Better for dancing!"

Leah turned away from me in a flourish of leggy movements that didn't entirely make sense to me and I had to remind myself repeatedly that I was in fact, very fond of her and that my friendship with her was totally worth being pushed – no, sorry, *catapulted* – out of my comfort zone. Threats to Natalie's life and all.

In a twist of unusual luck, the ladies room was blissfully empty. Not a tinkle to be heard or a thorough lipstick application to be seen. I didn't need to pee, but I *had* needed some peace and quiet. My bag remained where it was when we'd left my apartment; slung across my body, tattered and fraying at the edges.

I looked away from it and back to my face, swallowing the lump in my throat and studying the haunted way I now looked.

Sometimes I looked at myself and had no idea who was looking back.

*'Breathe, Pen.'*

I could hear my brother's voice in my head as clear as if he were sitting next to me. I let my eyes close against the pressure that bloomed behind them. Pressure, but never tears. Not for as long as I could remember.

*'Big deep breaths like you're about to blow out all the candles on your cake, but don't release it so fast. Breathe out like it's your*

*breath moving through the trees outside. Slow and steady.'*

As a kid I'd always been easily overwhelmed and just like everything else, Casimir had always known what to do. As I got older, he'd obviously stopped talking to me like I was eight, but no matter what those were always the memories that surfaced first.

I had makeup on my face but it seemed like an inconsequential thing to be concerned about over needing to feel the cold water on the heated skin of my cheeks.

When I opened my eyes again they were clearer. The light amber color seemed brighter and their identical nature to that of my brothers didn't create a yawning chasm in the pit of my stomach, but rather made it feel like he was looking right back at me. The pink tint to my cheeks made me look pretty, like I was happy to be at this very shitty bar.

Running my fingers through my long chestnut waves, I took a final deep breath, popping all the overwhelming thoughts and feelings back behind the door in my mind they'd managed to creep out of. A practiced mental maneuver so familiar to me it had become second nature over the last decade.

Only then did I head for the door, sure that I might be able to get at least another hour out of the evening.

Maybe.

Thirty minutes for sure.

My eyes were glued to the toes of my own boots and it became evident that, when a much larger pair of boots I didn't know entered my line of sight, I'd just encountered my first roadblock of the evening.

"Excuse me," I said. The perfect picture of politeness.

"I was dancing beside you on the dance floor just before." The voice held the gruff timbre you might expect from a man who smoked too many cigarettes. Like someone with a sort of hacking cough that walked around smelling like a suffocating blend of ashtray and Axe body spray.

"Excuse me," I said again, finally lifting my gaze to look at his face. I think he could have been handsome, maybe he even had been once upon a time. He wasn't anymore.

"I wanna buy you a drink." He delivered the words with a slur and an outrageous amount of confidence. I sort of wanted to ask him if he had any tips on how I might lift my own.

"Oh," I gave a small nod. "No, thank you."

"That's no way to thank a gentleman." He lifted his arms up and placed them on either side of me against the walls. A trifecta attack of displaying the pit stains of his flannel, providing me with a fiercely unwanted odor, and blocking me in even more than he had been before.

"I'm here with someone," my voice sounded as impressed as I was, which was not. At all.

"I think she's just fine in the company of her dance partner."

"I wasn't talking about her." That was a big fat lie. I was quietly impressed with the way it rolled off my tongue.

"Who, then?"

"He's over there," I gestured in the vague direction of the bar with my heart hammering in my chest.

Just as I'd hoped, the oaf turned to get a look at who I was (not really) gesturing to.

I didn't waste the opportunity to duck under his arm, getting a real heady whiff of the stale smell that I was certain would impact the results of my next eye test on account of the burning that ensued.

"Hey!" he called from behind me.

The tone change of his voice made my heart pick up. I tried my best not to run and held in the scream that wanted to purge itself from my soul at the feel of phantom hands grabbing for me.

I was panicked. I was actively *panicking.*

The part of the bar that was closest to the bathroom was occupied by someone who I hadn't noticed at first, but judging by the way his head hung low and how he nursed his beer I'd wager he'd been there for a while and wanted nothing more than to be left alone.

Dark brown hair that looked almost black peeked out from under a baseball cap that didn't really look like it fit with the rest of him. He wore a leather jacket that spanned the broad expanse of his back, leading down to black jeans and black boots.

My only regret was having to ruin his evening. "Excuse me?" My voice sounded more sure than I felt about actioning this plan.

He didn't move other than a slight tensing to his shoulders.

I took that like I hoped it was intended – a better sign than being told to fuck off – and let the rest of the words practically fall out of my mouth, "You don't know me but my name is Penelope, or Penny or Poppy, most people just call me Poppy and I really need your help. Would you mind, uhm, quickly kissing me?"

Well, that got his attention.

"I–what?" His face angled a little more towards me but he still didn't look at me.

"Please? I–" My heart was going so fast I could feel myself immediately starting to sweat, and not in a cute way. "There's someone…" Words had escaped me entirely and it seemed I'd also begun to forget all the words in the English language. "He smells terrifying. *Please* kiss me?" There was a desperation in my voice that I was sure he heard as clearly as I did.

"Hey, you!" The rumbling baritone of the guy sounded behind me.

"Oh, crap." Nope. That was a bad plan. A very, very bad plan. I decided to tell him that and make a run for it. "This was a very bad plan. I'm really sor–"

Baseball cap dude only hesitated for a second. He moved so quickly I didn't get a chance to see his face and then his lips were on mine.

I wasn't sure who was more shocked, him or me.

In the same moment my entire body melted against his. His hand, rough and calloused, reached up to cup my face. His thumb pressed against my jaw with just enough pressure to angle my head in a way that gave him better access to my mouth and I was suddenly made entirely of fireworks. I was an actual open flame.

His tongue swiped at my bottom lip sending a zap straight down my spine.

*Woah. Woahwoahwoah.*

A small sound escaped me, half surprised shock and half surprised whimper, wholly enough to snap him out of whatever was happening.

He pulled back with a jolt and dropped back onto his stool. He gave off a shocked, surprised and concerned vibe that made me feel like I'd approached him without pants on. The way he pulled his hands from me abruptly left me in a freefall straight onto the stool next to his.

My lips tingled from the fresh memory of where he had just been. Oh my *God,* I just kissed a stranger.

"I just kissed a stranger," I mumbled against my own fingers, frowning to myself. The path-blocking-oaf no longer a thought in my head. "I just–"

"Actually," I could hear the smile in his voice even though he still hadn't looked at me. "*I* kissed *you*."

I gripped the lip of the bar and turned myself around, resting my elbows on the sticky surface that was arguably worse than the dance floor, "But I asked you."

"I've never heard someone say an individual 'smelled terrifying' but oddly enough, I knew exactly what you meant. Plus, you asked me *twice*," he clarified.

"Thank you for that." I dropped my head into my hands.

"Which part?"

"That guy was…" I trailed off, equally as grossed out of his existence as I was with the surface beneath me.

"Yeah, I figured." He took a sip of his beer.

I took in his profile while he pulled his cap lower over his eyes.

"Can I buy you a drink? To thank you properly?"

"Not necessary." His decline wasn't rude, but more unexpected. It was obvious to anyone with eyes he wanted to be left alone, but I clearly had zero social reading cue skills.

"You kiss a lot of distressed women, then?"

*Wow, smooth Poppy.*

"Only those who ask me twice."

"Ah." I nodded. I felt my face relax into something that resembled a calm, natural sort of comfortability. Was I flirting? Was it *working?!* "So, that's your angle, then?"

"Good cop, bad cop. You're familiar I'm sure."

"Oh yes, you make a great good cop."

"Oh?"

I saw just the hint of a tug at the corner of his mouth.

"Very soft lips," I whispered at him conspiratorially.

The tentative tug at the corner of his mouth got more pronounced and it felt like I had a wild horse galloping in my chest.

"Do you make a habit of not ever looking at the people you rescue?"

"Oh, not really," he said the words on the back of a sigh. Not so much weary as it was knowing. "I was enjoying this conversation though."

"And if you look at me, it will become…unenjoyable?" I frowned. Maybe it wasn't working. The flirting, I mean. I instinctively leaned closer. Baseball cap dude had piqued my interest.

"No, it will be different though." He sounded reserved, maybe even a little disappointed. That was the moment he angled his body towards mine and looked directly at me.

# 2

# January 5th

**Poppy**

I was certain I was going into shock. My fingertips started to tingle and I wasn't entirely sure I could feel my nose on my face anymore.

"Oh my–" my voice cracked on the second word.

"Please don't scream," he implored, genuine worry on his face. His tone was calm and gentle like he'd done this before; soothed women on the edge of a mental breakdown.

"*Oh my God,*" I whispered this time. "You're–"

"Yes," he nodded, looking at me like he still wasn't sure I wasn't going to scream.

"Do you have any idea who you are?" I couldn't stop whispering. Did my voice box even work anymore?

"That feels like a loaded question, Poppy."

"Mother of pearl," I felt my eyes widen. "You know my name." For some reason that startled me, and my hand flew to my chest.

"Yes, you told it to me when you asked me to kiss you."

*Right.*

"Twice."

*...Right.*

"Great balls of *fire,* I just attacked Asp–"

"*Please*, don't say it," he whispered with a small amount of distress. Eyes pleading. Whole *face* pleading.

"Say what?" It was very hot in here. "Are you hot?"

"My name, and like, thermally?"

"Please don't arrest me. I didn't know you were…you. Is it a crime? To have come up to you like this? Oh my God, I'm a felon. Do I need to address you with a title?"

"Give me a second, I'm trying to unpack everything you just said." His brow was still furrowed in concentration, like he was trying to take everything I said seriously, but also trying very hard not to laugh.

"I don't think my legs are working. Am I walking?" I couldn't tear my eyes from his face.

He leaned back to get a better look at the stool I was sitting on and, by default, my legs that were still clearly dangling.

"I don't think so, but I've been wrong before."

"I'm so sorry, I really didn't know you were…*you.*"

"It's okay, no one's ever told me I have soft lips before so, I'd say this was a win-win."

That had to be a lie.

"I think I'm melting." I was still whispering.

"You're not melting." He grinned at me and my heart did a big, massive belly flop into my chest.

"I can't look away from your face," I admitted in a hushed tone.

"That's okay. If it helps I can also look at yours until you're able to?" he whispered back.

"That's—actually, that would be great."

So, there we sat. Staring at each other like this wasn't one of the most peculiar moments of either of our lives.

"…This is actually really cool for me," I broke the silence, unable to stop the way that very feeling took over my whole face so much my eyes crinkled, despite the context of the entire situation.

His lips tilted up in almost a bashful smile.

"Am I coming across cool?"

"Super cool." His face turned implicitly serious.

"You're sure?"

"Absolutely." His lips twitched once before settling back into his serious expression. "You know, you don't have to whisper anymore," he said, picking up his beer to take another sip, not breaking our eye contact for a single second.

"Oh, this is my voice forever now," I said.

"Well then, here's to hoping you never need to call out for someone across a long distance."

"I figured there would be people surrounding you."

"Like members of the public?" He quirked a brow.

"Or security," I countered.

"Ah." He nodded, "Usually, yes. His name is Jason, but I snuck out."

"Woah." My eyebrows lifted in surprise, "That's very bad cop."

"You assumed I was a good cop in the first place."

"Touché." My eyes relented their need to mentally grip onto his face and I finally blinked. It occurred to me then that I'd just had a conversation with a man for what must have been a good couple of minutes without blinking.

Wonderful.

Right, if I'd ever had a cue to leave, that was it.

"Okay, well," I cleared my throat and started to reach into my bag for my phone. "I am *very* sorry, again, for asking you to kiss me. Had I ever thought about this actually happening," I gestured between him and me, trying not to let my stomach flutter at the quick glance I gave his mouth. To lips that had just been pressed to my own. "I assure you, with great sincerity, that was not how I would have gone about it."

"That's okay, Poppy. It was fun, I've never rescued someone from such terrible peril before." His smile was so genuine it was hard to resist the urge to inscribe 'national treasure' onto his person. "Did you need a lift or anything?" He finished the last of his beer and stood up.

"Oh, no." I didn't think I'd ever been so flustered in my life. "That's alright. I'll just find my friend and—"

**Leah McDonaugh:**

Alright you social butterfly!! I am looking right at you with some fella at the bar.

**Leah McDonaugh:**

I refuse to salt your game, so I'm going home with Hank.

**Leah McDonaugh:**

Henry?

**Leah McDonaugh:**

Harold?

**Leah McDonaugh:**

Harry! It's Harry

**Leah McDonaugh:**
It might be Hunter actually

**Leah McDonaugh:**
Don't wait up sissy, love you! (super proud of you!!!!)

Leah had sent those messages ten minutes ago and if her lack of presence in this crappy bar was anything to go by, she'd ditched me.

"Great." I shoved my phone into my back pocket, hopping off the stool and mentally calculating the odds of me getting home safely on my own. Between Mr. Ashtray-Axe and the general vibe of the perimeter of this bar, I'd say they were fairly low.

"You sure you're good?" I hadn't realized he'd moved to stand beside me. His hat pulled down low once again, hiding every part of his face.

"Yeah, I'm–"

"Come on, I'll give you a ride." He nodded his head towards an emergency exit door to my left.

I was already shaking my head, "I can't ask you to do that."

"You didn't. What's a ride between two people who've kissed?" He looked up enough to shoot me a wink that caused every part of my body that had skin on it to flush.

"I don't know you, though." I was grasping at straws for reasons unbeknownst to myself.

He was trying his best to take my words seriously, but it was clear he was getting a kick out of this. "If I had a pension for never dropping women home after offering a ride, I would have picked a drastically different career path."

Well, he had me there.

I hesitated, knowing I'd already infiltrated what I was sure was meant to be a quiet evening just for him but torn with the reality that Leah had left me here all on my own.

"Really?"

"Really. Fame and crime aren't super complimentary as far as I know." He'd already started walking, reaching the door and pushing it open before I finally convinced my feet to move.

Alright, this was happening. It was really happening.

Aspen Smith, the drummer of the biggest rock band in the world, *Lady Luck,* was driving me home.

# 3

# January 5th

## Poppy

I trailed behind Aspen walking down the dark alley next to the bar and finally taking him in. He was tall and broad and looked like he smelt *very* nice. But I already knew all that.

It was weird that I knew this man more than strangers should know each other. I knew that his eyes were green and his hair was a dark brown. I knew he'd played the drums since he was in single digits and that he liked to bake sweet things. I knew he and his brother started a band that was now that band was the most popular rock band in the world and that even though he could sing, he never did and always declined with the most dazzling smile I'd ever seen.

My eyes lingered on the broad expanse of his shoulders and they didn't stop until they had landed right on his–

"I can feel your eyes either burning a hole into my back or really enjoying the shape of my ass," he called out over his shoulder. "I can't quite be sure of the placement." There was just a hint of a smirk flashing from under the brim of his hat. He walked with his head down and his hands in the pockets of his jacket. It was the walk of someone familiar with remaining inconspicuous when needed.

I pulled my coat around me tighter, blushing like it was what I did for a living and jogged up the extra couple of steps so that I was walking next to him. "Sorry, this is kind of nuts though, you're...*you.*"

"That's true," he said. Not in a conceited egotistical way, but rather just acknowledging that what I said was just factual.

"And you were just *here*, or I guess *there*." I nodded my head back towards the bar and watched him from my peripheral vision.

"That's also true."

"And the bar we just walked out of was...well, it was pretty dingy."

"True again."

"Goodness, I don't think I've ever been so right in my life." I turned to face him fully and couldn't stop the grin on my face, or how it widened impossibly when he chuckled quietly. I felt the sound seep into my skin, making me shiver. My body immediately wanted to draw closer to it. To hear it again.

We reached the end of the alley and I stopped, looking for the sort of car that I figured would belong to a rockstar. What I hadn't anticipated was the car that he walked up to.

I rocked back on my heels as if I'd been punched right in the sternum.

My heart lodged in my throat when he stuck the key into the door and thumped his fist just above the handle twice while rattling the key and for a second I was fifteen again, watching my brother do the exact same thing.

*"I don't know why we can't get a new car, Cas," I'd said, sliding into the passenger seat when he finally got his door to open.*

*He got into the car not a second after me, the frame creaking and groaning as it adjusted to bear his weight. Casimir reached across the center console to flick my forehead before tsking. He shoved the key into the ignition, turned on the car and put it into gear. "Just because it doesn't work perfectly doesn't mean it doesn't work well," he replied and peeled out of the parking spot.*

The memory was over as fast as it arrived.

My face must have said it all because Aspen looked up and immediately frowned, tentatively walking back towards me. "Are you alright? You look…" He didn't finish the sentence, he didn't have to. I already knew how I looked.

"This is your car?" It sounded like my throat was closing up, like I was struggling to breathe. I think I might have been. I started to count my breaths, trying to calm my frantic heart.

He looked back over his shoulder with a little smile on his face, "Isn't she a beauty?" He asked the question but voiced it as a statement. It was clear that this particular mode of transport meant a great deal to Aspen and the idea of that made something in my chest tighten. He blew the car a kiss before turning back to face me.

"When did you–" The words got stuck in my throat. I swallowed and tried again, unable to tear my gaze from the car. "When did you get it?"

He didn't reply for a little while, long enough that I forced myself to drag my eyes back to his face. His head was tilted to the side. The expression he wore was curious, as if trying to figure me out was suddenly at the very top of his priority list.

"It was Wyatt's first." The way he spoke was unsure, like the words he was speaking were private things he didn't ever share, but for some reason he'd decided to trust me with them. "He got it when he was eighteen and when he headed off to college a year later he gave it to me. Having the car helped with not having him. Been in the family ever since."

Aspen frowned immediately after the words left his mouth, dropping his gaze to his boots. Any other time I might have struggled to keep my eyeballs in their sockets at the casual reminder that Aspen's older brother was Wyatt Maddox Smith, the frontman of *Lady Luck* but out of everything he'd just said, it seemed like the least important part to me.

I nodded my head, trying to get my shit together so that this person I'd literally just met didn't think I was deranged, or for some undisclosed reason repelled by 2000 model Ford Tauruses.

But I *knew* that car.

Not just in the way that you know metal cases that moved around on wheels. No, I knew *that* car like the back of my hand. Or, at least, I'd known one like it.

"Do you…have a thing against geriatric sedans?" He quirked an eyebrow and tucked his hands back into his leather jacket. It was cold, but I'd forgotten about the bite of the air around us.

"No, I—" My voice sounded far away, like you could tell it was traveling from whatever distant memory I'd been captivated by just to spill out of my mouth. I lifted a hand to point in the general direction of the vehicle in question. "My brother used to have a car just like that."

"Oh," he nodded, glancing at the car again. "A man of good taste, then." Aspen's grin was so bright, it was hard not to feel its warmth even when the chill around us had started to make my eyes water. "Come on, it's fucking freezing and I like all my parts attached."

I snorted, "I'm sure you're not the only one."

I started to walk towards Aspen and couldn't help but think how weird this was for me. I thought of my brother every single day, sometimes they were happy thoughts, sometimes the memories were so debilitating it knocked the breath right out of me and I couldn't speak through them. Something like seeing a car that was the same color, make and model of the one he had loved so much would have sent me into a spiral that could have lasted days, but Aspen's cracking laugh reached across the distance between us, wrapping around me like a lasso. It yanked the first step from me, coercing every other that followed until I was standing in front of the passenger door.

I pretended not to notice the little tremble in my hand when I reached for the handle. The part of my brain that couldn't help but highlight it for once didn't put up a fight as I deluded myself into rationalizing the shaking as a mere repercussion of being out in the cold and my total lack of gloves.

"*Shit!*" Aspen yelled. The sound unrestrained and propelled from his vocal chords with the entirety of his lung capacity.

I screamed like a banshee and turned to take in my surroundings so quickly my head swam. "What?!" I panicked further when I couldn't immediately identify the threat he so clearly had.

"*What?!*" I said again, giving up on looking around me to settle my panicked gaze on him. But he wasn't across from me where he should've been, getting into his side of the car.

"Penelope," Aspen's voice came from directly beside me and

I screamed. Like, unrestrained with the entirety of *my* lung capacity.

"What," *heave,* "in God's name," *heave,* "is *wrong* with you?!" I smacked his chest in outrage before I took in his face and he was, well, he was outright beaming at me.

*Shocker.*

I smacked him again but this time he held my hand in place against his chest and I felt the rumble of laughter that shook his body.

"Sorry, *sorry.* I realized I didn't open your door for you. My mom would have had me by the balls. Actually, maybe not my mother, but I'm sure someone's mother would have."

"Sounds like you're incredibly comfortable with a lot of mothers," I mumbled, still

scowling at him.

"Oh, very. I share bathwater with them all on rotation." He reached in front of me for the handle of my door, still smiling like he was having the time of his life. I tracked his movements with my eyes until he was back in his original position. "Your chariot awaits, milady," he bowed, flourishing his hand a little.

I tried to hold back my eye roll and failed, "You're not what I expected, at all."

"And what did you expect?" He sounded genuinely curious and so I thought about it for a second before answering. It was important to me, for whatever reason, that I was as honest as I could be with him.

"Well, aside from never expecting to actually meet you, ever, I thought you might have a little more ego. Definitely a more environmentally damaging car. Definitely some sort of security team that you couldn't give the slip. Some ink. A deviated septum, maybe."

"Ink?" He was very clearly trying not to laugh.

"Yeah, you know, like maybe some dice on your bicep, or a spider web on your elbow."

"Like the fuzzy ones that hang from your rear view mirror?"

"I was thinking more like your band logo."

"That would make more sense, yes," he laughed.

I tried to keep my face as relaxed as possible even though my blood pressure was spiking to no doubt incredibly unhealthy levels at the feeling of another rumbling laugh beneath my palm.

"Well, no deviated septum here." He jumped to another of my previous assumptions. "Though it's oddly flattering that you've thought about my nasal cavity," he replied without missing a beat, and then he frowned. "Do you think lots of people have thought about my nasal cavity?"

Aspen looked so genuinely concerned about that reality that I couldn't stop the laugh from bubbling up and out of me.

*Definitely not what I'd expected.*

"Come on," he said, eyes twinkling and looking at me like he'd won something precious just by making me laugh. "Get in and I'll take you home."

"I can't," I said, my turn to set my gaze on him.

"Why?" A crease appeared between his dark brows, making me notice just how green his eyes were for the first time, even in the dim light from the street lamp nearby.

"You haven't let go of my hand," I said, dropping my gaze from his face to his mouth briefly before settling on the hand he still held beneath his, pressing it to his chest.

"Oh," he sounded as surprised as he looked, which made

me smile, *again.* He released his hold on me and stepped back a little, opening the door wider.

Buckling my seat belt while he walked around to his side, I did everything in my power not to observe the interior of his car. Not to look for things I knew wouldn't be there, like the rip in the roof at the back, or feel for the bubble stickers I had placed under the glove compartment as a kid.

Aspen knew the way to my house without even needing to put my address into maps on his phone.

"That's kind of impressive," I said, looking at him with raised brows.

"It's been known to happen once or twice," he winked at me before turning his attention back to the road. He held the steering wheel in one hand and let the other rest on the gear shift.

There was only one word for how he looked right now and it was fucking *delicious.*

I'd been doing a stellar job not thinking about how he'd kissed me for the whole drive. I hadn't thought about the warmth of his lips on mine, or how they felt, or how his thumb had dragged along the edge of my jaw and–

"Penny?" I didn't need to look at Aspen to see the amusement that would no doubt cover his features. I could hear it plain as day in his voice. I knew immediately he'd said my name more than once. It also occurred to me that it was the third version of my name he said, like he was trying them all out for size.

"Mm?" I was glad for the darkened car so that he couldn't see the blush that encompassed my entire body for the second time that evening.

"We're here," he said. His eyes flicked to the little town

house right across from us. The porch light turned on, just how I left it. The windows were dark so I knew Leah wasn't home yet.

"Oh," I wasn't surprised by the disappointment in my voice, I was surprised by the real, honest to God knowledge that I'd just said it that way out loud.

*Out. Loud.*

"Oh!" I said again. Entirely overcompensating and noticing, with no small amount of horror, Aspen physically jumped from the exclamation.

"Thank you, for the lift and the rescue. This has all been incredibly bizarre." I meant it only in the best of ways.

"I've enjoyed our time together equally as much, sweet Poppy." He turned the car off then turned to face me. The total absence of the engine rumbling made the silence seem much heavier.

"Sweet, huh?" I asked, my voice entirely too loud in the confines of his car.

"So far," he replied, his eyes twinkling with laughter.

I watched Aspen in the same way he watched me, with curiosity and bewilderment and a touch of confusion. It made me wonder what he saw, because I was always careful to keep myself in check. To keep all the heaviest and most desperately broken parts that had never healed no matter how many years passed in a safe place, away from direct sunlight. Where the things that I felt too strongly waited with years of learned patience for me to let them out. To give them space to breathe when I didn't need to worry about being seen or heard or noticed.

I'd tried a few times at the start, to feel them in front of Leah, but it hurt her to witness that in me. I knew it did and

I was so blindingly terrifying that I'd scare her away that I just…stopped.

My mind had learned when it was best to keep that part of myself quiet, to only let that side of myself show when it was safe to do so, which was when I was alone. When it was dark and the entire world around me was quiet.

It was probably the car, with its all too familiar interior that somehow convinced me to speak. To let a trickle of the words that circled around my mind relentlessly out in the presence of someone I didn't really know at all.

"It was nice getting to ride in a car like this again," I admitted. I'd been thinking that the entire car trip. Ignoring the pressure in my eyes every time it surfaced, knowing it would never amount to anything.

It was just that the seat beneath me felt so familiar. The smell of this car, though different, somehow seemed to still have the undercurrent of pine and vanilla, Casimir's favorite blend of air freshener that he religiously kept stock of in the boot. I felt convinced at that moment that if I got out and checked, there would be a box tucked in the back right filled to the brim with them.

"Your brother doesn't have his anymore?" His question was so innocent, and I never wanted to answer it because right there, in that question, my brother was still alive. He was still breathing, and blinking and *living* inside of Aspen's mind and it made my chest cave because it had been almost thirteen years since he'd been any of those things in mine.

"Casimir died when I was sixteen." I was struck stupid by the oddity of feeling brave enough to say the words when I was looking at Aspen. This person I didn't know, this stranger I'd met in a bar. Like I could say the words and not hear the sound of the gun going off as acutely as I usually did. Not feel the way the same bullet that ended the life of the only person who'd ever been just *mine* also embedded itself into me. Not feel the slight pinch in my shoulder every time I moved my arm that existed because of the bullet that had never been removed.

"Poppy." I could hear the sadness in his voice for me and it was clear then that was the name he had settled on.

Even though I'd just met Aspen Smith, I knew that making him sad was the very last thing I ever wanted to do, so I smiled.

"It's okay," I whispered, just like we had in the bar. I pretended not to feel the phantom weight of the tears that never surfaced well up in my eyes.

He didn't tell me he was sorry for my loss, or that he knew how I must have felt. He just looked at me and it was enough.

"This has been incredibly bizarre," I said again, still whispering. My chest felt a little lighter at the slight lift of the corner of his mouth.

"Certainly was a first for me," he whispered back.

"Bye, Aspen." I reached for the door.

"Ap," he said, his voice not a whisper but still soft enough not to pierce the night around us. "All my friends call me Ap."

I turned to look at him, keeping my face serious. "Friends, huh?" I asked.

"For now." His lips lifted in a shy sort of lilt and I wanted to commission paintings in its honor.

"You say that to all the girls under duress you rescue with a kiss." I opened the car door and stepped out, taking one last moment to lean down and look in at him, knowing full well it would be the last I'd ever see him like this.

"Only the ones that ask me twice."

# 4

# January 6th

**Aspen**

"You alright, Ap?" My brother's voice sounded in my headphones from behind the glass of the recording booth.

"What?"

The metronome counting the beats for the song we were recording stopped at the sound of his voice. I realized at that moment that I had absolutely no idea what song I was supposed to be drumming to.

"You're distracted," Dax frowned.

To everyone all over the world, he was Wyatt Maddox Smith. Lead singer and rhythm guitarist for *Lady Luck*. But to everyone who really knew him, who really loved *him*, he'd always been Dax. I knew my brother, and he was about to say that I'd been working too much and I needed to take a break.

"You're working too much," he heaved a heavy sigh, like he should have noticed that already. "Let's take a break."

*Told you.*

"I'm good. Sorry, just lots on my mind." I let the drum sticks roll between my fingers.

"Oh, I bet," Rip, the lead guitarist in *Lady Luck*, said from his spot next to Dax. "I take it that's code for 'yes Rip, the date you set up was incredibly successful.'"

I gave my friend the middle finger before signaling to run the track again.

We were in the middle of recording our next album. It was past midnight and our producer and longtime friend, Adrian Douglas, had long since headed home.

We met Adrian when we were just starting off as a band. A bunch of kids who knew nothing about anything except how to play the instruments in our hands.

Adrian had just welcomed his second baby into the world and was running on less sleep than any human ever should. We sent him home early when he went to the bathroom and found him half an hour later asleep on the toilet with his pants around his ankles.

The plan had been to record the drums for at least half the songs we'd already established the rhythm guitar and vocals for. That meant eight songs needed to be done before we could wrap things up.

We were done with five.

I'd long since rid myself of my shirt and sweat was dripping off the end of my nose. I took off my baseball cap to push my soaked hair back before readjusting it backwards and starting the song again.

It was a real honest to God effort to push Penelope-Penny-but-everyone-calls-me-Poppy from my mind. To quiet the chatter of every thought that raced through my head like they were on a loop pedal. It was an effort, but as soon as I pushed all the noise away and let myself lower into that place I always descended to when I was drumming, where I was in control and integral and my purpose was crystal clear, the next two hours flew by.

Dax walked into the booth with a towel and handed it to me. His face was the picture of pure elation. Stepping back, he leaned against the door frame and ran a hand through his jet black hair. "That was good, Ap. Really fucking good."

"Yeah?" My own smile matched his.

Nothing had ever felt quite as *right* as making music with my brother. As feeding off the excitement we both shared when things were going the exact way we had imagined. When a song came to life that had been only four notes strung together or pre-recorded in the voice memo app on Dax's phone. Or a drum pattern I'd been tapping out over breakfast while absentmindedly scrolling on my phone that Luke, our second rhythm guitarist, had recorded without me knowing.

There was nothing I loved more than playing in a stadium of thousands and thousands of people and meeting my brother's eyes, knowing that we did it. We fucking *did it.*

"This album's going to be next level," I said, unscrewing the top of the water bottle he tossed to me and drinking down the entire thing.

"Fucking wild," he laughed, shaking his head before heading back out to Rip.

I followed behind him, running the towel over my hair and flicking off the lights.

"So," Rip said from his spot on the couch, "How was the date?"

"You waited that whole time just to ask me that?" I threw

the damp towel right at his face.

"Dude, what the fuck?" Rip threw the towel off him so fast it was a testament to his fight or flight instinct. "Just trying to help you get laid. Sue me."

"Maybe you shouldn't think about my dick so much, it's weird." I dropped down beside him, closing my eyes.

"I only think about it because I care about you." He said the words with a genuineness that told me he was being a hundred percent serious.

"I want you to try and listen to the words that exit your mouth," Dax said, eyes alight with delighted entertainment as he swung from side to side in the desk chair across from us.

Rip just flipped him off before turning back to me. "Come on, Ap. Give me something. She seemed really into you."

I peeled open one eye and shot a quizzical look at my friend, "That so?"

"Yeah, I mean," he frowned, "Why? Was it really that bad?"

"Well," I hesitated for only a second, flicking my eyes to my brother who was looking at me with the same level of excited curiosity before I looked back at Rip, "It certainly wasn't *good*."

"Was she wearing lime green?" he asked with complete seriousness because I had once, *once*, mentioned that the color had made my head hurt when I looked at it for too long.

"Hated the drums?" Dax chimed in.

"Thought Narwhals were mythical creatures?" Rip asked, making both Dax and I give him a double take.

"What? No, she–" God, I really didn't want to say it. My eyes flicked to my brother again and I saw the moment it clicked for him.

"No," he said, face darkening with the sort of sad anger it

always did because unfortunately, this had happened before. A lot.

"I believe her exact words were, 'So, when you say *married,* you mean he's totally not seeing anyone else?'" My impression of her voice was probably off, but I'm sure they got the gist.

Rip's eyes widened comically and Dax just rubbed a hand down his face.

"But she literally said specifically that 'If Mr. Smith is open to a date, I'd love to meet him!' That's what she said."

"And it didn't occur to you to double check which Smith she was referring to?" Dax asked incredulously.

"You're *married!*" Rip exclaimed like no one in their right mind would assume she meant Dax, and that was because our friend was about as descent of a guy as you could get.

"Hey, it's okay, honestly." I closed my eyes again, wishing I could just fall asleep there. "I ended up sneaking away for a beer at that bar *Cherry's,* and—"

Poppy's name was on the tip of my tongue. Her hand beneath mine, against my chest, and the way I knew she didn't think I'd be able to see her blush in the dim light of my car. The feeling of her body melting against mine, molding to me so perfectly that I'd never felt more wanted in my life.

I got up abruptly. "I'm gonna head home." I walked back into the sound booth and grabbed my shirt, tugging it back on along with my hat.

"And what?" Dax asked, confused eyes assessing me.

"And it was nice to have a quiet beer for once." I gave him a little shrug before grabbing my keys where I'd dropped them on the table next to the couch. I didn't want to tell them about Poppy. I felt protective of the memory of her in my head even though I'd only met her once.

She'd been my peaceful moment. My rare blissful quiet at the end of what had been a very loud day and for once I wanted to be selfish. I wanted to keep this one, incredibly *good* thing for myself.

"Message when you're home, boys," I said over my shoulder. "Hi to Allie from me too, please," I tacked on, not waiting for either reply.

Dax and I used to live together before he moved out of our penthouse and into a place with his wife, Allie. I'd lived in the penthouse alone for a full six months before I realized how much I hated it. At first, I thought it was just because I'd lived there with my brother, and then I didn't, and that was why it felt so...*off*. So, I moved into a new penthouse in a different building. Smaller, with less rooms but bigger windows.

I pulled into the mostly empty second basement of my building that only I had access to and punched the code into the elevator that would take me all the way to the top floor.

When the doors opened into my apartment, I was greeted by a dense sort of darkness only broken apart by the glittering lights of the city that trickled in from the windows. I didn't even bother turning on any lights and headed straight for my bedroom, not bothering with the lights there either, instead going straight for the shower.

Every time my brother, or Allie, or Rip, or any of the guys in the band asked me about the new place I told them it was perfect. Bachelor life was much better now that I lived somewhere that was just mine.

That was a year ago and I think they all still asked me from time to time because they knew it was a lie every time I delivered the same practiced reply. They knew in some way that it covered a blistering truth that reared its ugly head every single time I came back to this empty apartment. That it didn't matter if I was here in the penthouse, in a house of my own or even in a studio apartment. It didn't matter if the furniture was new or secondhand or if the entire place smelled like a home cooked meal, because I was still the only one there. It was still *silent*.

I didn't like silence, and the longer I was in it the harder it was to tolerate. It made room for unruly and unwanted thoughts to circulate and accumulate and get louder and louder and *louder.* I hated the quiet almost as much as I hated sleeping.

To be fair, I hadn't always hated sleeping, but over the last couple of years it had gotten worse and now I only did it when I physically couldn't keep my eyes open any longer, like tonight.

I'd been up and drumming well before the sun rose and met the guys at the studio barely after first light.

I let sleep take me simply because I had no choice. No choice but to be consumed by the silence. No matter how much the frantic, racing beat of my heart protested against the very idea of it.

I'd woken three hours later heading straight for my sound-proofed drumming room with twitching fingers. Beats and patterns already built up in my head to an unbearable point to compensate for the absence of noise that surrounded me in every corner of every room.

The moment my drum sticks were in my hands my body started to relax. Only feeling completely at ease when my body was dripping with sweat and my muscles were screaming with the victory that there was no longer space for silence to exist around me.

# 5

# January 11th

## Poppy

"And you wonder why I didn't tell you in person." I rolled my eyes, picking all the best parts of the stir fry out of the container.

Leah was doing the same from where she sat in the form of FaceTime in front of me.

Alright, she *had* been doing the same thing. *Now*…she sat with her mouth wide open and half chewed Chow mein on full display.

"Leah, your mouth. Close your mouth," I said around my own chews. "Also, I thought you got all your wisdom teeth removed?" I squinted close to my phone to get a good look.

"I can't," she said, eyes wide with disbelief, "You've blind-sided me. And only the top two."

"I haven't blindsided you."

"Is nothing sacred anymore? What happened to the best friend code, sissy?" Her eyebrows were now almost one with her hairline.

Dropping my chopsticks back into my stir fry, I set the container to the floor beside me and heaved a breath, giving my phone my full attention. "Okay, I'm *sorry*. But I don't know what you expected me to do even if I did tell you. You got home at like 3:00 AM and fell asleep on the couch with your jeans halfway down your legs. I'm not entirely sure they were up when you walked through the door." I gave her a pointed look which earned a sly smirk.

"I can't confirm or deny that theory but you're right, I was in a sex haze."

"Precisely."

"I could have seen him before I left." That little smirk disappeared immediately, replaced once again with a scowl.

"How would you have managed that?"

"You could have called him!" She sounded truly incredulous now and it wasn't like I didn't know why. Leah, like me, and honestly like most young girls and women...actually literally *anyone* of any age, loved *Lady Luck*. Leah had a poster of Wyatt at the back of her closet that I'm certain she's kissed on more than one occasion.

"And how would I have done that?" I crossed my arms over my chest, ready for what was coming.

"Have you suddenly forgotten how to use a phone?"

"I actually didn't get his number."

Leah didn't reply. She didn't even *blink*.

I leaned in closer to my phone to see if she had actually frozen. "Leah? Are you there?"

*"YOU DIDN'T GET HIS NUMBER?"* she screamed into the line.

I'd gotten so close all you could see was my forehead. I was sixty percent sure I'd peed a little. "No, I —"

"You're saying, you bumped into *Aspen Fucking Smith* outside that dilapidated bar and you *didn't get his number?*"

"No. It seemed redundant." I was putting on a confident exterior but I'd thought the same thing over and over and *over* since Friday night. I'd never had any intention of asking for his number, it didn't mean I hadn't wanted it though.

"Penelope." Her tone had changed completely.

She said my name in the same way she'd said it when we were eight and I told her that Tommy Green said he didn't like me back. Or like when we were eleven and we'd found out she had made the volleyball team and I hadn't. Or like when I moved in with her and her family after I'd lost Casimir and on the six month anniversary of his death I admitted to her in the quiet dark of her butterfly decorated bedroom that I didn't really want to be here anymore.

"It was nice though," I cleared my throat. "You know? Like one of those passing moments between two strangers. Like the universe knew what you needed even when you didn't and then you part ways, forever changed by that single encounter."

Leah's face softened more with every word I spoke. "Forever changed?" There was no one in the world who had known me better than my brother, but Leah had always come in at a very close second. "You like him." She was beaming at me so big it was like she had marshmallows stuffed into her cheek. Or maybe a buttload of Chow mein.

I rolled my eyes, "Everyone likes him."

"Mmhm, but you like *him.*" She wagged her eyebrows, funneling another dumpling into her mouth.

"We interacted for like, an hour."

"Stranger things have happened," she countered.

*Preaching to the choir, sister.*

"I can't believe you met the drummer from *Lady Luck*," she said again in a quiet reverence that I'd once shared with her.

But when I thought of Aspen Smith now, I didn't think of him like that. The man I'd collided with, who I'd asked to kiss me twice. Whose laughter had reverberated beneath the pads of my fingers and wrapped around my nerve endings, setting every part of my body alight. He was so set apart from the version of him I'd thought I'd known and all I wanted to do was learn all the other things I didn't know about him now too.

They were all just big, crazy 'wants' though. Things I wanted for myself but knew I'd never have.

"I miss you already," I said, wishing she was right beside me again so I could wrap my arms around her.

"Me too, sissy," she said, blowing me a kiss. "Not long now until your birthday, will you come home? We missed you over Christmas and you know that Mom and Dad would love to see you."

"I'm not sure yet, but I'll let you know as soon as I do."

"Alright, sounds good." She smiled at me the same as she did every year, knowing those words were just a cover for the answer I eventually gave, which was no.

I would always be grateful for the way Leah's parents took me in. The way they had made space for me in their lives when they hadn't needed to. When my own father hadn't wanted to.

But no, I wouldn't go back.

We said our goodbyes and I cleaned up my apartment on autopilot.

I had picked up a new wisteria plant for Nat's fish tank

and quickly posted about it, typing out the caption that sat below her cute little face: *I am officially a crazy plant fishy #mymombuysmyplants #isthatweird?*

It was only once I was in bed did I let myself think about the one word that always rattled around in my head. It felt like a song I had heard once and loved, but now struggled to remember the way it began.

*Home.*

People threw that word around too much without really knowing what it meant to them; it was their hotel room on holiday or the city they were born in and moved from at age one. The first apartment they rented for three months on their own with a terrible upstairs neighbor and the bathroom with no door.

I didn't think any of those definitions were true.

To me, home was a feeling. It was so consuming and overwhelming and the very act of leaving it shook the foundations of your whole entire world. It *hurt* to leave it.

It was the hardest goodbye that ever existed and the happiest hello every single time.

I didn't have a home now, but I knew that feeling because I had it once before. I knew what it was like to have it with every cell of my body, which was why I knew what it was like to live without one.

It was the driving force behind my need to move so frequently.

I managed to wake up and move through life every day because of the rules I had put in place for myself. I called them 'Poppy's Life Rules'.

The first of many was keeping myself firmly split in two. It didn't sound healthy, but it simply just *was* and had been since I was sixteen. One half was for me, the other for the world. I had as much interest in sharing that part of myself as I was certain people wanted to witness it.

People were uncomfortable with pain. There was never the right thing to say, or do, or way to act, and soon enough it became too hard for everyone and people did the only thing they thought they *could* do, which was step away.

And away, and away. Then they were gone and that was it.

The second was that I always, *always*, made sure to call Leah, or at the very least message, no less than three times a week.

The third, and most important, was never to stay in one place for more than a year.

As soon as I'd set off on my own, I had needed something to hold on to. That 'thing' became a fierce determination to find that feeling again. There was only one way I figured how to do that, and that was to chase it. To cover as much ground as possible as fast as I could.

It made sense to just move on every year on the date I moved first.

April fifth.

It was three months away and it was coming too fast and too slow all at the same time. I didn't know where I was going next, only that I was going.

I had to go. It wasn't a want, but a need. I *needed* to find that feeling again.

Home.

The very idea of being without it for the rest of my life terrified me right back into my sixteen year old self, admitting my darkest secret into the quietness of the world.

So, that's why I moved. Because everyone deserved that feeling, even me.

I hoped by the time I found it, I'd believe that.

# 6

# January 12th

## Poppy

I saw him coming out of the corner of my eye and I knew exactly the sort of expression my face was making and I couldn't do a thing to change it.

"Woah, there she is!" Todd said and I immediately wanted to throat chop him. "Popsicle, give me some." Todd held out his knuckles to me and like every time he did that, I stared at his hand with immense confusion.

"Heavens," I mumbled, pressing my thumb against the pressure point that existed between my eyebrows to alleviate the immediate headache that surfaced.

I knew what a fist bump was, I'd given and received many in my life. I would even go as far as saying that I was a *fan* of the fist bump. I just refused to A: acknowledge that's what he was asking from me and B: respond to the nickname 'Popsicle'. Ever.

"C'mon, Popcorn, I explained it to you yesterday." His eyes

narrowed a little but his classic smile that showed too many teeth stayed firmly in place.

I wondered then if the casual use of a term of endearment usually reserved for one's father sat as uncomfortably between us for him as it did for me. My guess was not.

"You did, Todd." I didn't deny his claim, he'd explained it to me everytime I didn't fist bump, which was always.

I drummed my fingers on the counter, doing my best to ignore his hulking figure next to me while I waited for the microwave to finish heating my food. I usually timed my trips to the staff kitchen perfectly, missing Todd at least three out of the five days in the working week. Todd reminded me of the sort of guys in high school that were cool because they were mean and then grew up but didn't grow *out* of any of their habits.

"So, when can I get that date?" He stepped a little closer to me and the same marginally uncomfortable feeling that washed over me as always arrived right on cue. I wasn't totally sure what it was about Todd, but from the moment I met him a little light flashed in my head with a voice attached screaming *'Alert! Alert!'.*

The most aggravating part of it all was Todd didn't even work near this kitchen. He had his own kitchen, all the way over on his side of the office which meant he purposely walked over here when he knew I was having lunch.

*Gross.*

I had immediately become a conquest for Todd from my first day here, and if I knew him (I didn't really, but from our contained interactions I sort of had an inclination) then I knew that Todd didn't particularly like the word 'no'. So, on the days that our schedules unfortunately collided, he cornered me in this kitchen and asked me out.

"Sorry, Todd. My answer hasn't changed and I still have a boyfriend."

There was no reason why he should have, but Aspen Smith immediately popped into my head. He just appeared right in my occipital lobes out of a puff of smoke. *Bam!* There he was.

He'd done that pretty much every single day so far this week. Like always, I delivered an appropriately placed mental flick to my own forehead at the swell of unruly emotions that surged at the very idea of putting 'Aspen Smith' and 'boyfriend' into the same sentence and relating them to me. It wasn't healthy for my lady bits.

It was also delusion. Those words *couldn't* exist like that.

*One moment delivered by the universe,* I reminded myself.

*Never to be repeated again.* I chanted over and over...*because you were the idiot that didn't ask for his number....even if you'd never use it.*

I gave Todd a quick tight lipped sort of grimace, clocking thirty seconds left on the microwave.

Fuck it, cold Thai was better than Todd and his overbearing cologne.

I grabbed my food, a fork from the drawer and made for the exit. The *only* exit.

Todd stepped in front of me, crossing his arms. "You know," he said like I wasn't trying to escape his presence, "you've said that every time I've asked you and I've never seen him. You don't even call him on your lunch break and I've never heard you talk about him to anyone."

Todd was a big guy. He filled up the entire door frame with his head almost touching the top. I had to crane my neck to the point of pain to see him and I knew nothing about the image I posed was intimidating.

I pushed every thought of Aspen from my mind and squared my shoulders, looking up, up, *up* at Todd, "The fact that you know whether or not I call my boyfriend on my lunch break is incredibly alarming."

"You know what I mean," he smirked, casually leaning his shoulder on the door like he wasn't actively demonstrating all the traits of a creep. "Go out with me, come on."

"Nope."

"Penelope—"

"I'd like to get by, please." I pretended not to notice the way his toothy smile stopped looking like a smile entirely and more like he was baring his teeth at me like a rabid dog.

Coming back to reality, I sat down at my desk and ate my leftover Thai in peace, deciding to work while I forked cold Cashew Nut Chicken into my mouth. I actually really liked my job and the thought of leaving it when I inevitably moved on sent a small surge of regret through me.

I was a transcriber. People submitted things like voice recordings, interviews, presentations, and I listened to them. Turning all their spoken words into written ones as I went. The only qualification I'd needed was an above average word-per-minute typing speed and the ability to sign an NDA.

It was a desk job just like any other, but there was also always something new to learn, too. For example, today I learned that Jupiter had a moon called Io and, unlike Earth's moon, that one actually had multiple hundreds of volcanoes. Volcanoes that *erupted,* making it the most active moon in the solar system.

Fucking, *woah.* That was something I'd definitely fist bump over.

"Hey, P," Jessica, who worked three cubicles down from me said. Just her eyes framed in thick, black rimmed glasses visible over the top of my cubicle wall.

Jess was an incredibly kind, single mother of two that had always been welcoming without being overbearing. She was the perfect sort of work friend and the total opposite of Todd.

"Hey, Jess." My smile was genuine and even though I couldn't see her face from the nose down, I knew she was smiling back.

She walked around to stand in the entry of my cubicle, her turtleneck a bright yellow under her long, crocheted overalls.

Yes. *Crocheted.*

"Oh, new sweater?"

"You like it?" She beamed at me before reaching up to fiddle with the collar.

"Very much," I beamed back. There was no need to let her know the bright, highlighter-like nature of most of her clothing had me fearing for the health of my eyesight. Jess loved in-your-face colors and if they made her happy I was convinced that was all that mattered.

"Get through much today?" I asked, noticing for the first time it was 5:30 PM and I was officially off the clock.

"I had a court case." She wagged her eyebrows at me.

"Ooo!" I gasped, looking at her with real, genuine excitement.

"We're talking about a granny running through not one, not two, not *three*," her voice rose steadily with every number, "but *seven* red lights. All within twenty minutes of one another."

I whistled. "Holy smokes."

"And the best part," she went on, whole body almost vibrating while she bobbed on the balls of her feet.

"I'm not sure I'm ready." I closed my eyes and pressed my lips together.

"Her first name was Ina–"

I cracked an eye to see Jess's face was going red with her effort not to laugh.

"—and her last name," the laughter broke through and she crossed her legs like she was trying really hard not to pee her pants, "was *Minit.*"

I gripped the armrests of my desk chair and released my own belly laugh.  Half from her story and half from the contagious effects of her own bubbling laughter.

That was precisely the state both Jess and I were in when our boss, Winston, a young man who was roughly six years my junior strolled over like he was already in on the joke.

"Ladies," Winston said, leaning on the top of my cubicle wall and smiling at us in a way that made his top lip completely disappear beneath his mustache. "This seems like the place to be."

"Oh," Jess struggled valiantly to collect herself. "Hey, Winny. Just telling P about the flatulent properties of cauliflower." She delivered that line with a wink that closed both of her eyes.

Winston, bless his heart, nodded before giving Jess a double take. "Oh," he immediately became flustered, "are you…are you alright?"

"Oh, yeah," she said, waving him off. Her cheeks reddened slightly and she dropped her eyes to the floor. "Just bloated."

Winston, *Winny,* nodded sympathetically and Jess looked mortified. It was well known in the office that he took the responsibility of the constitution of staff members rather seriously. A weird thing for any workplace superior to hone in on and make their niche, but Winny was a weird guy so it sort of made sense.

Rumor had it that one time, Rahoul from accounting was having some serious bowel issues and Winny passed him a diluted gentle laxative under the lavatory door.

"Well, I just wanted to see if Poppy was coming to the staff Say No To The January Blues party, but actually, Jess you haven't RSVP'd either."

"Undecided," Jess said in a perfect blend of kind yet confident.

"Same," I jumped on the back of her self-assured train, "but I'll let you know soon."

Jess waited for me while I packed up my stuff so we could leave together. She asked me about my week, I asked her about hers, and it was perfect because she didn't push when I offered her the surface level pleasantries that only an acquaintance required.

Todd called out for us to hold the elevator from across the office and Jess responded by hitting the 'close door' button with vigor.

We parted ways in front of the building, her going one way and me going another. Forty minutes later I was sliding my key into my front door, shooting off a quick message to Leah in response to her last text at lunch time on whether or not it would be possible for Aquaman to *actually* exist.

**Me:**

Yes, I'd like to think somewhere out there, Aquaman really does exist.

**Leah McDonaugh:**

Superman?

**Me:**
Of course.

**Leah McDonaugh:**
Ant-Man?

**Me:**
God, I hope so.

While that conversation was happening via text, I also hopped into Instagram to send her a couple of memes I'd saved about never growing out of our emo phase and how, weirdly enough, the crossover that was happening between country songs and punk rock music was totally our vibe.

"Hey, Nat." I leaned down to plant a smooch to the glass of my goldfish's tank. Natalie was fourteen years old and, besides Leah, the closest thing to family I had now. She had been a gift from my brother on my fourteenth birthday.

I sat in my apartment eating one of the pre-made meals I'd spent last Sunday prepping for the week (a new thing for me, I'm not entirely sure it's going to stick), laughing intermittently at the meme's Leah was sending through, and then proceeding to share that humor with Natalie.

I'd just gotten into bed when my phone rang.

"Hey sissy," Leah said around a yawn with her face far too close to the camera, her hair twisted around a pair of tights in what was her fourth attempt at getting those heatless curls that she'd yet to have any success with.

"Hey sissy," I said back, peppering my phone camera with kisses.

She gave me the run down on her day first, telling me about how she was determined to learn calligraphy before the new year but couldn't figure out how to use a quill.

Leah was a photographer. She had stayed in our hometown and exercised her personable, approachable and people-loving qualities to build a thriving business that specialized in newborn photo shoots. In her spare time, she was on a never ending search for the perfect hobby. Calligraphy, it would have it, was next on the list.

"I feel like if you attacked these things alphabetically, it would create some order to your chaos."

"You make a valid point," she conceded, but made no further comment, letting the conversation end right in the middle of its existence. My friend danced to the beat of her own drum, and for a long time she had taken me by the hand, keeping my feet moving along with her own when all I'd wanted to do was stop.

Aside from those couple of times in the first year I'd officially become a part of her family, I hadn't said a thing to Leah about any of what reeled in my head. The whole new version of myself that coexisted with the person I used to be, that just constantly screamed behind that door in my mind. But Leah had done her best, and it had been enough for me.

Sometimes I would be bursting at the seams with it. With all these emotions and feelings and anger. Things that made me mad and hateful and painfully sad. I was always unwilling to unleash it upon her, unable to fathom the concept of hurting someone else I loved in any capacity in any way, ever again.

The thought I might do that still filled me with obscene

amounts of guilt at random points in my day, but I was selfish with Leah. Utterly unable and unwilling to let her go.

"And your day?" Her eyes had already started to droop. "Quickly, tell me about your day." Leah reached up and pinched her eyes open, reminding me of that scene in the Mr. Bean movie where he used toothpicks to keep his eyelids from closing.

"I have a good one for you," I said around a bubble of laughter, diving into the tale of Ina Minit, Todd, Winny and the January Blues party I didn't think I would go to.

"How's Rahoul?" she asked.

"I think he goes to the bathroom on a different floor now."

Leah nodded her head like that made perfect sense to her.

I almost told her about my thoughts of Aspen. *Almost.* But I didn't.

When we hung up after a very dragged out series of air kisses, I ended up just laying there, wide awake and thinking solely about Aspen Smith.

'It was hard to be gentle with myself when my stomach was in knots and the very idea that I'd somehow mistaken this universal gift as a once off when it was intended to be something more than that. It made my hands clammy.

*Something more.* What did that even mean? It meant everything and nothing all at the same time.

It was helpful when I reminded myself that while I didn't ask him for his number, or fax number or what direction of the city I should be directing my smoke signals, he also didn't ask for any of those from me.

And then I felt stupid and naive all in the same breath because he was a man that actively had thousands of pairs of underwear thrown in his general vicinity more times than I really wanted to think about on a yearly basis…and I was me.

My lungs filled only to expel a heavy sigh and the sheets that clung to my legs were now too stifling.

Of the things that I'd learned about Aspen in the hour that I'd met him, *really* met him, it was that he was a decent human. That, for some reason, he'd needed to sneak away from his own security guy to have a quiet beer in a crappy bar and had been too nice to tell me to get lost. And he kissed me to save me from a man who had smelled terrifying and had somehow known exactly what I meant.

There was also the asking twice thing.

I could still feel the swipe of his tongue along my bottom lip. I hadn't been able to *not* think about him without my stomach tightening and the severe and sudden urge to squeeze my thighs together. It became abundantly clear that a single kiss from Aspen Smith had been more satisfying than some of the actual sex I'd had.

By some, I meant all of it. All twenty minutes of every combined encounter.

All four times it happened.

You know what, make that three and a half. I still couldn't fully comprehend the five seconds and single thrust delivered by Henry Lexington in the backseat of his beaten up truck the day after my seventeenth birthday constituted as actual sex. Leah still couldn't contain her laughter even now, doing what I'd never actually admit was an impressive impersonation of his high pitched, *'oh, yeah!'* that spanned the duration of both the start and the end of my very first time.

It made me think about the way my body had buzzed to life with Aspen and how, for that moment, it was as if I'd never known what it was like to be awake before. That another person could make me feel like that. That if having the bare minimum of Aspen did that to me, what would it feel like to have him do *everything* to me?

I'd known him for a heartbeat and already he'd pulled more from the dark, quiet part of my mind than anyone ever had.

That terrified me for two reasons: the first was that I wasn't sure I would survive reliving the things Aspen seemed inclined to pull from me, knowing or not. The second was that I knew, without a shadow of a doubt, that the only thing sharing those things with him would achieve would be to hurt him, just like they'd done to Leah.

My thoughts were a broken record that had played on repeat in my head for the last six days because the only way I'd ever see him again was from the nosebleeds with him on stage.

And, you know, maybe in that moment it might feel like he looked my way, squinting into the farthest part of the stadium. For a second he might remember the girl he drove home in a car she secretly loved more than he did.

*That's enough,* I thought to myself. Rolling over onto my side and closing my eyes. *That's enough because it has to be.*

# January 13th

## Aspen

I knocked my boots against the side of Dax and Allie's house. The snow fell from my shoes in clumps and the sign I had gifted my brother and his wife for Christmas last year rattled from the impact.

The hand carved – arguably priceless – artifact read *Wallie's Place*, where it had been lovingly nailed off center and on a bit of a slant right next to their front door.

*"It's off center, Ap," Allie had said, trying to line her body up with the part of the house it should have been positioned in.*

*"And it's...I think it's crooked," Dax said, chewing on his bottom lip while he tilted his head to the side.*

*"So, perfect?" I asked, standing next to them in their front yard while it snowed.*

*They both walked over and wrapped their arms around me, sandwiching me between them.*

*"Perfect," Allie said, looking across me to give Dax a watery*

*smile.*

*"Perfect," he said, looking at her in the same way.*

The memory settled against my heart as something warm and familiar as I stepped inside and let the door close behind me.

"Heyo!" I called down the hallway, the gentle sounds of classical music and laughing trickling down to me.

"I called it!" Savannah, the girlfriend of Angus, *Lady Luck's* bassist, and Allie's best friend shouted with tremendous passion.

"You're two minutes late, that means Luke wins," Allie said, the image of her poking her tongue out crystal clear in my mind.

"I won?" Luke sounded delirious, "I never win!"

"You didn't win," Savannah deadpanned. "*I* won."

"I guessed your arrival time, Ap! *I won!*" Luke flew around the corner, charging at me with such intensity that all I could do was move my hands to cover my balls and brace for his weight when he jumped onto me.

"You didn't!" Savannah yelled after him a moment before I saw the bright blonde of her hair charging at me. I released an *oof* at her making what had to have been a running jump onto me as well.

"*Hey!*" Sav's voice was incredulous and I couldn't help my smile, "I'm light as a feather."

"Yes, ma'am," my voice was muffled by Luke's arm in front of my face.

I spotted my brother from the end of the hallway, his black hair still damp from a shower and his eyes glinting with mischief.

"Wyatt, no," I pleaded, moments before he launched down

the hallway, calling for his wife and adding himself to the pile.

"Fuck me," I grunted. "I'm going down."

"Not without me!" Allie called, and the top of her brown hair was the last thing I saw before my knees buckled beneath me.

"I got that one!" Angus called from the direction of the living room, the pride at finally managing to capture a photo of the 'Aspen Pile', as it had been so lovingly dubbed.

"Did she make it?" Savannah called from somewhere in the pile of people above me.

There was silence while we waited for the result.

"She made it!" Angus yelled, throwing in a few *'woop*'s and *'fuck yeah*'s.

He was, of course, referring to the amount of people I managed to hold up before we all fell. Last time, I crumbled like a shortcrust moments before Allie had managed to add her weight to the pile. This time, I'd held out.

"Why do we do this again?" Luke asked, offering me his hand to help me up.

"I—" Allie started but stopped immediately and looked back at me from halfway down the hallway. "I actually have no idea."

"Neither," Savannah said, grinning at Allie while she fixed her brown waves, stopping her from looking like she'd just been electrocuted. we

"It just makes sense," Rip called from the living room. "Now hurry up, this game won't play itself."

It was Friday night, which was games night and the one night a week, when we weren't touring, we made sure we all got together as a family. It was something we had sort of tried to do a couple years ago, but Luke's ex-girlfriend had never really cared for them. They always ended up being a boys hangout which wasn't any different from what we always did anyway.

When Angus and Savannah moved in together, Luke moved in with Rip and suddenly family games nights became everyone's favorite part of the week.

Our game of choice had always been charades. It continued to baffle mostly everyone present because none of us could actually act that well. Allie, on the other hand, had held tight to what she continued to describe as 'her truth' that she was exponentially gifted at this game. Any time anyone even attempted to allude to her that she was just as bad as the rest of us like, for example, pointing out to her that penguins didn't *skip*, Dax either threatened or followed through on grievous bodily harm.

Teams were decided based on couples and households, but Luke and Rip just sort of adopted me into their duo. I knew the question was coming, I saw it in four sets of jittery stares that made the spot right next to me appear a thousand times more vacant than it actually was.

"So," Luke started, completely ignoring the elbow to the ribs delivered not so subtly by my brother, "where's your girlfriend?" He wagged his eyebrows at me.

I felt the same pressure on my chest that made itself known every single time I was placed into a situation where I didn't think I could follow through in the way people expected. I didn't want to answer the question, wasn't really sure *how* to answer it. How to do it and not picture his face falling. So, I did what I always did. I gave him my biggest smile. The one with the dimples.

"Oh, I'm sure she's somewhere out there," I huffed a laugh

and settled back into the couch, tucking my hands into the front pocket of my hoodie.

The moment the words left my mouth, 'somewhere out there' came to me vividly in the form of the back alley street outside of *Cherry's*. I felt the moment my mouth went dry, filled with the remains of every word I had wanted to say to Poppy but held back for fear of *what*, I wasn't exactly sure.

Fear of everything, probably.

I thought about her and it felt like I was falling, like the ground was racing up to meet me over and over again but I never made contact.

Poppy. *Poppy.* I liked the way her name sounded in my head almost as much as I liked saying it out loud. She'd given me three different names to choose from, like she'd wanted to let me make up my own mind of who she could be to me.

She hadn't known me at all when she'd stumbled to my side and asked me to kiss her.

The look that took over my face was utterly involuntary at the memory. That she had taken the time to introduce herself with three different names in the midst of what I could have only assumed was a great and terrible panic. I'd thought about the way it felt to have her pressed against me more than I'd thought about anything in a long time.

"What's that look?" Allie had come to sit next to me without me even realizing it. She spoke quietly, considerate of the incredibly attuned listeners around us.

"What look?"

"*That* one." She pointed right at the middle of my face.

"Just thinking." I let my head drop back to the couch. "Not something you witness frequently, I'm sure. Living with he-who-must-not-be-named."

"It does always look painful when he does it," she frowned, nodding her head in agreement. "Like a cross between trying to focus his eyes on something too close to his face and remembering how he called the moment wrong when our neighbor Mike was trying to hand him something but Dax thought he was going in for a hug."

My head rolled to the side with laughter, able to imagine that exact moment perfectly. "What a dingus."

"The biggest dingus." Allie's smile was bright and clear as she stared at my brother across the living room with nothing but pure, unfiltered love on her face. "So," she continued, "that look?"

It had been a long time since I was caught between not wanting to let someone down and wanting to keep something for myself. I didn't want to lie to her, but I *did* want to be selfish with the thoughts in my head.

*Selfish.*

The very idea of it pushed me to say something.

"I met a girl," I whispered the words to Allie in the same way that Poppy had whispered to me, and I cursed myself for the thousandth time that I hadn't asked for her number.

*You assumed she wanted to give it.*

I did, for a second. And that had been all for me, I thought. So, I didn't ask.

"Oh?" Allie whispered back. "Just once?"

"Mm," I hummed, focusing on something in the bookshelf across from me. "Just the once."

"No number?" She quirked a brow, remembering that when she and Dax had met, they faced a similar issue.

"Must run in the family," I winked at her and she rolled her eyes. The truth was, I'd almost driven to the bar three different times on my way here but I reminded myself that even if I went back there, she wasn't going to be there.

That wasn't the first time I'd managed to have a beer at *Cherry's* on my own without anyone seeing me or following me there.

There were paparazzi almost permanently camped outside of my apartment building and even though they tended to leave us all alone, at least when we were home, only snapping a photo of us coming or going and no real pursuits of any kind. One of the biggest selling points for my new apartment was that there were two exits: one went out onto the public street, the other was a little bit of a maze to get through with a fence that spanned back almost a whole block and three different gated entrances depending on where you were going. That's the way I usually went when I really didn't want to fuck with them.

Namely when I was heading to *Cherry's.*

Even if they did catch on and happened to be at one of the other gates, I usually had enough time and skill to lose them without much effort. The Taurus had never let me down.

"She's not going to be there, if I go back," I mumbled, my eyes darted to my sister-in-law who had really become more of a best friend to me in the last three years.

"Might not be," she nodded, "but she might be, too."

I thought about not at least *trying* to see her and the idea made my chest ache. It made my body hurt all the way to my fingernails.

"Yeah, she might be."

If she wasn't there, I'd let it go. I'd give it one shot and then I'd force myself to stop letting her consume every single thought I had.

"Thanks, Al." I gave her a quick kiss on the top of the head before I headed for the door.

"Hey, where are you going?" my brother called from behind me.

"Out!" I called back, the word not even fully out of my mouth before the door closed shut.

Not even ten seconds later my phone was buzzing in my pocket. I reached for it on instinct, to pick it up, to be there for whoever it was that was calling, whoever it was that might need me. I knew, rationally, that it was probably Dax, and that he was inside his own house with all of our friends.

Safe.

I knew he was safe, but the panic that started to claw at my throat at the reality that I was seriously considering not picking up was making me feel sick.

I had just gotten into my car when the buzzing stopped. All I wanted to do was turn the car on and put it in drive.

*Poppy. Poppy. Poppy.*

Her name was echoing in my pulse. I could feel it in my fingertips.

I couldn't do it.

*"Fuck,"* I grunted between clenched teeth, digging my phone out of my pocket and pressing redial immediately on my brothers name.

"Ap?"

"Hey!" I shoved every ounce of cheerfulness into that word. "You all good?" I kept the smile on my face because it made it easier to keep the smile in my voice. To keep it from cracking and letting the panic that was clouding my vision seep through.

"Yeah, I just...you sure you're okay?" He sounded worried,

and suddenly I had gained a bit of clarity. That I hadn't thought about how he'd feel, any of them really, if I just walked up and strode out. No explanation, no nothing.

My gut twisted.

"Sorry," I said, rubbing my eyes. "Sorry, Dax. Yeah I'm good, I just—" I started to explain but it was Allie who cut me off, pulling the phone from my brother.

"I can't believe you called him." I could hear her frown as she attempted, and failed, to keep their voices from traveling through the phone. "He's a grown man, Wyatt. He doesn't have to always explain to you where he's going."

"He just stormed out without even —" Dax's voice cut out completely.

"Aspen?" Allie asked, calm as ever. "We're all good here, I promise no one will call unless it's an emergency. And we'll text first."

"You sure?" No one had ever come quite as close to seeing through me as Allie did. I think it's because, in some ways, we were the same.

"I'll use the emergency word."

"Schnauzer?"

"Schnauzer," she repeated in confirmation. It had been her idea to implement an emergency word. If I was ever unable to pick up her call, if the call was followed by the emergency word then I'd know it was important. If it wasn't, I didn't have to call her back. She suggested it one time, ever so casually, first saying she wanted to do it for herself.

She said she panicked if she couldn't answer the phone for whatever reason.

That was a lie.

Allie had suffered a car accident so bad I couldn't even

recount to you all the injuries she'd sustained. The experience had left her with PTSD which had, more often than not, sent her into these debilitating panic attacks.

It had been almost six months and she hadn't had a single one. After years of working hard on her own and then, eventually, going to see someone again.

So, panic from the sound of sirens and headlights? Sure. Unanswered phone calls? No. That was all me and she knew that I knew, but we'd never spoken of it aloud.

"Schnauzer," I repeated, double checking.

"That's the one. Have fun and good luck." She hung up the phone and I waited another five minutes to see if any other calls would come through.

I heaved a heavy breath before turning on the car, remembering my single minded focus from before.

*Poppy. Poppy. Poppy.*

I'd built it up in the twenty minutes it took to drive there. Built it up some more in the five it took to park the car, then I waited for the feeling of panic to go away. To do this one thing for myself. To go in and see if she was there.

She could be. She *might* be. But that meant in some roundabout way I was assuming I deserved this. Deserved to get to know her, or to take her out to dinner. To put her number in my phone under one of the three names she'd given me to choose from.

I wanted to. I really fucking wanted to. But I couldn't get out of the car.

I sat there for twenty three minutes before I finally made myself turn the car back on to head home.

The head lights shot out in front of me, immediately illuminating a small frame with heaving shoulders.

She stood there like she'd come running from wherever she'd been. Like she was equally as shocked to find herself standing in front of my car as I was to see her there.

"Poppy." Her name just fell out of my mouth, like the word wanted to run straight for her and bring her back to me. Seeing her standing there sent every single thought flying from my head, draining every drop of panic that had been poisoning my body from the moment I walked out of my brother's house.

It was just her. All of a sudden exactly what I wanted became very clear, and it didn't seem so selfish to reach out and take it.

I opened the car door, the frame creaking as I stepped onto the road. I didn't stop until I was standing right in front of her. Amber eyes, wide and unsure, looked back at me. Her hair in a plait down one side.

"Poppy," I whispered into the space between us.

"Hey, Ap," she whispered back.

"I want to have dinner with you," I said, not entirely sure on the logistics of how that would work, but she nodded anyway.

"Okay," she still whispered, her breath making a cloud between us.

"And I'd like your number," I added quickly, "please." My eyes darted between hers and the lips I was doing my very best not to think about, especially when they started to curve into a small smirk.

"That delivery felt weird," I said, reaching up to push my hair back from my forehead. "Let me try again." I turned around and walked back a few steps before facing her once more and reapproaching.

Her lips clamped into a tight line in an attempt to take this as seriously as I was.

"Don't laugh," I said, turning around and going back to try it for a third time.

"No laughing," she replied, shaking her head with a small frown.

I walked up to her again, stopping only when we were toe to toe. "Poppy," I started, "can I please have your number?"

Her eyes didn't dart around my features but instead they glided, like she wasn't in a rush. Like she wanted to remember what she was looking at.

"You can," she said, "but only because you asked me twice."

# 8

# January 19th

**Poppy**

I didn't know that he was going to be there. I actively convinced myself that he wouldn't be, and if he was, it wouldn't have had anything to do with me.

Every time I reached for the door to walk into *Cherry's* I turned around and walked away. I ran into three patrons on three different occasions who I was sure thought I was in the process of losing my mind. It took twenty minutes of hardcore talking myself in, then out, then back into the idea again before I walked in.

It had been this blinding sort of panic when my eyes went straight to the stool he'd been at and it sat empty. The very first thought that entered into my head was '*no*'. Powered by genuine disbelief that he *couldn't* be there. That was when I'd run. Moving through the bodies of Friday night clientele and sparing only a single thought as to how, in all the world, Leah had found *this* bar and decided it was the place to visit. This place I'd never heard of in a part of this city I'd never even thought of going to.

*A universe moment.*

The thought seeped through no matter how many times I knocked it away, only disappearing completely when I found myself standing in front of Aspen's geriatric sedan, right where I knew it would be. I didn't need more light than the same faint glow of the nearby street lamp that had made his eyes glitter like stars to know the body behind the wheel was his.

My heart had been galloping so fast. Thumping like the beat of a drum I was sure he'd hear, and then he turned on the car.

I'd been able to admit to myself in that breath you take between big moments that it seemed this was the first time in a very long time that I'd run *towards* something instead of away. It was terrifying and exhilarating and made my heart ache with a mixture of joy and betrayal when I watched him step out of his car and realized that I was precisely where I needed to be.

Aspen's number was now saved into my phone as 'Ap'. He'd handed me his phone right

there and watched as I entered it. I then watched as he changed the name from Penelope to Poppy. When I added him into my phone as Aspen, he'd plucked it immediately from my grasp and changed it to Ap.

With every conversation we had it became more apparent that I actually didn't know anything about Aspen. That knowledge thrilled me. He continued to be unpredictable, never doing or saying or replying with anything I remotely anticipated which meant I was constantly grinning at my phone like a fool.

At the start of the week I hadn't been able to focus on a single thing. So, in a compromise to myself, I put my phone face down next to me on my desk. It did nothing for my productivity because my eyes darted to it multiple times a minute waiting for the telling buzz that indicated a message.

The first time it had been Leah, just as it had been the second time. That was when I decided to put myself out of my own misery and text him first.

**Me:**

I've tried to write the word 'bio' three times and each time somehow managed to write 'nip'

He replied immediately and it sent my heart careening right into my esophagus.

**Ap:**

Extraterrestrial communication? Are you wearing your foil hat?

**Me:**

I thought I was wearing it when I left the house, but now I can't remember…

**Ap:**

They're onto us

**Ap:**

Hide in the men's bathroom immediately

**Ap:**

The last stall (very important)

**Ap:**

I'll be there with provisions and you'll know it's me because I'll knock three times in quick succession

I'd snorted so loudly that Jess thought I was choking on my food and ran over in terror, immediately delivering the Heimlich without first confirming my ailment.

"Breathe!" she yelled with alarming vigor. *"Breathe, god dammit!"*

Jess had arrived with a small bell the next day and sat it on my desk. "Just so that never happens again," she muttered, "this is the choking bell."

I could only nod and watch her leave, but not before she stopped in front of my cubicle and with only her eyes to be seen murmuring a reassuring, "I have one too," and headed back to her desk.

Leah demanded a choking bell for Christmas that evening.

I was sitting on my couch last night when my phone went off again, my heart role playing a prison break the same way it did every other time Aspen messaged me in the last week.

**Ap:**

Roughing it without support of, or access to, amenities humankind has developed to make life a breeze?

In full fledged fool mode, I grinned at my phone. Aspen had taken to sending me definitions through the day of different things. I assumed it was a way of him just letting me know what he was up to when the first few had been the definitions of 'studio', 'drums' and 'burrito', but now I severely doubted it.

> **Me:**
> Camping?

**Ap:**
You've been practicing, Poppy

I read my name like I was hearing him say it and my body erupted in goosebumps. I could practically feel the way he'd whispered it against my skin, like a question and an answer all rolled into two syllables.

**Ap:**
Liquid substances falling from great heights?

> **Me:**
> Oh no :[

**Ap:**
I believe in you

> **Me:**
> I'm perplexed

**Ap:**
Your vocabulary is so hot

At least no one was around to deliver the Heimlich on account of my howling laughter that time.

**Me:**
I believe you're flirting with me

**Ap:**
It's become my favorite thing to do

*Holy balls.*

**Me:**
Either rain, or maybe a waterfall?

**Ap:**
You're very good at this game

**Me:**
So you're saying I won?

**Ap:**
A really close second :D

It was the first time in a while where falling asleep had been difficult on account of something positive. I wanted to meet every single one of his messages with a reply of my own that went off just as fast as his came in, but I always seemed to fall asleep first. It was like the man didn't rest.

My favorite conversations were the ones where he called, and he did that a lot. Aspen was an incredibly entertaining text-volley partner, but it was easy to pretend he wasn't making me feel the things I was starting to feel when they were words on a screen.

Hearing his voice come through the phone was like being struck by lightning. It woke me up.

"Picture this," he said, voice clear and unburdened by sleep like I thought it would be so early in the morning. Yet again, not what I'd expect from a rock star though I'm fully able to admit I was leaning into a stereotype there.

In my defense, I'd never met a rock star before.

I had just stepped off the train and was making my way up and out of the station, a smile already on my face. "Occipital lobes at the ready," I replied immediately.

"You're so smart Poppy..." he paused for only a second followed by a sound that resembled severe devastation. "Oh my *lanta*."

"What's wrong?" My chest swelled with panic.

"I don't know your last name. We've been talking all week and I never asked your last

name. This is so much worse than forgetting your car door," he grumbled.

All that did was make me smile wider.

"I won't tell the mom's you have on rotation if you don't want me to."

"You really *do* like me."

"Hart," I laughed, replying to his dramatics. "That's my last name."

"Your name is Poppy Hart?" He sounded in awe and my eye role was unstoppable. "That's a beautiful name." His voice was full of a quiet sincerity that I was coming to understand as his default setting. Aspen Smith, I realized, was a labrador.

"Thanks, Ap." It had always been my name, but all of a sudden I liked it a whole lot more.

"Do you have a middle name?" It sounded like this was equivalent to Christmas for him.

I couldn't not laugh, "Yes. It's Elizabeth."

"You have *got* to be joking. I think I'm dying."

"What's yours?" I giggled. *I giggled.* I was giggling? I think I needed to add a new rule to Poppy's Life Rules but I was, all at once, finding any of them difficult to recall.

"You don't know it?"

"I'd like you to tell me," I slowed my steps, knowing my office building was coming up but not wanting the conversation to end.

"Okay Poppy Elizabeth Hart," his delight was an audible, tangible thing through the phone, "my name is Aspen Killian Smith."

"Well," I said, doing my absolute best to remember everything about this moment and the man I was talking to. To remember that no matter what, I had felt like *this*, "That's a beautiful name."

Aspen had texted me the entire day meaning I had gotten zero work done. As soon as I was off the clock and out the doors of the building, waving to Jess as she headed off in the other direction, my phone rang with an incoming call.

He spoke, continuing our text conversation, as soon as I picked up.

"Hiking to a waterfall," he said, sounding like he was playing a video game in the background, "that's what I think we should do."

Now all I could do was imagine Aspen playing a video game, maybe just in sweats? Maybe he might not have a shirt on.

I cleared my throat, "I thought the answer was camping?"

"It was. However, upon further pondering," he paused to swear softly, "sorry, zombies. Anyway, I figured being out in the middle of nowhere in the dead of winter was probably not ideal for your toe tips."

"You might be the first boy who's ever thought about my toes tips."

"Boy?"

"Sorry, man."

"*Man?*" His voice rose a full octave on that single word.

"Guide me, please," I laughed, stepping onto the train.

"No," he sighed, "man feels right. I might just need to do some pull ups against the window in the nude to earn the title."

"What an interesting definition."

"It's either that or lather myself in baby lotion and pose for a charitable calendar."

"Option B please." I was joking, of course. In saying that, I was also grateful that he couldn't see the way my face had flushed raspberry pink at the thought of him covered in oil.

We'd spoken about absolutely nothing, but we did talk.

I'd realized I didn't really find myself caring that nothing more had been said about his proposed dinner date or that his sidetracked comment on hiking to a waterfall was equally exciting as it was unanticipated. Talking to Aspen had been consuming all of my thoughts. I couldn't even recall everything I'd transcribed in the last five days when normally I'd have learned at least a handful of new things by now.

It really was all I'd been thinking about with every single part of my brain so when I sat down and stared at my laptop with the web browser open to potential rentals available in three different cities, my heart sank.

Because I was leaving.

It didn't fully register in my own brain what I was doing until my phone was pressed to my ear and Aspen was picking up on the second ring. The words just poured from my mouth.

"I've seen you in person twice."

"That's true." Aspen seemed to have a knack of picking up on whatever I was feeling, his tone was soft but serious.

"Maybe I don't know you that well," I said, staring at the listings of apartments I already knew I'd hate on the screen.

"Oh, I know what this is about. You missed the column about my favorite color combinations in *Rolling Stone*."

"I must have," I said, the grip I had on my panic slipping just a little.

"The one about my taste in music in *Mojo*?" he went on, his voice full of feigned outrage.

"No, I caught that one."

"Perfect!" It sounded like he slapped his hand on his leg. "You're half up to date."

My quiet laughter fluttered between us and I could picture him so clearly, somewhere, anywhere, sitting down and smiling into his phone.

"Ap," I whispered.

"Poppy," he whispered back.

"Are you busy?"

"I am not."

"Would you like to come over?"

"More than anything, yes."

I had no idea where Aspen lived, but thirty minutes later there were three knocks in quick succession at my front door and there he was, right in the doorway to my house.

"Hey," I sounded breathless. I *felt* breathless.

"Hey." His responding grin was something that I wanted to see everyday. It was like looking right into the sun and I wanted nothing more than to always be able to see the imprint of it when I closed my eyes.

He brushed so close to me when he walked in and I'd never been so aware of someone else's body, clad all in black as he was and smelling faintly like pine and violets. Aspen was tall but it didn't hurt my neck to peer up at him in the same way it did to look at Todd. He moved like someone who used their body, who was comfortable in it. Someone who didn't really like to sit still.

I didn't like where I lived. In fact, I hated pretty much every place I'd ever rented but looking at Aspen Killian Smith standing in my living room, it was like the walls of my little town house sagged in relief in the same way I did.

Right in that moment, of all the places I'd lived since I was sixteen, this one had just become my favorite.

# 9

# January 19th

**Aspen**

It occurred to me moments before I knocked on Poppy's front door that I'd gotten myself out of the house so fast that I forgot to put on both underwear and deodorant. But I wanted to see her.

Actually, I wanted to see her again the moment I dropped her off at home last Friday. From the literal second she closed her front door with a little wave and an uncertain tilt of her head, but I didn't want to be *that guy*.

Too forward and pushy.

So, I waited. I waited for her to say outloud what days suited her for dinner, or if hiking to a waterfall was what we were going to do on the weekend. If she had asked me to sit on her couch and hold her yarn while she crocheted, I would've done it.

Being in Poppy's orbit was where I'd wanted to be all week, and I'd never wanted to be anywhere else when I was behind my drum kit. With drum sticks in my hands and a beat in my head.

We'd been in the recording studio every day. Long days that were tiring but the songs were coming together in a way that surpassed even our last record, and that experience had been borderline religious. There was only one thing that was stumping us so far, and all five of us agreed that we'd yet to find what was going to be our first single for the album.

The first song we were going to release. We had a bit of time, it wasn't planned to be released until the start of April and we were only halfway through January. Dax just thought we needed some perspective and so the call was made that we would take the week off. We'd worked right through Christmas and New Years and he'd declared that what was missing was our ability to 'chill'. That's where hiking with Poppy was meant to come in.

Poppy was still staring at me, her back pressed to the front door, her hands ringing nervously in front of her.

"Shoes?" I asked, pointing down at my boots.

"No, they're fine," she smiled at me, but it was timid. I'd seen Poppy look shy before, but never worried, not like that.

"I wanted to see you." I couldn't help the single step I took back towards her.

"You did?" Her eyes widened a fraction and I'd bet if she could've, she would have stepped back.

"Yep." I sunk my hands into the front pockets of my jeans and rocked back on my heels. "Pretty much since I dropped you off at home last week." I let my eyes wander, trying to figure out what it was about being near Poppy that made it impossible to not say the things that were in my head. To not *do* the things I wanted to do.

Both habits I had rid myself of a very long time ago.

She just watched me, unmoving, and so I took the lead feeling weirdly confident about every step I took further into her house. It was small and…bare.

It was not the sort of home I had imagined for Poppy. I'd thought of colors, of patterns that didn't match and paintings either too small or too big for the walls she'd put them on. I had imagined carpets so fluffy they swallowed your feet and plants that crept along walls and window sills.

Instead there was a serious absence of color, like she'd intended for it to be plain and unwelcoming.

That's when I noticed the boxes.

There were some in the living room, some to the side of the kitchen, some at the base of the stairs.

I felt her eyes taking in every movement I made while I took in everything around me. I pointed to the boxes, "Going somewhere?" I flicked my eyes to hers and found her already looking at me. Our eyes clashed for a second and it seemed to be enough to break whatever trance she'd fallen into.

"Oh. No." She pulled the sleeves of her sweatshirt over her hands, crossing her arms over her chest. There was more to that answer than that but it felt like a violation of her privacy to ask, even though every part of my brain screamed for me to find out.

*Why the unpacked boxes? Don't tell me you're leaving when I've only just found you.*

No, I wasn't going to do that. Instead, I did what anyone else would do in my position. I focused on the fish.

"That," I pointed at the tank and walked over to sit on a stool at the breakfast bar of her kitchen, "is a lovely fish."

Watching Poppy right then was like seeing the moment the

sun had finally burnt away the remaining clouds after a storm, showering everything in light again. She beamed at me with pure, undiluted joy and it was like I'd been punched right in the chest with a flaming fist. I would have everything I'd ever need if I could have this girl look at me just like that for the rest of my life.

Poppy was beautiful. Like she was the very image of a spring day with her bright amber eyes and chestnut hair.

"Aspen," she said, walking over to sit on the stool next to me, both of us just there looking at her fish. "Meet Natalie." She looked at me like I should be extending my hand towards the tank.

I did the next best thing I could manage in a pinch and bowed my head in reverence. "Natalie, the pleasure is mine."

"Nat," Poppy leaned towards the tank, "this is Aspen Killian Smith. We like him."

"We do?" Her words had taken me off guard and now I wanted more of them. I wanted *all* of them.

"Oh, she likes you," Poppy said, conveniently hurdling right over my question.

"How can you tell?" I leaned in as close as she was, peering at the little floating orange sparkling blob.

"She's fluttering her fins extra fast," she murmured, her nose almost pressed to the side of the tank.

"Is it some kind of mating call?" I mused,

"That's definitely one possibility," Poppy nodded.

"Should I be doing it back?"

"Not on the first date, Aspen!" She looked at me in mock horror before a small laugh escaped her.

The noise triggered something in my mind, notes forming into the beginnings of the sort of song Poppy would be. The longer she looked at me, the more somber she got, like that brief moment of sunshine was only a sliver between thick, rain heavy clouds.

"There was a reason I thought you should come over," her voice was unsteady and I wanted to reach out to touch her.

"You *do* want to ravish me." The corner of my mouth tipped up at the way a light pink flush made its way up her neck. I wanted to follow its accent with the tip of my tongue.

"No? Okay," I tried again, leaning my elbow on the counter beside me. "You've heard about my baking ability?"

"Well, it *was* in *The Stones*."

"You did read it!" It had worked for a second, her eyes brightened and the crease between her eyes smoothed out, but only for a second.

"Aspen," she said my name the way you'd read the start of the last sentence of a book. It had this note of finality to it that made my hands feel heavy and my teeth ache. It felt very much like this was going to end before it ever really started and suddenly I couldn't breathe.

I was under water and she was above the surface, just out of my reach.

"I'm leaving," she pushed the words at me unceremoniously, like they frightened her almost as much as they frightened me. And they did, those two previously insignificant words strung side by side had become terrifying.

I felt my smile falter. I'd never been so taken off guard that I'd let it slip before and the moment her eyes flicked to my mouth I saw her own expression fall too.

"It's a rule that I have. For myself, not for, like, the general public." She was ringing her hands in front of her again. "I don't stay anywhere more than a year," she explained, and I was trying really hard to hear the words.

I swallowed, bringing my attention back to my own expression, keeping the right one in place. I didn't know what else to do, everything felt too loud.

"Okay," I whispered.

Silence so heavy and claustrophobic settled around us like a blanket. It was the first time I hadn't ever wanted it to end. I didn't want the words to fill it that I knew were coming. I wanted to sit in it, before things changed and the possibility of Poppy becoming mine was still a reality.

In the absence of noise, Poppy frantically started to fill it. "I've moved every year since I was eighteen," she said with rushed words like they explained everything.

"Why?" The word was out before I could stop it.

"I'm —" she cut herself off and I knew she'd pulled some invisible leash on herself. "It's complicated."

I nodded even though nothing had ever made less sense to me. "How long have you been here?"

She knew as well as I did that what I'd really asked was how long until she wouldn't be anymore.

"A little under three months," she whispered. "Until I go."

"Where are you going?" Another mental check that my expression was still relaxed. Calm.

"I don't know," her voice shook and her chin quivered and I couldn't take it. All I wanted to do was *fix* it. Poppy's eyes fluttered before she dropped my gaze and I knew, before the words even left her mouth, that they were a lie. "It's complicated."

"Okay," I whispered.

"You make me," she started to talk, her wide amber eyes flittering around my face with uncertainty until a look of determination set her brows in a small furrow. "You make me feel *a lot*. More than I have in a long time and I wanted to tell you right away because I, well, I'm sort of a one woman band."

"You're using a band related metaphor?" I smiled at her. I couldn't help it, even though every word she spoke was equivalent to a paper cut between my fingers.

"What do you think?" She grinned too, and I knew it was despite herself.

"Impeccable decision making. Please, continue."

"I'm…I'm a…"

"…One woman band?"

"Yes. *Yes*. And you're sort of…*challenging* all of that which I think…I *know* will end up with you getting hurt and the thought of that makes me sick, Aspen. So I needed to tell you now." Poppy stopped only to take a big breath and kept talking. "I don't date, like, at all. It's never really been something that's made sense with my lifestyle. I've just never been anywhere long enough for it to matter, and it hasn't mattered really, until recently. I just don't date. See people. Have relationships. Except for Leah…and Nat." Her hand flew up and gestured helplessly at her fish.

"Okay," I said again. I was trying to take in everything she'd said and I was trying to do it calmly because I was confused and worried and not really okay at all and Poppy was very clearly nervous.

"*Okay?*" She didn't whisper back that time, the word came out in full force. Whatever she'd expected from me after her one-woman-band explanation, that hadn't been it.

My ribs groaned at the effort of keeping my lungs from exploding. It felt like I'd inhaled a big breath and couldn't let it go.

I picked my next words for Poppy, not for me. "That's okay."

She just nodded, clearly determined to be pleased with this conversation regardless of the small crease still lingering between her brows. Just like when we were standing in front of my car, the consequences of my own wants didn't seem to cross my mind.

"Can I still see you, until then?"

"You…are you sure?" Relief and shock colored her words in equal parts.

"We're friends, Poppy. Plus, it's surprisingly hard to find a fellow Taurus enthusiast around these parts." I reached my hand out, palm up between us because I couldn't stop myself anymore. My entire body seemed to thaw against the chill that had unknowingly settled in when she didn't even seem to think about it and placed her hand in mine. It stung, the warmth of her hand against the coolness of mine. Her skin was soft, fingers unhurried as they traveled over the calluses on my hand over and over.

"I can believe that," she nodded.

"You're a dime a dozen," I still whispered because anything else felt too hard.

"Now you're just trying to ravish me." She lifted her eyes from our hands. It felt like I was getting another peek of sunshine and all I wanted to do was bask in it.

I had thought about Poppy in every way a man could think about a woman. I wanted to walk down a busy street with her tucked into my side. Arrive home and find the lights already on and Poppy curled into the corner of the couch. I wanted her hair fanned out across my pillow, her hands fisting my sheets and my lips on every single part of her body.

That was when my control slipped and I finally, *finally*, just let my eyes roam over her. Thick socks revealed the expanse of her golden legs. Her shorts looked soft and well loved and disappeared under the oversized sweatshirt that devoured her whole.

"So," I swallowed, needing to change the direction of my thoughts before I did something incredibly inappropriate in front of her fish. "About dinner. I don't think it's such a good idea."

She nodded even as her face fell. It happened so fast I don't even think she realized it. Seeing it happen was equivalent to the ground slipping out from under me. "Unless you're partial to a camera in your face along with your entree."

"Oh." Her eyes flicked back to mine. She'd forgotten that was a reality for me, because even though she had known who I was when we'd met, she didn't look at me in the same way she had when the realization hit her. Poppy looked at me like she could see behind the curtain that separated the Aspen the public knew and the other parts of myself that not even my family saw. Like she could see every part of me, even the parts made completely of glass and prone to shattering and wanted to keep me anyway.

"Mm," my voice was rough, my head filled with images of Poppy beneath me. Above me. Of all of her *everywhere*. "So, how about hiking?" It was a small grace that I was sitting down.

"Does a waterfall exist somewhere in there?"

"You *are* very good at that game and here I thought you were just Googling the answers."

"I like to hike," she said, her attention focused on where her hand still rested in mine.

I had her for three months.

It made it easier to think of what I wanted knowing that I was never going to be able to keep her.

"Hiking it is, sweet Poppy."

She looked up at me resembling the loveliest version of the Cheshire Cat, "Sweet, huh?"

I wanted to run the pad of my thumb over her bottom lip, to trace the shape of her face and never forget that if nothing else, someone had looked at me like Poppy was looking at me right now. Like she'd follow me anywhere if I only asked her to.

"For now," I said, squeezing her hand and letting the smile on my face turn into something real, something hers.

# 10

## January 20th

**Poppy**

The request for Aspen to stay with me had been on the tip of my tongue. It seemed absurd that he didn't feel the way even my house wanted to keep him, his warmth and sunshine and goodness. But, that would have been cruel.

I had asked him to come to tell him I wasn't staying. To do the right thing, and be upfront about my situation.

Well, as upfront as I could have been.

Aspen was the sort of person you wanted to trust fall into. He was solid and present and if I let myself want him like that, it would only end up hurting him. I was already breaking so many of my own rules by entertaining the idea of a friendship with him.

I could admit that even though I had Leah, I was lonely. I was always achingly aware of that fact but I forced myself to endure it.

It was what I deserved, what was for the best. It was what worked *best*.

So, when my eyelids had started to droop shut and he tucked the blanket up further around me that we'd been sharing while watching a movie, he stood up to leave.

*Ask me.*

That's what his face had said when he tucked a strand of hair behind my ear. When his fingertips blazed a trail with the lightest touch down the column of my throat.

*Ask me to stay.*

But I didn't, and I knew he wouldn't ask to stay either.

That seemed hard for him, asking. That second time outside of *Cherry's* when he'd asked for my number I thought at first it was nerves that made his eyes uncertain, maybe even a little afraid. I was sure now that wasn't it at all. Ever since then he hadn't asked for a single thing more, not like he'd asked me for that one thing.

Aspen leaned forward, pressing a kiss to my cheek, lingering for only a breath too long before his long legs led him away from me.

I gripped the blanket he'd tucked around me so tightly my hands began to ache, just so I wouldn't chase him down. I was about to fold, to give in and demand he come back, even if it was just to sit with me, just to *be* there, when my phone went off with a new message.

**Ap:**
   I'll see you bright and early, we're going
   to hike the shit out of that waterfall trail.

**Ap:**

Goodnight, Poppy.

And then not a moment later,

**Ap:**
Goodnight, Nat.

I cursed my alarm to the deepest, darkest pits of hell when it blared *'I'm walking on sunshine'* directly into my right ear at the butt crack of dawn. For some reason I felt optimistic about the act of waking up if the thing to *wake* me up was a bright, happy diddle I felt fondly about.

I now hated that song with the ferocity of a hard done by hedgehog.

My eyes were still pretty much closed when I locked the door to my house and followed the sound of the rumbling engine that idled out front. That's why it had taken me a full three seconds to realize that was *not* the sound of Aspen's car.

The passenger side window was already down and he was grinning at me so wide his eyes were almost closed.

"Aspen," I said, my voice full of the sleep I had been very much still in only fifteen minutes ago.

"Poppy, have I ever told you that you look the *most* beautiful in the mornings?" He sounded genuine and I wanted to flick his nose.

"Aspen," I tried again, "this isn't your car."

"This is my *hiking* car," he corrected. "Actually, It's my brothers but he keeps it parked in my garage.

I was silent while I just took in the hefty piece of machinery that was his Jeep Wrangler, but then he added on, "and that was absolutely not a euphemism."

As hard as I tried, the smile I'd been holding back tugged at the corner of my mouth while I just stared at it.

His car, I mean. It was huge, I wasn't even sure I'd be able to get in without looking like I was trying to mount a horse. "Guess I was right about one assumption," I said, rubbing my eyes. "You do own a less environmentally friendly car."

Aspen leaned over just as I clicked my seat belt in, leaving a chaste kiss on my cheek like it was something he'd done a thousand times before and I felt the contact of his mouth on my skin all the way to the ends of my eyelashes.

"This," he put the car into drive and peeled out of his park, looking no less delicious than he had in the Taurus, "is not my car. So technically you're still wrong. But if it makes you feel better, this is a hybrid." He shot me a quick wink before focusing his attention back onto the road.

Aspen was dressed precisely how you would expect for someone going hiking in winter and not at all what you might expect someone who favored jeans as tight as the ones he wore. Aspen was decked out (still all in black) with hiking boots that looked well worn, black, form fitting cargo pants and a sweatshirt under his winter coat. His dark hair curled around his ears under his beanie that had a big *Lady Luck* logo on the front of it.

"So, Poppy Elizabeth," he said after a minute, the barely

noticeable tug at the corner of his mouth let me know he had been very aware of my perusal. "What is it that you do?"

Aspen didn't manage to run out of any questions for the entire hour and a half drive it took to get us out to what he had only divulged as 'his spot'. Insisting it was like a family recipe, only passed down when you became of age.

He'd said that right as we passed by the sign that said 'Frosted Lakes Hiking Trail'. By the time we were there he knew almost everything about what I did Monday to Friday, including the story of Miss Ina Minit and Jupiter's Moon, but minus Todd.

With my hand held firmly in his grip, Ap led us through overgrown terrain to get to the hiking trail he insisted was a much easier walk. I could tell he was excited, mainly because he was narrating almost everything we did.

"We're just going up this hill now, you okay?" He checked over his shoulder, giving me a little grin before tugging me along. He followed it up only moments later with, "We're going down this hill now. Oh, hey look, that's one of my favorite trees! See the roots? They're so twisty that if you look at it from right over...*here*," he held me in front of him so close my entire back was pressed to his chest, his arm wrapped around me and resting on my collarbones, "it spells 'Ap'."

I turned my head to peer up at him, catching another of his big, bright smiles that I knew were real, knew were all Aspen. I had never been that great at reading people, but it was right then that I had the sort of realization that took your breath away. It was knowing that he was choosing to share something he loved with *me*, of anyone, anywhere, ever. It made me think that maybe one day – if we'd had the time –

I'd have known this big, hiking, drummer with glittery eyes and rough hands better than I knew myself.

"That's pretty cool," I said, my voice suddenly thick and I didn't think too much about what it meant when my own hands came up to grip the arm he had wrapped around me.

We made it to the path, known not only by the well worn dirt that spanned either side of us and the snow that dotted the edges left from a fall a few days ago, but also by Aspen's announcement.

"We've made it to the path!" He held both arms out to either side of him, as if this wasn't a public trial but a place that was all his, that he was proud of.

The path was wide enough in most parts that we could walk side by side, only going single file in the tricky bits. Ap made sure he was in front of me when it was a steep decline, or that he held my hand and led the way on any rough uphill parts.

It made my body want to turn to jelly.

I had to make it a rule for myself that any time I felt like removing any article of his clothes I would chant *just friends* six times in my head.

It had, thus far, not worked in the slightest in deterring any such mental behavior on my part.

"So," I said, a little out of breath. A little from him and a little from a particularly tricky bit. "You know what I do, now you have to tell me what you do."

"I thought you read my articles?"

"Mostly everything I know about you I knew before I met you. That's weird, Aspen," I said.

"Alright, what's something you know that's weird you didn't find out yourself?" He held a hand out to me and helped me over a log.

"I know one time when you were really drunk, you went to pee but missed the toilet and ended up going all over Angus."

"Ha!" He barked a laugh so loud birds flew out of trees around us. "I totally forgot about that. Okay, yes those are the sorts of war stories that regular people might not know about one another, but that has nothing to really do with *me*."

"Alright, I know you love to bake."

"That phrase lives on half the shirts I own. Try again."

"That you thought swapping places with your sibling didn't only apply to twins and you tried to get Wyatt to take your math test in the second grade."

"I've forgotten all about these! Poppy, keep going, this is wonderful."

"You're not seeing my point at all," I scowled at him.

"Please?" He jutted out his bottom lip and I immediately wondered what it would be like to take it between my teeth.

"I know your preferred brand *and* style of boxers." I didn't meet his eyes on that one, because I knew for a fact, knowing that about a stranger was definitely not normal.

"Oh?" I could hear the mischief in his voice.

"See," I said, "the only way I should know that is if I'd seen them myself."

"Are you picturing me in my underwear, Poppy?"

"I--*No*."

*Boy was I ever.*

There were so many other things I could have said, but I went for the option that sat closest to his genitals.

"It's okay," he leaned in to whisper in my ear and the heat of his words made me shiver. "I've pictured you too." He pulled back just enough to shoot a wink right at my shocked face.

Aspen took my hand in his after that, doing me the favor

of not making a note on how I was flushed from head to toe, and proceeded to tell me as much about himself as he could.

Aspen hated running, he *loathed* it and he was terrified of publicity events because he was constantly nervous he'd say something that would upset someone without meaning to. He'd always liked avocados from his earliest memories, his parents were nice people, but they weren't a close family and he and Wyatt didn't ever really go home. He'd been a theater kid at school which was why it was common knowledge that he could sing very well, though he'd decided that when it became his brother's thing, he just wouldn't do it anymore.

"Do you sing in the shower?"

"Loudly," he slung an arm over my shoulder and smirked down at me.

"That's something I didn't know." My arm wrapped around his waist on instinct. "Can I hear you sing?" I asked the question not thinking it would be a big deal, but I felt him stiffen at the question and the very moment I was about to take it back he spoke.

"I mean, sure, maybe if it's just the two of us I could —"

"Why did you do that?" I asked, more curious than anything. His face completely transformed with the weight of his frown.

"Do what?"

"Say yes when you didn't want to? It's okay that you don't want to, Aspen."

We'd stopped walking, locked in this stare off where he was trying to find an answer to whatever questions he had running through his head in the same way I was trying to find the answer to mine.

Then my stomach growled. This big, grumbling, echoing sound.

Just like that, his very real, very Aspen grin was back in place and that conversation was going to have to be left for another time.

"You're in luck, Poppy Elizabeth Hart." He swung his backpack around to his front and pulled out two ziplock bags containing sandwiches with the crusts cut off.

"You cooked lunch!" I was absolutely as excited about that reality as I sounded.

"No cooking involved, sweet Poppy."

"I can't believe you packed lunch."

"I figured you ate food."

"First you think of my toe tips, now my stomach? Is this how friends are supposed to act?"

"Where we're concerned, absolutely."

My cheeks hurt from the way my smile took over every muscle in my face. "You cut off the crusts."

"I didn't know your preference, so better safe than sorry." Aspen suddenly looked incredibly shy.

"Well, you were right. I don't like them," I said, taking the one he handed to me.

"Like I always say," he said, sitting down on a rock off to the side and patting one next to him for me to join, "trust your sixth sense."

"When do you say that?"

"That would be the first time."

We ate in companionable silence until three quarters of my sandwich was gone and Aspen had moved onto his third granola bar. We tried to be oblivious, but it was hard not to be conscious of the day getting away from us.

I handed him my empty ziplock back, intending on finishing the last few bites of my PB and J on the hike.

Silence with Aspen was like knowing you'd locked the deadbolt of your house without second guessing it when you were on the cusp of sleep. It was certain and safe and the sort of silence that I imagined people thought of when they were looking for a quiet moment to ground themselves, to regroup. The only downside was the racing thoughts in my head.

A tug of war of joy and dread that I wasn't doing the right thing by being there, but in the end the side of my brain that insisted I lived in the moment won. Mostly because I knew that there would come a time I would recall moments like the one we were in and I'd be glad I kept it close until I could see the imprint of it on the palms of my hands, even long after I'd let him go.

"Are you waterfall ready?" Ap reached his hand down, pulling me up effortlessly.

"I've never been more —" The words got stuck in my throat and then a scream ripped from me with such jarring brutality I was sure I saw the trees tremble around us.

My scream didn't stop. As if it was being pulled right out of my fucking *soul*, it just got louder and louder. The sandwich went flying out of my hand in what direction, I had no idea. Aspen made some maneuver with his hands that looked like he was all at once trying to punch the air and grab some invisible perpetrator.

"*SNAKE!*" The word finally burst out of my mouth in a frequency that could be heard by human ears. "*SNAKE!*" I repeated, like it was suddenly the only word I knew.

I didn't think another second on my decision to launch myself directly at Aspen.

To his credit, he didn't even seem remotely phased by what was happening.

My hands grabbed at his backpack, at his jacket, at his arms and shoulders and chest. Things that I would have really liked to have taken my time in touching for the very first time, but this was life or death and I was in pure flight mode. I didn't stop my ascent up his body until one of my legs draped over his shoulder and my hands were holding onto his head while he turned in a circle trying to get his bearings without being able to see.

"You know," he reached up and parted my fingers so he could see out between them, "in a weird turn of events, I feel like I've been training for this exact moment."

"It's winter, there shouldn't be snakes in winter, Aspen!" My voice was nothing more than a pathetic rasp.

While I did my best to keep the next lot of screams secured in my chest, he explained a number of things to me. The first being that it was, and he stressed this as being really important, the size of his forearm.

"You have massive forearms," I squeaked, keeping my eyes locked on the beast.

"I'll be honest, that's a brand new compliment for me, Poppy, and I would like to take the appropriate amount of time to unpack that later." His voice was still muffled by the part of my hand that covered his mouth. "The sun's out, love, it was probably just trying to catch some UV." Aspen delivered that fact like it was cute.

*Cute.*

I didn't take a single breath while I watched it start to move, slithering away like it hadn't just shaken the foundations of my sanity. It was at that point that I realized that it was very, *very* silent and I was very, *very* wrapped around Aspen's still form.

He moved slowly like he didn't want to startle me, reaching up and around for me in the same way he had done for his backpack, pulling me around to his front. The light green of his eyes had all but disappeared on account of how large his pupils had become.

His eyes were half lidded and his mouth parted while he kept me pressed to him in a hold that was both too strong and not strong enough.

My heart started to pound for an entirely different reason than it had before. Images of the sort of underwear I knew he was wearing filtered into my mind, of how solid he felt beneath my hands, how he still smelled like violets and pine trees even after we'd been hiking for hours.

Aspen started to let me down. He did it so slowly I'd become hopeful that it would never end. On my way down I felt every single part of his body with every single part of mine. I wanted to climb back up just so he could do it again.

And again. I wanted the fast pass and to only ever do this for the rest of my life.

The way he was looking at me didn't lighten up, the heat in his eyes or the way his gaze dropped to my mouth didn't change.

"I feel like you handled that with incredible grace," he murmured. Even though his words were supposed to be light, there wasn't any humor in his voice. It was strained with whatever he was battling against in his own head.

"I appreciate that," my voice was so gravelly that it hurt to speak but I was glad for the cover up, otherwise it would have been very clear exactly what I was thinking.

"Poppy," Aspen whispered, his hands still holding my waist, the tips of his fingers digging into the side of my ribs like he was desperate to hold me there, to keep me close and all to himself.

"Yes?" There was no mistaking the shake in my voice that time.

"I think I'm going to kiss you now." He was already leaning in.

"This is breaking so many of my rules." I was impressed with myself that I'd managed to say that much. At least I couldn't say I didn't try.

"Which ones?"

"Pretty much all of them," I swallowed.

"I think I'm still going to kiss you," he said again.

I'd spent so long telling myself no. Reprimanding myself over and over for *wanting* more than I had, even as I'd continuously tried running towards that very thing without any hope of ever finding it.

"Okay," I said, knowing it was wrong, knowing that I shouldn't. "Yes," I said again. "Okay." Just as his lips met mine.

I had tried my very best to remember what it felt like to be kissed by Aspen.

Tried to remember the way his lips fit against mine and how it felt different to exist in my own skin when his hand came up to hold my face. I had been so far off pinpointing the remnants of how it felt now that I was comparing the memory to the real thing.

I wasn't ready for it like I thought I'd be. The feeling of his rough, calloused hands moving to both sides of my face.

The first kiss was gentle.

He pulled back to look at my face. Eyes darting to the points where his hands touched me before moving back to my eyes and then down to my mouth. It looked like he was trying to convince himself it was really happening. I knew that because I was doing the same.

"Friends don't kiss like this, right?" I whispered, because I knew that they didn't and I wanted him to help me break my rules. I moved my hands up to hold onto his wrists, to keep him in place.

"It's different in every part of the country but I'm pretty sure it's standard here," he said, lips breaking apart into a little smile that made his eyes shine a brighter green than before.

"Okay," I said, falling into the lie and lifting up on my tip toes, "that's good."

This time when Aspen kissed me, he did it like he was trying to tell me a secret.

His lips were *so soft* and every swipe of his tongue against the seam of my mouth made my body jolt with little zaps of pleasure, going off behind my eyelids and traveling down the length of my spine to settle low in my belly. Every touch of his lips on mine overwhelmed me. I was completely made of helium right then with no hope of ever being a regular woman ever again.

Aspen's hands shifted, one sinking into the roots of my hair, gripping hard, and the other to the middle of my back, pressing me further into him.

I couldn't help the sound that escaped me. I tried to hold it in but I was becoming a person I didn't recognize with every second that his hands were on me.

I stiffened, completely embarrassed that that had just happened. This was not something I had experience in, feeling like I was being unwrapped in the best way (cue all three and a half of my sexual experiences, please).

I tried to pull away but Ap's grip on me tightened, "No," he said, his lips hovering over mine. "Don't go."

"I—" I wanted to explain to him that the noise was an accident. That I hadn't meant to, but I didn't get a chance before his lips were back on mine and I was suddenly no longer standing on the ground.

Aspen moved us around like someone who knew the trail we were on like the back of his hand, leaning me against a tree with my legs around his waist and I could feel *everything*. His hands were slow but seeking as they made their way under my coat. The expanse of his broad palms against ribs, the very tips of his fingers skimming the underside of my breasts.

It was involuntary the way my hips started to circle. Moving and seeking the friction he had made me absolutely desperate for and, *sweet slipping sanity*, this man was well endowed.

"Poppy," he said my name like a curse word and all it did was serve to short circuit whatever parts of my brain still worked the way they should've been.

"Yes?" That didn't sound like my voice, it didn't feel like my hands that were hungry to touch the warm skin I knew lay just under his sweatshirt.

"I have to stop touching you, but I can't," he admitted, like it was a truth he hadn't ever wanted to share. "But if I don't," he continued, his mouth tracing a line along my jaw before it settled against my ear, "especially with you doing *this*," he dropped his hands to my hips and delivered one, mind altering grind of his own, "I'm probably...I'm *definitely* going to do some very bad things to you."

"Bad?" The word was an incoherent gasp. What I actually meant to say was, 'yes fucking please'.

"Yeah." Aspen was breathing hard and my eyes were

completely focused on the way his throat worked as he swallowed. His eyes were looking down to where he was *still* grinding against me. "I can think of at least four different laws I'd like to break right now that include both you and this tree, but I'm not sure you'd like that."

"Is that what friends do here too?" My whole body was shaking. Could he feel it?

"Oh, I'm pretty confident it is, yeah," he said, voice strained, "but not on public hiking trails and not before dinner."

This man had the willpower of a saint.

"I'm not that hungry and I've always liked nature," I said, still breathless and gulping and wriggling against him.

He nuzzled his head into the side of my neck, releasing his laughter in warm bursts against my flushed skin that made me dizzy. He started to pull away slowly and it injected this bizarre fear right into my blood that this would be the last time I'd be held like this, looked at like this, by him.

"Ap." What was I supposed to even say? I wasn't sure, but whatever it was I wanted to say it all.

He rested his forehead against mine before lowering his mouth to me again. Testing and tasting and exploring, pulling more of those noises from me that I was coming to realize he liked. Aspen pulled me from the tree and slid me down his body once again like he'd heard every wish I had thought.

"You're actually killing me," he said.

I was shocked because they had been the words on the tip of my tongue. In the end, I just stood there looking like...well probably like I'd respectfully been ravished by the drummer of the biggest rock band in the whole fucking world.

Aspen turned away, his hand already reaching into the front of his pants to sort out what had to be the biggest penis I'd ever almost come into contact with.

I took the opportunity to drop my hands down onto my knees, bending at the waist. I was wheezing, I could hear it.

It was an involuntary reaction at the reality of what had just happened.

I didn't manage to collect myself in time to play off that entire experience as anything but religious. I righted myself after he'd already turned back towards me, a sly lift to his lips lingering, probably because I no doubt resembled a range of blush colored produce and that was perfectly acceptable to him.

"What if we see another snake?" I said, lips still tingling and head still swimming while I tried to take steady steps on wobbly legs to slide my hand into the one he held out for me.

"Then we'll resume our previous positions." Aspen started dragging me along behind him before stopping abruptly. In the same movement he turned around in, he reached for me, taking my face with his hands once more and kissing me in a completely different way than he had just moments ago.

This one was desperate and wanting and achingly familiar to all the knotted, messy emotions that were currently learning the choreography to *Footloose* inside my stomach.

"Friends?" he asked in a whispered tone after letting go, his tall frame bent over with his forehead resting on my shoulder.

"Definitely," I said back, unable to stop the smile from creeping into my voice.

# 11

## January 24th

### Poppy

"You know it's not common practice to take your goldfish to the movies, right?" Leah asked around a mouth full of popcorn.

"Of course." A small frown formed between my eyebrows at her need to state the obvious. Natalie was tucked under my arm hidden gently beneath the confines of my jacket in her travel tank while I walked with practiced ease that meant her water didn't slosh at all. "I'm not sure what that has to do with anything, though."

"No, all good, just checking." Leah was chewing so loudly it wasn't like she was just in my ears but actually living inside my brain.

"I'm walking in so I'm going to have to hang up in a second." I headed to the back of the theater and claimed a seat in the back left corner and set Nat up on her own chair.

"God, I am *SO* excited for this movie, Miles Teller can come to mommy."

"Leah, you can't keep referring to yourself as 'mommy'." I scrunched my nose up. "We've talked about this."

"It will scare the children. Yes, yes. I know." I could practically hear her eyes rolling.

"Okay the trailers are starting, call you after."

"Love you, sissy," Leah whispered as they started on her end too.

"Love you more."

I quickly snapped a photo of Nat in her theater chair and posted it to her instagram: *Just a fish, ready for a little Miles Teller. #cometomommy*

I snorted to myself and decided to let Leah find that one all on her own. Most of the captions I wrote were in some way inspired by my best friend.

We tried to do this once every couple of months. Leah and I would find a movie we both wanted to watch and search high and low for theaters in our own cities that were playing them at the exact same time. She would go on her end, and I'd go on my end and it would be sort of like we were doing it together.

I started bringing Nat about four years ago when I was overwhelmed with unyielding guilt at leaving her out of all the fun. That's when I discovered travel containers. I always just moved her from house to house in a big bucket that sat in the passenger footwell of whatever moving truck I'd rented, the whole travel container thing totally changed the game for us.

I wasn't as big of a fan of bringing her out nowadays given she was going to be fifteen in April (sort of, that was when Casimir had gifted her to me. I wasn't even sure Natalie was a girl, it was just the vibe I got), but every so often I made an exception.

Leah had been pleading her case, leaning really heavily into the 'pros' of her 'pros and cons' list on why *Top Gun Maverick* needed to be our next movie. Most of her points revolved around the actors Miles Teller and some other guy named Glen.

I admittedly was enraptured with the movie and, after it was done, proceeded to talk animatedly to Leah about it all the way to the station, on the train and right to the front door of my house.

"This is going in my top five," Leah said, her own keys jingling on the other end.

"Like, life moments?"

"Bless, sissy, but no," she sighed and I could tell just by the disjointed sounds on the other end of the phone that I plopped down on my couch almost the exact same time that she plopped down on hers.

"Fair enough. I suppose you do have a more exciting life than me."

"I actually reject that statement. Right now, at this moment, you have the number of a famous drummer right in your phone."

My immediate reaction was to exclaim some sort of profanity and tell her she was losing her marbles, but then I remembered that actually, that was true. It wasn't the reason why I'd struggled to stay focused at work for the last few days, though.

No, that was more along the lines of still coming to terms that I had left his body pressed against every part of mine and just the thought of that made every part of me, mind body and spirit, erupt into tingles. That I was all but a stiff wind away from collapsing into a heap of goo if I really let myself remember the way it felt to have him speak words that had no business being as sexy as they were against my skin. That my stomach had learned all on it's own how to do the Can-Can when I remembered his laugh, his hands, his warmth, his *hands*–

"Poppy?" Leah called through the phone like she was projecting her voice through a megaphone.

"And now I'm deaf." I scowled even though she couldn't see me.

"You didn't answer my question," she whined while I reached for my laptop and lifted the lid.

Every warm and tingly sensation went cold at the web browser pulled up for apartments in Banks City. It was about a six hour drive away from where I was now in the city of Blazewood and the destination I'd decided on.

"I didn't hear your question, but I need you to help me look for apartments. Nothing I've looked at is decent," I grumbled, refreshing the page and looking through the same listings I'd looked at last night.

Leah was quiet on the other end for so long I pulled the phone from my ear just to see if we were still connected.

"Sissy? You still there?" I clicking over to page two. "I can send you the link."

"Poppy," she started, speaking slowly and with just the right amount of hesitation that I knew immediately what conversation she was going to broach. It was one we'd had many times before. "You just settled into the place you're at now. Actually, that's a lie, most of your stuff is still in boxes and you have one glass unpacked. We had to take turns drinking water when I was there."

"Leah, you know I don't like to stay put for longer than a year." The words were rehearsed. They were the same ones I said every time we had this conversation because this need to keep moving was connected to the part of myself that lived behind that huge, metal, impenetrable door in my mind. The one I only unlocked and opened when it was just me and I didn't have to worry about what came out or who would see it.

My voice sounded calm but also like I'd just sat bolt straight. Muscles locked to brace for an impending attack, but even I could tell I was exhausted.

"Yeah," she started, and I could picture her chewing on her fingernails. "I know but I just thought that eventually, you'd…" She didn't finish that sentence, but I knew what she wanted to say. That eventually I'd settle down, that I'd find somewhere that stuck. Eventually I'd stop searching, or looking, or seeking, or running.

"He wouldn't want you to be living like this, Penelope."

"Leah." Her name was a warning not to keep going. Not to push. Her simple mention of my brother made that door in my mind rattle.

"No, I have to say it because I'm it." *Push.* "I'm who you have and if Casimir was here he'd kick my ass for not saying the words out loud. He'd hate this for you, Poppy." *Push* "All of it. Always moving, never settling down, never just *stopping*. And I think you hate when I bring it up so much because you know I'm right."

My eyes stung with the tears that weren't there and my chest was heaving with so many things; with anger, and hurt and sadness and guilt. Aching with the need to release words

I didn't mean and things I'd never in a million years would ever want to say to my friend.

I bit my lip hard enough to draw blood, until I was sure I could speak without my words being overpowered by one of the hundreds of choking hollow sobs I'd swallowed down in front of her.

This was why I'd split myself into two. I knew she wouldn't recognise me if she saw the person I became when all of the darkest things I felt and carried came out, and I knew she wouldn't want to stay.

"But he's not here, Leah. So, I guess it doesn't really matter what he'd say." I ended the call and did my best to forget the words so full of truth she had spoken, and the words so full of lies I had spoken back.

It would matter.

There were so many things I needed to tell him. To hear him say back. But that was impossible.

I spent the rest of the night staring at listings for apartments I already knew I hated before even stepping foot into them, still surrounded by boxes I hadn't unpacked for so long that I really didn't remember what was even in them.

I walked into the staff kitchen the next day at work on autopilot feeling like everything was wrong after my conversation with Leah the night before.

We hardly ever fought. It was almost impossible for there to be anything said that we couldn't fix right in the moment with either a sarcastic quip or a dose of reality in the form of calling the other person out on their shit. I know that's what she did last night and even though there was a big part of me that knew what she said had some truth in it, it wasn't the same. She didn't know the whole story and I knew that was my doing.

I knew that she hurt when I hurt. That was just one of the things that her heart was made of. Leah was an empath of the highest level, another reason why I'd made the decision to deal with all the very hardest things that had ever happened to me in the way I had. I'd always had Leah, before I'd been stupid and selfish and impulsive and the sole reason my brother had lost his life. For a long time I think I felt like if I didn't have Leah, if she hadn't been there for me the way she'd been, I'd have disappeared completely.

So, that's pretty much the way things were going so far today. Sad, lonely, guilty. All those wonderful things were what made up the Poppy of the present, which explained entirely why I had to sit on the floor of the train and fix my shoes after putting them on the wrong feet before I left the house.

My phone started to buzz in my hand. My heart immediately started its departure from the vicinity of my body when it was Aspen's name staring back at me.

"Hello, Poppy," his voice rang through crisp and clear.

"Hello, Aspen." My smile spread across my face like perfectly, ooey-gooey melty butter on warm bread because I couldn't help myself. This, *this,* was the Aspen-Effect.

I put my leftover spaghetti that I found right at the back of my fridge from so long ago I actually couldn't remember when I'd cooked it, into the microwave and punched in two minutes for it to heat up.

"I'm calling about our second date." He delivered the words so casually it took me a second to realize what he'd said.

I completely missed the bench I intended to lean on again.

"*Fuck me,*" I mumbled, catching myself before becoming intimate with the floor.

Aspen gasped dramatically, "But you're at work?" The sounds of cymbals and movement came through the phone. "I haven't ever had an office job. Do they let you do that sort of thing now?" He was laughing without laughing, I could just tell. "Is it too forward of me to say that your assertiveness is a real turn on? I think I'm turned on."

"You think? Like you're not sure?" I could feel the heat taking over my face, so conflicting at the laughter trapped in my chest and the guilt from my conversation with Leah that lingered at the back of my throat, sour and upsetting.

"No, I'm sure," he said. "Very, very turned on." His voice was full of the things he was feeling. The perfect sound to the look that I knew would be on his face.

That one so like the sun.

"Aspen," I sighed, "We're just friends, remember? Friends don't date."

"That's not true," he countered.

"It's not?" I knew it was. I also knew friends didn't kiss pressed up against trees or know all the places one another might be soft or very, very, *very* hard.

I'd learned that as well as hiking and a penchant for creating peculiar definitions for common words, Ap enjoyed toeing what had fast become a very murky line, one we'd both been walking since last weekend. The problem was, I really, *really* liked how murky it had become. Especially when I let myself forget all the reasons I drew it in the first place.

"Why do you think brunch became such a big thing?" Aspen delivered that line like it was a truth as old as time.

"That's not at all true."

"I wholeheartedly disagree. Friends have been dating since the 30's," he said around what now sounded like a mouth full of food.

"The 30's?" I wondered when I would stop being surprised by this man. Probably never.

"Now," he continued on, undeterred, "our second date."

"Popsicle, my girl!"

My stomach dropped immediately at Todd's arrival. I feel it pertinent to mention once again that his desk was so far on the other side of the office that you couldn't even *see* this kitchen. Actually, I knew for a fact that you had to first walk by the kitchen on *that* side of the office to get to *this* one.

"Lord, no," I mumbled into my phone, turning the screen protectively in case he tried to see who I was speaking to for some unhinged reason, not that I expected him to know who 'Ap' was.

"*Whose* girl?" Aspen sounded curious, but there was something in his voice that sounded like raised hackles.

I could see it now, how he'd save me from this incredibly unwanted and recurring life-mare. The scene played out in my head immediately; Aspen would appear out of nowhere, stepping into this office kitchen that always smelt faintly of corn, and in a strange but not completely unwelcome chain of events, he'd fling a drumstick like a throwing star. It would embed itself perfectly in the wall between Todd and I like an impassable barrier. I'd be speechless, maybe taken aback, but still impressed and Todd would fall through the floor.

I was losing my mind.

I cleared my throat, "Hi, Todd." I wonder if he could tell how uninvited this conversation was.

"Who ya speaking to, Poompaloompa?"

"Did he just call you *Poompaloompa?*" Aspen asked, sounding absolutely affronted for me, I did my best to ignore him in favor of getting rid of Todd.

"I'm on the phone Todd, do you mind?" If I sounded like I'd just sat on a thumb tack, it's because that's how Todd made me feel most days.

"Is it that elusive boyfriend of yours?" He said the words in that sort of exaggerated way that you used when mimicking what your siblings said in an effort to piss them off. I really hoped Aspen still spoke to me after this.

"Yep." I felt like I shouted the word. Delivered it in the sort of way that made me feel like I should have accompanied it with a fist pump or a high kick.

"Oh my god," Aspen whispered, sounding like he was bouncing up and down with excitement.

"Yes, that's exactly who I'm speaking to." I tried to keep a pleasant look on my face but it really felt more like a cringe and suddenly I really needed to pee.

"Oh, Poompaloompa. This is a real gift, what you're giving me right now. Maybe even the best thing I've ever witnessed." Aspen's delighted laughter trickled through my phone and now I wanted to steal a single sock from each of his pairs and hide them from him forever for being entertained by my misery.

Todd's face did a lot of things in that moment and the few seconds that followed, none of them good and all of them made my palms sweaty.

"I don't believe you. Come on, let me see your phone." He actually went to grab for it.

"What? *Hey*—" I took a step to the side just as the microwave beeped with the now heated pasta I no longer wanted.

"Is this dude serious?" Aspen's voice was harder now. No trace of the light hearted joking from before.

"Ap, I'll call you back." My feet had gotten so hot they started to slip around in my socks and all I really wanted to do was run to Winny and report that Todd has intestinal issues of his own and personally requested his assistance.

"Penelope, don't—"

"I finish at 5:30," I whispered quickly. "I'll call you then." I ended the call before I could hear his reply, ducking around Todd to grab my food so quickly he didn't have time to block my path with his bulky frame.

The entire ordeal had turned my stomach so bad, every bite of my pasta tasted sour. In an effort to prove how much Todd *didn't* get to me, I ate every last bite.

*Take that, Todd.*

Like when most things set me on edge, I poured every ounce of brain space I had into doing my job right until the clock on my desk showed 5:30 PM on the dot.

The seconds waiting for the elevator to arrive left my mind wandering to the conversation I had with Leah again. The reminder of how things had ended made me feel sick to my stomach. I couldn't remember the last time we'd fought like that. That was the exact moment Todd called out to hold the elevator and I once again pretended not to hear him.

I tapped the call button again frantically, breathing through the swirl of nausea that refused to dissipate by clinging to the idea of calling Ap back to talk about our friend-date as soon as I was out the doors of the building. It was completely inappropriate (Poppy, meet line-drawn-in-sand-you-drew-yourself-with-purpose-and-good-reason) but the thought improved my mood drastically. I was so improved that I didn't notice the black sedan parked just outside my building, or the tall, dark figure that hopped out wearing sunglasses and a baseball cap and a thick winter coat that was way too heavy for the mild day we were having. Not until he was standing right in front of me.

"Hello, Poppy," he said, grinning down at me in a way that made my knees wobble and my heart stop.

# 12

## January 25th

**Poppy**

"Oh my god, Aspen!" My hands fluttered haphazardly on either side of his face like somehow that would help disguise his identity to the outside world. I really couldn't say why, but it felt helpful. "*You're outside my building!*"

Those were the actual words that came out of my mouth. Not '*seeing your whole person with my own eyes is the biggest relief I've ever known*' or '*is it weird that I've thought of you so thoroughly I accidentally signed off an email with your name instead of mine today?*'.

"I told you where I worked once, and only sort of, how, *how*, did you even remember that?"

"It may surprise you to know that I listen to the words that come out of your mouth. Also, typing into Google 'transcribing company on Eastborne Avenue in Blazewood' produced exactly one result so, here I am." He paused for a second, a small frown growing bigger by the millisecond between his brows, "That's creepy, isn't it?"

"In a very flattering way, yes." My reply seemed to be good enough for him because he looked utterly delighted at that. The look on his face did its job in distracting me from my panic, but only for a second.

"Aspen," I whispered to him frantically, "you're still *here*, at my *work*."

"Yes, I thought we already covered that in a creepy but flattering way," he leaned in closer to me, whispering back.

"But what about the—" It was at that moment I noticed them from the corner of my eye. The paparazzi.

"Shit." He'd noticed what had captured my attention and pulled his hat down lower over his head, like that would all of a sudden convince the men in the distance with the very big camera lenses that Aspen was not in fact who he really was. "Sorry, Poppy. I thought I lost them."

It was at that exact moment that Todd exited the building. He looked up from his phone and came to a standstill right in front of us.

"Pop tart," he said, adding yet another name to the ever growing list of things that made me want to scream into a trash can in an effort to curb my desire to kick him in the balls. "Who's this?"

I'll admit, I froze.

In my freezing, I considered for one, teeny weeny moment saying that Aspen was my boyfriend, because then Todd might actually leave me alone. Here was a real life man who knew my name. First, middle *and* last. What more proof did Todd need than that?

My stomach lurched with a serve and soul shuddering wave

of nausea so intense I reached out to grip Aspen's jacket sleeve on reflex. But then I thought of the men with the cameras, and the fact that Todd was probably a whole four seconds away from realizing who was standing in front of him. I forced myself to swallow the feeling down as best I could.

The real issue here was that Aspen was clearly thinking of a plan of his own.

I knew that he'd probably put two and two together, realizing that this was in fact that hemorrhoid of a human he'd overheard on the phone.

It should have surprised exactly zero people that at the exact same time that Aspen said, "I'm her boyfriend", I decided to deliver a cool and collected, "He's my cousin."

...*Super*.

The only way to describe how I was feeling was sort of like how someone *might* feel when they knew they were about to be electrocuted. My grip on his sleeve tightened so fiercely I was worried I'd never be able to unfurl my fingers. We'd have to cut off his jacket sleeve and I'd forever be forced to walk around with the reminder of this exact moment clenched between my phalanges.

I turned to look up just as Aspen looked down at me. Just in time to see his green eyes, so bright they looked luminescent, widen to a comedic size and his lips thin in what was a very valiant effort of keeping a neutral expression. He was *enjoying this*.

I could tell my own expression had turned incredulous because he had to close his eyes, shaking his head minutely as if fighting every urge he had *not* to burst out into tear-filled, joyful laughter.

"Woah," Todd sounded like he'd just been tasered. "You're...

you're *dating* your cousin?"

I was really going to throw up. "Hold on. That's actually not —"

"Holy shit, Poppy? You're dating your cousin?" Todd cut me off with the same exact question I'd been trying to answer which seemed on all accounts unproductive to me.

On instinct I moved a little closer to Aspen, the gentle woodsy pine scent with his signature hint of violets made me feel a little less like I was about to barf my brains out. It was getting so bad I could feel the sweat starting to pebble on my hairline.

I'd been anxious before, but never like this.

"Your friend looks a little green, Pop tart," Aspen's voice strained with the obvious effort of trying not to laugh. Meanwhile, I was panicking because his casual use of the color 'green' sent a jolt through my whole body and my hand immediately clamped over my mouth.

Satan's blazing balls, I was *really* going to throw up. Really, really, *really*.

Just when I thought all hell was going to break loose and my soul was screaming for someone, *anyone* – I might've even settled for Todd at this point – to help me, the barnacle in question finally looked right at Aspen.

Ah. We were so close. *So, so close.*

There had been a minute there where we'd have been able to get out of this without Todd looking at Aspen and realizing that the drummer of *Lady Luck* was standing two feet in front of him, and as far as Todd was concerned in that moment, dating his own cousin.

There was no way he wouldn't have noticed.

Todd was a firm believer in casual Fridays at work, and

I could remember maybe one time where he hadn't worn a shirt that had something to do with *Lady Luck* on it.

Todd's mouth went slack at the same time as his nostrils flared. The exact moment he realized who Aspen was.

"Ap," I whispered, knowing he could hear the stress in my voice with a hint of relief, the latter from the miracle that it was words that came out of my mouth, not regurgitated spaghetti.

"Yep," he replied, letting me know that he too saw how this was all about to backfire a lot faster than perhaps originally thought. With his arm still around my shoulder, he backed us up towards the Taurus.

From then, it happened very quickly.

The passenger door opened, firm but gentle hands pushed me in, Aspen's mouth close to my ear whispering a rushed *"Go, go, go!"* And then he was running. Sliding across the bonnet of his car like he was James Dean reincarnated, with a grin so big I took another mental snap. Another moment for me to hold, hopefully tight enough that even when I closed my eyes years from now I'd see it as clearly as I did right then.

"You have absolutely no idea how much I've wanted to do that my whole life," Aspen panted, out of breath and sparkly eyed.

Todd had his phone pulled out just as we were pulling away from the sidewalk.

My face was frozen in place as I tried very hard to think through exactly what happened, but my spiral was interrupted by a loud, unrestrained laugh from the man beside me.

*"Did you see his face?"* Aspen wheezed with both hands gripping the steering wheel.

I also wanted to laugh. Sort of. I was dizzy, so I also wanted to lie down.

Mostly, I wanted to empty the contents of my stomach but the very chaotic way things had just descended out of control momentarily pushed that unfortunate desire from my mind.

"Aspen, he thinks I'm your cousin." I was unable to do more than whisper.

Ap did a double take at the look on my face. I was certain he was confusing my need to hurl with fear of the hole that we'd both just happily plopped ourselves into.

"Well, on the upside, maybe if he thinks your sexual desires are a little under the burrow he might leave you be? From what I heard over the phone–Poppy? Woah, *hey*...are you okay?" He reached over to tuck a loose bit of hair behind my ear and if I hadn't been in absolute peril I might have lost my *ever loving mind*. Maybe, I would've had time to bear witness to the opposing parts of myself partaking in some serious hand to hand combat. Fighting over being wooed and reminding myself this was absolutely not what friends did.

"He thinks I'm having sex with my cousin," I said the words out loud and couldn't stop the immediate onslaught of full body tingles that pushed me over the edge into hysterical laughter. That's when it really hit me. It hit me in a very big way. "Aspen, I'm going to throw up." My hand clamped over my mouth.

His face fell instantaneously. "Wait, really?" He looked at me with serious concern and even though he was double checking, he'd already pulled the car over to the side of the road. "Poppy, it's not that big of a deal, I swear–"

I didn't get to hear the rest of the words that came out of Aspen's mouth, because every single bite I ate for lunch was suddenly staring back at me from the road in front of me.

"I'm going to puke in your bed." The words were a pathetic grumble that I pushed out of my mouth for the third time. The room was spinning faster than I was sure anything had ever spun in the history of time and space. All I really wanted to do was keep my head tucked firmly beneath Aspen's jaw while he carried me through the elevator doors and into his penthouse.

It was silly, maybe, but I'd imagined walking into this very place so many times. Thought about how it would look and feel and smell. Wondered how Aspen would decorate his home and if I'd be surprised or proven right in any of my predictions.

Let's just say being carried bridal style while fretting that there were chunks of spaghetti on my shirt was absolutely not how I had envisioned it coming together.

*At all.*

"That's okay," he said, dropping a gentle kiss onto my forehead and heading straight for what I assumed was somewhere I could wrap myself around a toilet and never leave.

"I smell like puke."

"A little."

I tried to whack his stomach but I'm certain my hand didn't move at all. "You're not supposed to agree with me." I wanted to cry.

"We're about to rectify the situation." He quickly opened a door that led to a clean, but clearly very masculine bathroom from what I could make out in the small crack between my eyelids. The second he did it, it was like my body knew it was safe to let loose again.

"Oh no." They were the only words that made it out of my mouth before Aspen set me right in front of the toilet and I tried not to think about the fact that I sounded like a pterodactyl screaming into his porcelain throne.

"Your toilet is very clean," I said between heaves.

"Thank you," he said, sounding close and far away at the same time. His voice too soft and too loud. I could feel his hands combing back my hair and wondered if it possible to be smitten and so embarrassed you could die all in the some moment? Because that was me.

"I think my soul is trying to leave my body." My voice echoed around the toilet bowl.

"The door is closed so it can't get out, we'll put it back later." Somehow, that was incredibly reassuring and all I could do was nod before I was hit with another round of wretches.

"Aspen." His name was a barely audible rasp. "You need to leave," I said when I could get in a breath.

"Not gonna happen." But then he turned around and went straight out the door we'd entered in.

Once he left, I was confused for a while before deciding I'd clearly hallucinated the last few minutes of conversation and had obviously reached the end of my tether. It was clear to me now that I was going to die from this.

I didn't hear him come back on account of the banshee that seemed to be squatting in Aspen's plumbing so I jumped with an undignified squeak when a cool, damp washcloth was pressed to my forehead. I didn't even have it in me to tell him to leave again, in either reality or via hallucination, because the small relief from what he was doing pulled a moan so guttural from my body it was possible to confuse me for a bison in heat.

He stayed there with me until my body was cramping with nothing left to expel and I was so exhausted I was pretty sure I fell asleep with my head in the toilet.

"Poppy," Ap's voice was gentle and soft and I wanted to wrap it around me forever.

I peeled open my aching eyelids to see a very concerned version of Aspen's face peering down at me.

"I think we need to get you cleaned up."

"What's happening to me?" I croaked out, letting my body flop to the tiled floor. "I'm dying."

"You're not dying." His hand was rubbing circles on my back, voice still gentle.

"This is karma."

"Oh? What did you do that was so bad?"

I knew he was joking, but if he knew what I'd done, he'd never look at me the same again. There was nothing that I could say, even if I wanted to, the words just wouldn't come out because more than anything, I was a coward.

I don't think Aspen thought I was a coward at that moment though, I think he just thought I fell asleep with my head next to his toilet for a second time because he whispered my name again, his hand still gentle on my back.

"Mm?" It was all I could muster to say.

"I think you have food poisoning. What did you eat today?"

Just the thought of it had my body heaving again, but nothing came out. "Oh no." I tried to drag in gulps of air.

"It was the spaghet—" Another heave.

"Spaghetti?" He said the cursed word for me.

"It was at the back of my fridge," I said, refusing to look up at him. "It tasted sour."

"You *knowingly* ate sour spaghetti?" He sounded incredulous but also incredibly entertained.

"I was sticking it to Todd."

"Oh, Poompaloompa," Aspen sighed, like he knew this had 'Poppy' written all over it.

"And now I am covered in barf and you're calling me by Todd's nicknames."

I cried. I really, truly cried. It had been the first time in over a decade and this was what got me.

His thumb swiped under my eye, catching a runaway tear. "How you haven't jumped his bones is beyond me."

Aspen graced me with a beautiful grin when I dared to finally stare up at him. "Do you think you can stand?"

I gave a small nod and accepted his help to get to my feet. The dizziness hit me immediately and I reached out unceremoniously for anything to hold onto.

"I've got you, Pop." And he did, his hold on me was firm and strong.

"Dizzy," I mumbled, keeping my eyes closed tight. "Just set me on the shower floor and turn the water on, I'll be okay."

"I can't stress enough how much I'm not going to be doing that."

"Aspen, you can't help me shower." It took all my energy to look at him with as much passion as I felt about that situation.

"Yes, I can."

"But you'll see me naked." Even as I said the words there wasn't any real worry to be felt. The idea of Aspen seeing me naked didn't scare me, it almost seemed inevitable. It was entirely possible that was the bacteria talking.

"Poppy, you need help because you're not well. I promise my eyes won't wander but if you really don't want my help I can call Allie." He sounded so genuine I didn't even consider the fact that he was only saying it to appease me.

"You're never going to be able to look at me again. All my sex appeal just, *poof*. Gone. You'll think of me and only ever be able to think of the words 'pterodactyl mating call' and 'toilet.'" I blame the delirium from two week old spaghetti bolognese for every word coming out of my mouth.

Aspen didn't say anything as he reached for the hem of my shirt, a silent request for me to lift up my arms. I didn't fight him because I knew I didn't want anyone else here with me but him.

My shirt dropped to the floor next to us and I could see through my half lidded eyes the way his eyes flicked to the scar on my shoulder. Aside from that moment, his eyes never left my face and he didn't say anything about it.

"Poppy," his voice was quiet but firm, "believe me when I say that I think you might just be the sexiest woman I've ever met in my entire life. That I've thought of you in ways a friend really never should, even in this part of the country, and that nothing about you being unwell because you decided to eat month-old pasta will change that for me. Except that I'm actually pretty impressed you downed an entire portion of something that no doubt tasted like actual feet."

"Two weeks," I mumbled half-heartedly. "And much worse than feet."

"I promise," he said again, "I won't look until you want me to. Okay?" He didn't move, not a single muscle until I nodded my head and then he reached for the button of my pants. Stripped completely down and not fully comprehending that it was the firm, rough, calloused grip of Aspen's hands around my waist keeping me up right, I was led to the shower.

I was certain that Aspen kept his word because his hands didn't leave my waist from where he stood at my back. Actually, I was pretty sure he still had all his clothes on as he murmured where to grab the soap and where to reach for the tooth brush prepped with a little strip of peppermint toothpaste, which he'd also promised was new.

The next thing I remembered was a big, fluffy towel that smelt exactly like Aspen being wrapped around me moments before a shirt that smelt just the same was pulled over my head.

My favorite part was the body, warm and solid that held me like I was this incredibly precious thing and I wondered then, because it had been so long since I'd known it and I couldn't be certain, if maybe this was what finally coming home felt like.

<h1 style="text-align:center">13</h1>

<h1 style="text-align:center">January 25th</h1>

## Aspen

Poppy was asleep by the time I tucked her into my bed. It was a weird realization that, as an adult, I'd never required the use of a bucket up until that moment. I opted for the next best thing and put my least used pot next to the bed along with a glass of water.

Poppy was restless. Soft little mewing noises coming from her every so often as she kept herself tucked into a tight ball in the middle of my bed.

I watched her feeling helpless and infinitely stupid. Because it *had* been a stupid idea to show up at her work. Stupid and selfish because she didn't realize it yet, but there would be paparazzi camping outside from here on out thanks to my reckless, impulsive decision. It was like my brain malfunctioned at the very idea of being close to her and every rule I lived by just went out the window.

I had spent a long time doing right by everyone around me,

regardless of what it cost me. Thinking of everyone before myself because the mere thought of *not* sent me into such an intense panic I was certain my heart would give out on me. The beats thumping through my body like a vibration so intense there was no way I could cope with it.

I didn't realize my hands were tugging so hard at the roots of my hair until another of Poppy's mewling cries broke the spell. There was a reason I was the way I was and this was the perfect example of why things were better when I thought of everyone else before myself.

I ran a hand down my face swallowing back a groan at the thought of how I was going to explain this to her when she suddenly sat up, eyes wide and terrified with a hand over her mouth. I sprang for the pot so fast I literally tripped on the edge of the rumpled rug that had never sat right beneath my bed, landing with a loud and painful thump on the floor. Scrambling to my knees I had the pot in her lap and her hair pulled back while she gripped it like a lifeline.

Poppy was a lot smaller than me, but it became that much more noticeable with her frame swallowed up by my shirt. It made me want to protect her at all costs. To make sure that she always felt safe and cared for and happy.

The thoughts came at me so abruptly my body actively jolted backwards. I had known Poppy for barely three weeks and already it was becoming increasingly hard to remember any time before where I *hadn't* known her. To imagine any time in the future where I would have to refer to her in the past tense as someone I'd known once. It sent an ache through my whole body so visceral I almost needed to use the pot she clung to.

Her body trembled through the contracting waves of her

stomach trying to dispel something that was no longer there for a while until slowly, she started to relax.

"I'm okay," she croaked, handing me back the pot and looking so defeated it made me feel helpless all over again. I reached for the glass of water and handed it to her.

"Just take a really little sip." I didn't let go of the glass as she did just that, a small thrill zinging through me at her trusting me to help her. "That's my girl."

The words slipped out. I was almost positive Poppy didn't really register them, not when she mumbled a small "Thanks," and started to settle back down into the covers.

In reality, Poppy was not mine.

Even covered in my shirt, in my bed. The very idea that she wasn't mine all of a sudden made my hands go numb. For fear of reaching out to hold onto her without any intention of ever letting go, I started to move back to my spot against the wall where I'd dragged a chair from the dining table just to keep an eye on her.

Her hand reached out to grip mine, holding on with about as much strength as a squirrel.

"Aspen," she whispered from her spot facing away from me.

"I'm here." I was ready to do just about anything to make her feel better.

"Do friends cuddle in this part of the country?" Her voice was raspy and weak but I could imagine the hint of humor she'd probably intended to ask the question with.

No. *Nope*. No, they didn't.

Not by any definition even I had of the word, but because there wasn't that much more damage I could do tonight, I lifted back the covers and climbed in behind her.

Poppy was warm and soft and smelt like my body wash as

she nestled back into me. I did everything I could to think about absolutely anything except the way her ass was now pressed firmly against my crotch. Her perfect, round, mouth watering–

"Is this okay?" she asked, still wiggling her hips. The movement made me hiss and I reached out to grip her waist in a very desperate attempt to keep her still.

"Poppy, if you do that again I think you might actually kill me this time," I said around the strain of keeping my own shit together.

In an effort to diffuse what was about to become a much less friend-like situation than we were already in, I grappled for anything to help. Somehow I settled on that one time Dax and I nailed an empty fruit crate to the top of my skateboard from the bottom and didn't think much about it when he stepped on it and immediately impaled his foot on a nail. There was blood everywhere. My little seven year old self had never seen so much blood all at once before. Dax was so worried we'd get in trouble that he used the hand he'd held over the hole in his foot to cover my mouth, thus transferring all his foot-blood right onto my face.

My body relaxed as any fear of Poppy feeling my painfully hard cock against her ass was completely and totally averted.

"Oh," she sounded a little more awake now. "Sorry."

"It's okay," I grinned, giving in to temptation and nuzzling into the side of her neck.

This was the sweetest sort of torture. Poppy was *right here* and still completely out of my reach. Her hands wrapped around my forearm that I'd wound gently around her, mindful of her stomach.

She was so quiet for so long I thought she'd finally fallen

asleep, but then she spoke softly into the darkened room around us. "I'm sorry I ruined our second friend-date."

"This was actually far better than what I had planned."

"Oh, good." It was incredibly satisfying that I knew without looking that she would have delivered that with an epic eye roll if she'd been well enough.

"I have a photo of you sleeping with your head in the toilet. I think I want to blow it up and hang it on my wall."

"That's really sweet of you, Aspen."

"I know." My voice was muffled from where it was still pressed to the skin of her neck.

Poppy's body relaxed further into me.

By the time I spoke again there was no space between us at all. "You didn't ruin anything," I told her and meant every word. "I'm sorry I showed up at your work unannounced and that your best friend Todd now thinks you're sleeping with your cousin."

Poppy's body shook with laughter until she groaned and curled in on herself a little more. "No," she gasped. "No laughing, please."

"Got it," I said, pulling her back into me like I'd held her exactly like this before. Because that's how it felt, like my body knew hers, like her being in my bed was exactly how things had always been.

"I can't believe you saw me naked and covered in puke," she groaned. Her hands left their place on my arm to cover her face.

"I promise that I kept my eyes directly on your shoulder blades." I dropped a soft kiss on the slope of her neck. "I feel compelled to let you know; you have sublime shoulder blades."

"Aspen," she started, her reprimand sounding only half serious.

"I'm glad I was with you," I said seriously. "The idea of you dealing with this on your own makes me feel insane." I let the truth of that statement hang between us, wondering if she was able to read between the words I had spoken to the ones that I hadn't.

"Aspen, what are we doing?" she whispered, "I told you, I'm leaving."

"Because you only stay for a year and then you move on because you're looking for something you can't explain because it's complicated," I finished the explanation for her, as if the words hadn't been burned into my mind when she'd said them the first time.

"Yes."

"Why?" The single worded question left my tongue like a slingshot. I was breaking so many of my own rules tonight. I hadn't really expected her to answer, so when she did I held my breath for fear she'd stop.

"Because I'm scared. Because —"

"Because?"

Just when I didn't think she'd reply, her whispered words pierced the quiet between us. "I'm not always good, Aspen. There are things that I've done that I can't forget."

I wanted to say so many things to her then. To break apart every word she said and have her explain to me *why*. To explain to me *how* she, this person that when I was around her I might as well be standing right in the warmest part of the sun, had ever been allowed to feel like that.

"Things are better this way," she said before I'd even had a chance to organize my mind. "And, you know, I get to see all these different cities, and meet all these different people and no one gets hurt. It's just better this way."

It sounded like a line she'd rehearsed in the mirror. The inflections of her voice so unlike the person I'd come to know.

"Poppy," I said, swallowing thickly at my own nerve, "I don't believe you."

"I know." Her whisper was gentle as it seeped into my skin and splintered right into my chest. In what was the most honesty I think I'd ever had from her she added, "Me either."

I wanted to push her, to tell her that it sounded to me like she was doing a whole lot of running in the wrong direction. That of everything she'd just said, there was only one part that was true, but I think she knew that. I could feel the beat of her heart as I held her, felt it speed up at the same time that she moved her hands back down to my arm and gripped it tightly, like she wanted to use me to anchor herself here. To this bed, to this apartment, to this city.

The grip she had on me said it all, that this was something that she had carried with her for so long that she probably couldn't separate herself from it. Suddenly, the very idea of her being in pain was completely unacceptable to me. Unbearable.

"You know," I whispered against the back of her neck, "this might be poor timing but you look really hot in my shirt."

Poppy snorted so aggressively I couldn't breathe through the laughs that rocked through me, unable to control it in the slightest even as she pleaded with me to stop, that when she laughed she couldn't promise it would be spaghetti free.

"The depth of tone you got on that sound was incredible," I wiped the tears from my eyes on the back of her shirt and moved up on an elbow to try and see her face.

"If my puke covered nudity didn't send you running, that'll do the trick."

"Actually, I think you just uncovered a new kink for me."

"You're saying all the right things to make me forget you're doing this completely out of pity."

"You think I'm *pity*-flirting with you?"

"Of course," she sighed and finally rolled onto her back. It was just her eyes that seemed to reflect the small amount of light getting into the room. Only the barest outline of her features were visible but I didn't need even that to know how beautiful this woman was and that it didn't have a single thing to do with how she looked on the outside.

"Penelope, I'm so confident that, given the opportunity, I'd seduce the shit out of you."

"You will find no arguments here, Aspen Killian."

That surprised me, "Is that right, Poppy Elizabeth?"

Her face morphed into the picture of cocky confidence that sent a zap of electricity right down my spine, "Aspen, I'm confident that you could seduce a wet paper towel if given half the chance."

"I'm oddly flattered by that sentiment."

"You can put it right in your 'flattery basket' next to all my thoughts about your nasal cavity." Poppy rolled her eyes and a small, breathy laugh left her igniting those same notes that rushed through my mind the first time I heard it.

We didn't speak after that. It wasn't unbearable or suffocating or seemingly louder than any stadium I'd ever played in, not like it usually felt when I'd laid in this exact bed without her.

I pulled her tighter to me and she seemed to hold me just as hard.

"Thank you for looking after me," her voice was so small and anything I wanted to say back got stuck in my throat because it felt like it had been a very long time since anyone had looked after Poppy.

I kissed the bare, warm skin of her shoulder and tried desperately for the right thing to say back.

Poppy fell asleep in my arms as the words continued to evade me, leaving me wide awake for the rest of the night, thinking instead about all the ways I would keep looking after her if she ever decided to let me try.

# 14

## January 26th

**Poppy**

The first thing I realized as I slowly woke up, was that it felt as if I had been hit by a relatively large vehicle. The second thing that struck me was that for one, weirdly terrifying moment I thought I was back in my childhood bedroom. The one with glow in the dark stickers on the ceiling and posters of all my favorite bands covering the walls top to bottom.

But I was in Aspen's room.

It was *his* glow in the dark stars on the ceiling but he was nowhere to be found. The room around me was so incredibly dark it seemed like it was the middle of the night. It was then that a minor wave of nausea pulsed through me. A gentle and completely unwelcome reminder of everything that had happened yesterday.

Me throwing up out the door of Aspen's car.

Me hugging his toilet bowl making enough noise to raise

the dead.

*Me needing to be showered with the support of the very man in question.*

"Oh, for the love of Pete," I moaned, sinking deeper into his bed. This was just freaking *dandy*. I mean really, just great.

He told me I had sublime shoulder blades. *Sublime. Shoulder blades.*

The only saving grace of the moment was that he wasn't here to witness me coming to terms with my reality. All I knew was that there was no way I was heading into work in my current state. If it wasn't from the residue of the sour spaghetti, then it would be on account of wanting to avoid Todd at all costs.

Swinging my legs off the side of the bed, my foot landed right in the cold metal pot that had been placed there. Was it weird that that made me melt a little? That's when I heard a loud and very unmistakable bang come from the kitchen followed by and equally loud, "*Fuck.*"

Standing slowly just to test the capabilities of my still tender body, I was glad to find myself without any dizziness or the need to throw up and set out to find Aspen.

And find him I did.

His penthouse was filled with incredibly comfortable looking furniture in creams and dark greens with big windows that let in copious amounts of light. I counted at least five sets of drum sticks on my way to wherever I was going and that made me smile too.

This was the way I had imagined getting to see his space. It made so much sense to me, somehow, that there was a set of drumsticks balancing precariously on top of a picture frame in the hallway.

Aspen's penthouse made it feel like we were right up in the clouds. Like we were in a bubble away from the world and that helped ease some of the tension in my shoulders.

He was in the kitchen, like I assumed he would be, wearing an apron tied at the back in a big red bow. Like, the waist straps of his apron were actually made of ribbon and tied in a huge, kind of poofy looking red bow. His hips were swaying from side to side and I knew in my soul it would be a real shame for me to make myself known and bring whatever was happening in front of me to an end.

Scratch that, it would be worse than a shame. A crime. It would be a crime.

That was the moment my stomach cramped, catching me off guard and causing me to squeak and Ap to turn on his heels. As soon as he saw me — I don't even really know how to explain it, but the way he looked at me felt like taking a deep breath when you really needed it.

"Hey," he said, waving a gloved hand my way and I finally got to see the front of his apron. It had a massive picture of his brother and sister-in-law on the front with a speech bubble from both of them that said 'Wallie loves this baker'.

"Hey," I grinned back.

"How do you feel?"

"Well, I haven't thrown up yet."

"An immediate win, then." He gave me a little wink before turning back to whatever he was doing. "Take a seat." He looked back over his shoulder and gestured towards the kitchen island which was…covered in baked goods.

"You have stars on your ceiling," I said, sliding onto the first stool I walked towards.

"Big fan?"

"The biggest. Hey, Aspen?"

"Mm?"

"What are you doing?" And I really was curious because there were enough baked goods in front of me to open a small establishment.

"Well, Wyatt called an emergency session because he had a dream about a song he thinks could be our single but I had to bail. I've learned that everyone's usually a lot more forgiving when I show up with The Goods." He was gesturing to all the things he'd baked; cupcakes, cinnamon buns, croissants, little tart thingies. I assumed they were 'The Goods'.

"Bailed on recording? Like your album?"

"That's the one."

"But why?"

"I couldn't just leave you here on your own."

"But I have to go to work?" I was asking a lot of questions, and as much as I didn't want to see anyone, I knew I still had to at least attempt to go. That's when Aspen turned around, putting whatever he'd been fiddling with in a bowl and covering it with a dish towel.

"Poppy," he started the sentence like he was worried I'd accidentally thrown up my brain last night. "What time do you think it is?"

"Seven?"

"Okay, look," he started, reaching behind him to untie his apron, "it's clear this is going to be a real shock to you...but it's half past one."

"In the morning?" I squeaked, completely choosing to ignore the very clear, bright blue sky outside of the windows. "Oh my god, I'm going to lose my job. I can't show up *and* be sleeping with my cousin in the same twenty four hour cycle,

Aspen!" I was panicking, clearly, but I had to hand it to him, he was oddly ready for this.

"Please don't be mad at anything I'm about to say."

"Well, that's a promising way to begin a sentence!" My voice was rising and my stomach was cramping and I really felt like I was about to shit myself.

"So your phone wouldn't stop ringing, and I tried to wake you up, but you were out cold. Like, *cold* Poppy. I stopped breathing while I watched to make sure you hadn't."

"Good grief." My hand unintentionally flew to clutch my non-existent pearls.

"I know," he waved me off, "it was terrifying. So, I picked it up. Your phone…"

"Dear god." I covered my face with my hands.

"Winny's great, and aside from asking me if I was your cousin, he seemed very understanding of how unwell you are. I explained everything to him in graphic detail. He seemed super concerned with your fiber intake, though, even when I told him all was well on…*that* end of things." Aspen frowned like he was still trying to make sense of that. I didn't have the heart to tell him he never really would, it was simply something that just *was*.

"Anyway," he went on, "I clarified I wasn't, in fact, your cousin and that you'd need to take today off because of the whole sour spaghetti thing. I also promised to sign his favorite pair of socks."

"Oh." I dropped my hands. "Well, that's not so bad."

"I'm hoping that if I arrive in the morning they'll still be relatively fresh."

"That's a good plan." I nodded my agreement.

"And then Leah called. Well, actually she FaceTimed."

I covered my mouth at the very real way Leah would have absolutely died.

"Needless to say she was *not* expecting me." Aspen's face said everything about how he was still recovering from whatever transpired.

"Did she pass out?" I was absolutely giddy.

"She excused herself out of frame to scream. It made me jump."

"You're an excellent spot, Aspen Killian," I beamed at him, feeling at least fifty percent better than when I'd walked out here.

"Thank you, Poppy Elizabeth." He bowed slightly and my heart did a flip flop. "I was a little scared for most of that conversation to be honest so I don't really remember much of it except that I nodded a lot and I promised to tell you that she said you guys were not fighting anymore and she misses you. Then I ducked out quickly to feed Nat, came home and started baking."

He breezed right over that last little bit so quickly I had to rewind in my own head to confirm it was really what he said.

"You—" I swallowed, "you left to feed Natalie?"

"Yeah, and before you say anything I know that's super weird but your keys were in your bag and after you fell asleep last night you kept saying 'dinner time, Natalie Jean. Dinner time!'" He cleared his throat and reached up to rub the back of his neck. "So, I just thought–"

I propelled myself off the stool and right at him before he could finish that sentence. There was no hesitation on his side in wrapping his arms around me and holding me close.

"Thank you," my voice sounded thick with the emotion that was making my eyes mist over. I don't think anyone really knew how much Natalie meant to me, including Aspen, but even without knowing, he *knew.*

It didn't feel so scary then to share a little more with him, to crack that door to the parts of myself I kept tucked away open and let this one story out. It didn't scare me to do it at all and I didn't think Aspen would mind hearing it. It took a few tries, but eventually the words came. Tumbling out like they had that first night I met him.

"On my fourteenth birthday I came home from school and Casimir had her tank set up on the tiny kitchen counter in our apartment," I whispered, the words to this story familiar but unused, like they were covered in a thick layer of dust. I gripped Aspen harder, ready for the shakes that would start to overtake my body like anytime I relived a memory that had to do with my brother but even as I gripped him, I didn't tremble.

I stayed right there with him, in the present.

"I'd asked him for a dog for months. I even wrote him a letter explaining in detail all the things I'd do to look after one." A watery laugh escaped me and I didn't realize until that moment that I was crying and subsequently soaking Aspen's shirt. I pulled back confused to see these phantom things that had never actually fallen real and wet on my face. "Oh crap, sorry." I reached out to wipe at his shirt but he just grabbed my wrists and pulled me back to him, wrapping his arms around me and kissing the top of my head.

"'*Goldfish are the dogs of the sea, Pen.*' That's what he'd said, and I didn't even care that factually everything about his statement was false." Aspen laughed at that. My eyes closed involuntarily at the rumble I felt reverberate through his chest. "I was so excited, regardless. She reminds me of him now, like

I still have some of him with me."

We stayed like that for a while, for so long that I wasn't even sure how to break the hug, so I just said the first thing that came to mind.

"I'm really glad you're not my cousin." I looked up in time to see Ap tilt his head back in a laugh. I made sure to soak up every rumble and sound, determined to add it to the growing list of things I never, ever wanted to forget.

"I don't have the words to say how glad I am you're not my blood relation, Poppy." He kissed the top of my head for the second time that morning and it had immediately become one of my favorite things he did. "Speaking of, if you're feeling better tomorrow, I have our next friend-date planned."

"Should I be scared?"

"Wasn't our last one wonderful?"

"I almost died via snake, but sure."

"That's right, you complimented my forearms."

"We remember that story in dramatically different ways," I grumbled, finally pulling away from him.

"Alright, time to get you fed, sweet Poppy." Aspen turned back around towards the stove. The mention of food, and namely the thought of consuming something sweet, made my stomach roll.

"Ap, this all looks amazing, but I'm not sure —"

"Oh, no pastries for you, Poompaloompa." He walked towards the stove and lifted off the lid of a pot containing a simmering, and incredible smelling soup. "You're getting homemade chicken noodle soup. Good for the soul."

It was very clear to me then that Aspen was the human version of chicken noodle soup.

I had no idea what I was going to do because I'd drawn

this line between us but somehow in the last nineteen and a half hours it had been criss-crossed over so many times that I was barely able to make it out. I'd told him right in the living room of my own house that I could only be his friend, namely because I didn't want to *just be* his friend, but I couldn't stomach the thought of hurting him in any way and I panicked.

I knew that no matter how many times I double checked, this wasn't something that happened to people on accident. That you just *found* someone who soothed your rough edges the way Aspen did for me. People didn't simply just *fit* together the way we did. Without force. With such little effort.

His hands on my waist, his teeth dragging along my neck, his declaration of imminent law-breaking activity. Not fast and aching like that, or even slow and patient like the strong band of an arm around my waist or his tender kiss on my bare shoulder.

I'd never wanted to be a fugitive so badly in my whole life as I had with him on that trail. I'd never wanted to stay *still* so desperately.

That Aspen would only ever be my friend seemed completely and totally ridiculous.

"Thank you for looking after me." It was all I could think to say, and I hoped he could see between the words I had spoken to the ones that I hadn't.

*You're soup, Aspen. You're good for my soul.*

"Thank you for letting me," was all he said, reading those unspoken words loud and clear.

# 15

# January 28th

**Poppy**

"**A**re you sure?" Aspen asked for probably the twentieth time just as he put the Taurus into park at the curb outside my house.

The porch light was on, just like I'd left it before heading to work Thursday morning. But now it was Sunday night and it was a little hard to believe how much had changed in such a short amount of time.

"It really can only go up from here." I looked over at him, at the crease that seemed to live on his brow permanently over the last forty-eight hours.

"You could relapse?"

"Highly improbable." I rolled my eyes. This wasn't the first time he'd mentioned relapsing as a possibility.

"Okay, but *if* —"

"If I feel unwell again I will let you know, yes." I couldn't stop the way my features softened.

"And about the paparazzi…" He let the sentence hang between us, reaching up to rub the back of his neck. He took his hat off, pushed his hair back and put it back on in its usual backwards state before he looked at me.

I knew he felt awful about it. I was positive that he'd been dangerously close to popping a blood vessel in his eye considering how constipated he looked watching me eat soup Saturday morning before I all but demanded he spill whatever beans he was coveting.

He first told me about the fact that now that they'd followed him to my work and seen us together, they would probably have an interest in me. *Then* he followed it up by saying there may be an interest because there were actually already photos circulating of the two of us.

I was completely and totally ill equipped at being able to manage media attention. I didn't even want my own phone camera in my face taking photos, let alone one that could capture the amount of detail the lenses I saw on Thursday afternoon outside my office could.

I was scared, nervous and irrationally worried that none of my keys would properly lock any of my doors or windows and I'd walk into my kitchen to find it littered with men armed with big cameras. But I'd meant what I said when I told him it was okay, and we'd figure out how to work through it.

"Ap." I waited until he looked at me, his eyes still pleading and full of guilt, "It's all going to be okay. The only issue is that I'm going to have to think a lot harder about whether or not I have panty lines in my work pants when I leave the house."

"Poppy." His head tilted to the side in a way that said *'be serious'*.

"Aspen." My head tilted to the side in a way that said *'I am being serious'*.

"Now," I unclicked my seat belt and turned to face him fully, "thank you again for looking after me in what was arguably one of the more embarrassing moments of my life. Good luck tomorrow, please tell your friends I'm sorry I kept you from recording and," I held up my hand to stop him from speaking just as he took an inhale, "yes, if anything happens with the men with cameras, work or Todd, I will call you."

"I've already sent Jane a message on everything, including what we can do to make sure they leave you alone for the most part but…"

"I know, you can't promise anything but Jane is the best and will do everything she can." I recounted the words he'd said repeatedly over the weekend. Jane was the manager of *Lady Luck* and apparently 'the best and most sparkliest human', according to Aspen.

"Okay," he'd said on the tail end of a huge exhale.

"Okay," I said back, giving him my best reassuring smile.

Aspen had a knack for taking care of people. It had been weird and awkward to be on the receiving end of that at the start, like hugging a stranger and being unsure of where to put your hands.

Letting someone take care of me when I could do it myself was something I avoided completely, but from the moment his smile reached all the way to his eyes upon the unveiling of his chicken soup, I'd been a goner.

I knew that he knew I was finding it…weird. To say the least. Not because it wasn't appreciated. Especially considering how lacking in energy I had been for most of our time spent together, dozing in and out of consciousness and completely unable to take care of any of my basic needs. It was just *foreign*. Even when I had stayed with Leah's family for my last two years of high school, I'd never let them take care of me like that, and they never pushed the issue hard enough for me to try and let them.

There was a part of me that revolted at the idea that I'd sipped on ginger ale and snacked on saltines that Aspen had left on his coffee table because he'd looked up the best things to eat to help a sensitive stomach. At waking up to find myself covered in a blanket that smelt like him. To wake up again halfway through a movie and feel the warm press of his body right next to me before his gently whispered question of, "You okay?"

Waking and not feeling him close but knowing he was near based on the sounds of him in the kitchen. Coming to again and trying my best to pretend I was still asleep so he wouldn't stop the way he was running his fingers through my hair.

Revolted because I was *relieved*.

Relieved to fall asleep and know when I woke up he'd still be there. To know his presence even when I wasn't truly aware of it.

To be around Aspen was to feel safe and cared for. Wanted. *Needed*.

I didn't deserve any of it. Still, I wanted to hold on to him with both hands in the same way I was doing to all the memories I'd been collecting. To feel its burning imprint on the very bones of me. Wishing for it to leave its mark because even though I didn't deserve any of it, I wanted it. I wanted *him*.

Before I knew what I was doing, I was leaning across the console. In my head, I was totally thinking about giving him a hug, but halfway across it changed to a *friendly* kiss on the cheek.

Once again, Aspen had plans of his own and somehow, some way, our faces ended up on the same flight path and then there I was, pressing my lips against his.

Yep, that's right.

I had my lips pressed right to his with my eyes wide open, staring right at his face so hard that he'd become a cyclops. There was a moment, probably more than one, where I could have – *should* have – removed my lips from his face and ran from my front door like my ass was on fire.

None of those things happened.

Aspen's hand moved slowly, like he was trying to be careful not to startle me. The tips of his fingers dragged up the column of my throat making my entire body erupt in goosebumps before settling on the side of my face, cupping my jaw with a grip that was both gentle and firm. I was so totally and completely lost to him then.

His lips moved against mine, coaxing them open and I could do nothing, *nothing*, except relinquish every bit of my control and just do as he bid.

Kissing Aspen again was nothing like it had been the first time or the second, and even then I'd been so helpless against him. So overwhelmed but the way it felt to be touched by him, even for the short time it had lasted. Shocked at how much more I wanted even knowing all the rules that I would break.

He wasn't in a rush now, not like he had been at the bar with my quiet frantic requests or the hike with the threat of being found at any moment. No, actually, he was taking his sweet time if the languid, exploratory strokes of his tongue had anything to say about it.

Every single movement set my entire nervous system into overdrive, until I felt every swipe and nip and flick of his tongue against mine in every part of my body. Until I was too hot and too cold.

I reached up to grip the wrists of both hands that now cradled my head, angling me in whatever way he wanted to kiss me deeper. To kiss me harder. To taste me in every way he wanted and I didn't do a thing to stop it. I don't think I could have even if I wanted to, and I'd never wanted to do anything less in my whole life.

It was like he was trying to figure out a way to imprint this moment in his mind, like he'd thought about that first time and second time almost as much as I had.

He kissed the corners of my mouth delicately, leaving feather light pecks and open mouthed kisses along my jaw.

He pulled back a couple times, his eyes moving across my face. That little crease between his brows was nowhere to be seen but instead replaced with a slight lift to his equally swollen and reddening lips before he pulled my face back to his.

I couldn't tell you how long he kissed me on the quiet, darkened street out front of my house. Couldn't really put into words the way my entire body ached at the sounds that rumbled in his chest. That climbed out of his throat and danced across my own tongue. Each reverberation sent a pulse through every bone in my body, imbedding himself there. Right in the very core of me so that I'd have no choice but to remember him for the rest of my life. Have no choice but to admit that two people had never fit better together as we did right then.

It could have been minutes. I hoped it was hours.

There was a tipping point, maybe a mutual understanding of how temporary this moment was and how much neither of us wanted to lose it when our hands became more frantic and I wanted more. I couldn't stop the way I reached for the hem of his shirt to tug over his head, which he obliged without any complaints. The material and his hat discarded somewhere in the backseat.

He pulled the lever beneath his seat sending it careening back as far as it would go, which was way more arousing than it had a right to be, and in a display of what could only be described as admirable upper body strength, he hauled me up and over to straddle him.

"Oh," I hiccuped. It was definitely a hiccup because I was entirely incapable of speaking any real words. In all honesty, I was having a hard time thinking about pretty much anything with the feel of Aspen, rock hard beneath me.

"You okay?" His chest was rising and falling as fast as my own.

"Super okay," was my well thought out reply and then my hands were in his hair and his were up the back of my shirt – *his* shirt – because I had been wearing his clothes all weekend even though mine had been washed and dried. It was like a frenzy. I had no idea how I could stop and I really didn't ever want to. Aspen was warm. He was this inviting, safe, solid person and it was as terrifying as it was a fucking respite to realize that I wanted to stay right where I was, in his orbit.

*I've never felt like this in my entire life*, I wanted to tell him. Willed the words from my brain to jump into his. *I've been running since I was sixteen and you make me want to stand still.*

"Poppy," his voice was a whisper against my lips, bringing

me back to the moment where I realized my fingers were aching for how hard they were gripping his shoulders.

"Yes?" My whole body was vibrating as if the tectonic plates of my soul were shifting.

"I—," he started then stopped. "Penelope I want…I want *everything*. I want to kiss you and touch you and *feel* every single inch of you…but not as friends." I saw his throat work on a swallow and mimicked the action.

All I kept thinking was *'how am I supposed to let him go?'*

"This is not what friends do, Poppy. And I know you made it really clear and I get it, at least I'm trying to but–"

"I don't want to be your friend, Aspen." The words were up and out of my mouth before I had time to think through the consequences of what speaking them to life would mean for me. For *him*. "I've never wanted to be just your friend but—" I interrupted him to say it all, or at least as much as I could.

That 'but' hung between us like a live wire. Its existence unwanted but absolutely necessary. That 'but' was every single part of me that lived behind that hulking, impenetrable door in my mind that I kept so much of myself behind. But some parts had snuck out, hadn't they? One I'd even willingly gone to retrieve. To share with him and somehow I hadn't fallen apart, and he hadn't run away. Not yet.

"Okay," he said, both knowing and not knowing everything that hadn't been said at the end of my unfinished sentence and still picking me anyway.

Aspen didn't even get to finish the word before his lips were on mine again. His hands were on my hips, encouraging me in a very valiant way to keep moving them the way I had been. It was a heady feeling, to know it was my body that his hands were trailing over. My shirt he was pushing up. *My* mouth that was capturing every sound that was coming out of his.

"Poppy." I felt my name more than I heard it. I wanted to feel him speak it everywhere, I realized. On every single part of my body.

"More," I gasped, "*please.*" I trailed my nails down his chest, obsessing over the warmth of his body. Aspen was lean and defined and fit. The body of someone who spent a very long time playing the drums day after day, year after year.

"*Fuck,*" he groaned into the crook of my neck. I had never been so turned on in my entire life. "Poppy, wait–" The words sounded painful as he gritted them out and my hands stilled on the button of his jeans.

"You don't want to?" I was so out of breath it should have been embarrassing.

"Oh, I want to." The grin he flashed me soothed the sting of his rejection just a little. "Believe me. But not here."

It sucked because every word that came out of his mouth just made me want to rid him of his pants even more, but he was right. I deflated immediately, my body leaning away and landing right on the steering wheel, eliciting a jarring and all too familiar blaring horn.

Casimir had what he would always refer to as 'gentle road rage'. He insisted on confusing people who made him angry by blaring his horn and then smiling and waving as he drove by them. The sound of that car horn was imprinted in my mind as much as the chipping pale green paint of our kitchen cabinets were and the mind numbing screech that the windows in our living room had made every time you tried to open them up even a little.

It was like a bucket of cold water had been thrown over me and I suddenly felt stupid for wanting things I knew I couldn't.

I climbed off Aspen and sat back in the passenger seat, embarrassed and ashamed of everything I had been so willing to do, the pain I had been so ready to cause. "I'm so sorry, I–"

"No," his voice wasn't harsh but it was direct, enough for me to whip my head around to face him. "You won't apologize for any of that, and neither will I." His eyes were *so* green, sort of like our old kitchen cabinets.

"I'm not usually like this," he said after a second, looking back at the dark street in front of us. "It's like my mind stops doing the things I've forced it to learn to do. To make the decision I've always forced it to make. With you I just keep doing the things I want even though I shouldn't."

He was so quiet, not saying a thing as he fixed his seat, grabbing his shirt and hat from the back and a hoodie that he must've kept back there, a very much needed addition now that the car had been off for a while and the cold was seeping in.

"So, before I do all the very wrong and dirty things I would like to do with you, we're going to sort out that 'but.'"

"You heard the 'but'?" Of course he'd heard it.

"Oh, yeah. Don't you worry though, I have a plan." His smirk was devilish.

Ever the gentleman that he was, Aspen walked me right to my door.

"Do I get a hint?" My stomach was in knots. It was fear and excitement all balled into one because I wasn't entirely sure what I'd agreed to when I spoke out in what had been a very thick haze of lust.

"Trust, Poppy. It's all about trust." He nodded like that one word held all the answers of the universe. His face betrayed nothing while I, on the other hand, was gearing up to scream into a vacuum.

"Goodnight, Poppy." Aspen left a lingering kiss on my cheek that gave me something akin to an adrenaline rush, no matter how much more tame it had been than what we were just doing in his car.

"Night, Ap." I practically slurred the words, my mind and body working against one another.

I stared at my phone all night waiting for a message to come through from him. Typing out my own and then deleting it entirely. Staring at my ceiling and hating that it wasn't home to glow in the dark stars. All I could think about was the sticky note that he'd taped to the side of Natalie's tank of a stick figure waving and the other sticky note on the counter right next to her explaining that he was worried she would get lonely and thought his drawing would keep her company until I came home.

I could think about very little else other than his declaration of never doing the things he wanted until me and how I hadn't thought much of it at the time but I needed to know what he meant.

The events of the last seventy two hours ran through my head as I got ready for work the next morning and made the journey on complete and total autopilot into the city, wondering what he was going to do. Feeling giddy and happy and excited.

I was all of those things, but they all held the bitterness of guilt and dread and fear and pain and it only subsided when I settled on the unwavering decision that I knew I couldn't just be his friend. And so, I would let myself have him in whatever way I could get him and then I'd let him go like I'd always planned on doing come April fifth.

*April fifth.* When I would leave. The day I hated and loathed and wished never existed.

It wasn't perfect as far as plans went, and I was certain now that I would hurt him but not so bad that he wouldn't recover.

That's when I heard someone yell my name from across the street a moment before their huge, massive, has-to-be-compensating-for-something camera lens came into view.

"Oh, crap," I muttered and ran like a bat out of hell into my office building.

# 16

## January 29th

### Aspen

"The prodigal drummer returns," were the words that my brother hurled at me moments before a pillow was thrown directly at my face. It was then followed by a notepad and someone's shoe.

"*Ow*," I moaned, huddling into the door frame I'd entered through and covering my face. "That could have resulted in a paper cut for crying out loud!" My voice was muffled by my hands, but I was definitely yelling, so I knew they heard.

"Guys, give him a break." Angus strolled over to hold out his hand to help me up.

"What do you mean, 'give him a break'?" Luke mimicked the words back in his best Angus impression which, actually, wasn't that bad. "You're the one who threw your shoe at his head."

And he was right. My hand was still hovering between us as I let my eyes fall on Angus's feet. One shoe clad and one completely bare.

"Dude." I felt my face scrunch up. "Who doesn't wear socks with their boots?"

"I was in a rush," he shrugged, sliding his hands into his pockets like he hadn't just basically admitted he was a psychopath.

"I'm incredibly alarmed that I didn't know this about you and we've been friends for, like, twelve years." I helped myself up and delivered a much deserved whack to his balls for the aforementioned shoe throwing.

Angus doubled over. "I don't do it often," he wheezed before falling right to the floor.

"You've never bailed on a recording session, ever," Rip announced from his usual place on the couch and I swallowed down the bile in my throat. Making the decision not to come to the studio when my brother called and asked had made me so sick I threw up. Twice.

"It's true, I thought you were joking at first," Luke chimed in, "but no cigar. Rip believed it so much he bet on it."

"Woah, big money exchanged hands then?" I said, settling in the tiny sliver of free couch space that Rip had left free and trying to emulate the picture of ease just as he gave Luke the finger.

"So," Dax said, swiveling to face me from where he sat in the captain's chair of the studio, "before Adrian gets here, and because you literally refused to answer any of my calls or texts –"

"You didn't use the emergency word," I rebutted immediately, trying to ignore the black hole of guilt that seemed to live in the middle of my stomach since the very moment I said I couldn't make it. Poppy had been sick in my bed and it had been between her and Wyatt. Between her and Luke and Rip and Angus.

These guys were my family and I'd be there in a heart beat for them. Drop everything and show up and fill in, and I had done that. In a lot of cases to my own detriment, because the very idea of *not* doing it sent me into such a panic I couldn't breathe. That if they needed me and I didn't go, something would happen. Someone would get hurt and I wouldn't have been there to stop it.

I'd done that since I was seventeen. But…*Poppy had been sick in my bed.*

So, I let my phone ring out every time. It was only when Allie texted that I replied.

**1/2 of Wallie:**

Not using the emergency word just triple checking you're okay?

**Me**

I'm okay. Poppy's sick…

**1/2 of Wallie**

Does she need anything? We can be there in however long it takes to get from our house to hers? Yours? The hospital?

**Me**

I got it, Al. Thanks x

**1/2 of Wallie**

xxxxoooo

"Or anyone else besides Allie," he finished with a scowl.

"Can't not reply to Allie," I said with a shrug, the justification backed by a choir of mumbled agreement.

"So, want to tell us why you bailed?" Dax leaned forward, his elbows on his knees. This was not like him, at all. It was *so* not like him, actually, that I…

I groaned, "You guys are such assholes, you know?" I gave my brother a flat look.

"I don't know what –"

"Oh, cram your cramhole." I pulled my hat from where it sat in its usual backwards position on my head, a must have to keep the messy waves out of my face when I was drumming, and pulled it down over my eyes.

"God, that's a good movie," Angus piped up from his position still on the floor.

"Totally. Dude, maybe our next game night can be a movie night!" Luke's eyes lit up like the fourth of freaking July. "I vote we watch *Dodgeball!*"

"We're getting heavily off topic here," Rip chimed in, which told me one important thing.

"Alright, so the bet was between you two then, huh?" I gestured between Rip and Dax, my hat still pulled down over my eyes. They didn't even try to deny it.

"So?" Rip nudged my knee with the tip of his sneaker.

"You're not going to let this go, are you?" I peeked from under my hat.

"Forty bucks says not a chance, buddy boy." Rip's grin was huge and I wanted to hit him in the balls too, but I knew he'd evade the attack and then get me back twice as bad for daring to try.

I heaved a deep sigh, my fingers starting to twitch with the want to play drums after so many days without it. I couldn't remember the last time I'd gone a single day without doing *something*.

"I was looking after my friend," I relented. "She had food poisoning."

"Your *friend*? Did you say 'she'?" Angus asked, sitting up but still cupping his balls, eyebrows scrunched together in deep confusion.

"But...all your friends are here?" Luke added, looking equally confused.

"That's not true," I said, moving my hat off my eyes.

"The girls are a given," Dax chimed in, equally as puzzled.

"I have...*other* friends." It was hard to not look at any of the four different pairs of eyes that were currently on my face.

"No, you don't," Dax said, leaning back into his chair and crossing his arms.

"Oh my god." Rip bolted into a sitting position and pointed a solitary finger right at me, "Aspen's got a girlfriend."

"No," I swallowed, trying very hard not to think about last night. The feeling of Poppy settled around me was a solace like I'd never known, and then me and my fucking big mouth told her to stop. "I have a *friend*...who is also a *girl*. There is a substantial difference."

"*That*," Luke said wiggling his finger in my direction, "is a substantial *lie*."

"You bailed because of your new girlfriend? He spent the weekend with his *girlfriend!*" Rip had a stupidly huge grin on his face. He didn't sound pissed in the slightest, he sounded fucking *elated*.

"She had food poisoning, and she went home Sunday night when she was feeling well enough so whatever's in your mind, cast those thoughts very far."

"I wasn't thinking about anything." The look on his face said otherwise.

"You were thinking about me having sex. It's written all over your face." My hand fluttered between us.

"How do you know what my face looks like when I'm thinking about sex?"

"Because you think about sex all the time, you pervert," Angus called out.

"Then it's settled," Dax said with a look on his face that gave me no confidence of assured good behavior before swinging his chair around to face the mixing console. "Aspen will bring his new *friend* to our next Fun Friday Family Fiesta night."

"I won't be doing that," I said to deaf ears.

"When the girls aren't around, I'm not sure it's entirely necessary for us to use their name for it." Rip had grabbed his guitar and started messing around with a tune I'm assuming had something to do with the emergency recording session on Saturday and just like that, the conversation was over.

I had a few rebuttals, but was it a little twisted that now I had a reason to push the topic of her attendance? At least, eventually? I knew Poppy kept to herself, that beyond anything she might outwardly defend, she *made* herself take a step back from people and places that might threaten her plans to leave. She'd already drawn a line with me even though it had been well and truly crossed now, by both of us. Maybe introducing her to the rest of the people I cared about would do more than I could in changing her mind.

The sound of a song I hadn't heard before trickled into the room around us. Dax and Adrian, who arrived around the time the word 'pervert' left Angus's mouth, were huddled together while everyone listened to what they had created over the weekend.

"Holy shit." It was really the only thing I *could* say.

"Dude," Dax said, beaming at me over his shoulder, "I told you!"

"For the drums we were thinking–" Angus started, but I cut him off almost immediately.

Already taking off my shirt and replacing my cap where it sat on my head, "No, no. Wait, I got something." Stalking straight for the drum kit, I gave the signal to my brother to start the track again, and then I just let loose.

Again and again the track ran. Listening and reworking different guitar riffs and solos, and even changing some of the vocal melodies as Adrian worked his magic, transforming the song from a general idea into probably one of my favorite songs we'd ever created.

We were in there all day, the outside world zoned out completely the way it always did when we worked together. When we played music together, we settled into this place where we were all in sync, knowing what one another was thinking and feeling.

"Hey, Ap," Dax's voice cut in through my headphones, "that was insane. Can you run that part just after the bridge again, but like '*dum, dahdahdahdah budum dum*' and then that thing you just did with the hi-hat but more intense and a little longer right until the quick stop for a beat before coming in strong for the last chorus? Does that make sense?"

"Yep, I think so. Like this…"

As soon as the song ended, I locked eyes with my brother through the glass and the grin on his face said everything I was feeling.

"That's our single, Dax." I knew my expression matched his own in every way.

"That's our fucking single!" he yelled, standing up with his arms stretched wide and head tipped back in howling laughter.

Luke and Angus had jumped on Rip where he sat on the couch and I took out my phone and snapped a photo of them all from my spot in the booth behind my drum kit. I quickly posted it to my Instagram profile, something I didn't do often but tried to do enough to keep engaged with our fans. Immediately, comments started coming in.

I just slipped my phone back into my pocket when Dax's phone started to ring through the open channel from his mic.

He picked it up which meant it could only be one person and then his laughter was bouncing off of every wall, louder than before.

Everyone was looking right at him when I'd finished pulling my shirt over my head and dropping onto my spot on the couch.

Everyone's eyes might have been on my brother, but his were on me.

He looked diabolically *jovial* as he spoke into his phone. "No, sweetheart," his mouth quirked up at the side, "I had no idea that Aspen was sleeping with our cousin."

# 17

## January 29th

**Poppy**

I'd rushed into the building with the sort of panic that you possess when you're out having dinner at a restaurant wearing that pair of white jeans you bought three years ago and hadn't been brave enough to don until that very day, and then realized half way through your tuna tartare that your period had arrived two days early.

That sort of blinding panic covered me head to toe in the form of a fine mist of perspiration. My heart rate had only started to calm down on my trip from the ground floor up the eighteen levels to the office. It was incredibly off base of me to think that everything would have been just as it was the last time I was here.

My heart rate skyrocketed all over again when I stepped out of the elevator and there wasn't a single set of eyes not watching me. I did this weird crab-style-grape-vine walk to my desk, thinking it would be more inconspicuous than just walking there normally.

I'd been also very off base with that assumption too.

Huddled down beneath the protective walls of my cubicle I pulled out my phone to…do what?  I could call Leah, but I genuinely thought she'd be more of the 'trust fall into this new adventure' mentality than providing me with anything remotely helpful, and there was no way I was going to call Aspen.  Not for something as inconsequential as creepy camera people outside my office and the skin-itching sensation of twenty different eyes staring at you unblinkingly all at once.

For one, twenty people would have been nothing to him. This man who had once agreed to sign the bottom of some-one's foot. For two, I knew he hadn't done a bunch of things he really should have done over the weekend for his new album and *Lady Luck's* next tour in order to stay with me. There was no way I was disturbing him now that he was actively doing those things. And third…well, we'd already spoken about this. About the cameras and the attention as a likely reality to whatever it was we were doing.

Our…*friendship*.

It would probably solve all my problems to tell him right then and there that it was too much and he needed to stay far from me because of some far-fetched excuse, like my gentle constitution couldn't handle the attention.

I knew that if I said words that sounded something like that they would seem stupid to us both but he'd believe me. Whatever the case may be, I was not going to be doing any of that, so I bundled up all the things I probably *should* do and shoved them behind that door in my mind to dwell on later. There was so much behind there now I half wondered how there was any room left. That's when my choking bell caught my eye from where it sat on my desk, right where Jess had left it.

I was teetering on the edge of an impending panic attack when I grabbed the bell and rang it like an enthusiastic town crier.

There was a loud thump, a surprised yelp that was more than likely Jess falling off her office chair and a handful of seconds before she flung herself into my cubicle.

"I'm here!" she panted, pushing her glasses up her nose. "I'm—" Jess didn't finish her sentence before I grabbed her hand and pulled her beneath my desk with me.

I started to explain everything to her before her ass even hit the carpet about what happened. A dam opened up and more words than I'd spoken to anyone that wasn't Leah in a short space of time since I was ten years old and explaining to my brother that I was certain unicorns were real and just in hiding from the world.

I told Jess everything because it felt like I owed it to her as my single in-office friend to reassure her that she hadn't put her constant attempts at companionship to waste on a real weirdo. I told her about Aspen, and Todd and how I was absolutely not engaging in coitus with my cousin. That there were people with cameras outside and they were calling *my* name.

"First of all, I'm trying super hard not to fangirl right now because I love *Lady Luck* so much I walked down the aisle to an acoustic version of *Feel the Fear* by them and even though that marriage was about as successful as trying to form a diamond by squeezing coal super tight in between your hands, I am confident the song is what enabled it to last long enough to give me my boys." Jess was talking very fast and I felt like I'd learned more about her in the last ten seconds than I had over the last nine months. "Second, I know he's not your cousin," she whispered, the corner of her mouth pulling up ever so slightly. "They stopped me when I was on my way in and asked me if I knew who you were and why Aspen Smith was seen here on Thursday afternoon ushering a young woman into his car. And that they'd spoken to a man named Todd who told them your name was Poppy." Like she couldn't physically contain it, her face split into this look of wicked delight that reminded me of Leah, "I told them that Todd had been caught multiple times in compromising positions with a toilet brush and often asked people around the office to neigh at him in greeting, so anything he said was likely unhinged garble."

"I am so impressed with you right now," I couldn't stop my own super look of impish satisfaction or the growing feeling of needing to laugh regardless of the current situation.

"But, that's not all, I have to tell you," she paused, her smile falling from her face, "I told Winny already in case he could help but he already knew. I —"

"There you are," Winny said, his head peeking down under the desk like Jess's mere mention summoned him, making us both jump. "Poppy, I think it's best you quickly come with me."

"Hummus?" Winny offered from the other side of his desk, a

look of serious concern in his eyes.

"I'm okay, thanks." I gave him my best *I swear, I'm regular!* smile.

Winny had a minifridge in his office full of a range of high fiber snacks, including some homemade chocolate peanut butter balls. "They're a family recipe," he'd said the first time he ever offered them around the office after I'd started. "My grandma used to make them for me."

It made a lot of sense that his fixation on healthy bowel movements was hereditary.

The cat was out of the bag, especially knowing that Winny had actually spoken directly *to* Aspen on account of my trying to exorcise the spaghetti demons from my body. Between him and Jess, I had quite the support system at work considering that Todd had, as assumed, flapped his massive pie-hole telling everyone that I was sleeping with my cousin.

"I sat down with him and explained," Winny said as soon as he ushered me into his office. "He was quite convinced that everything I was saying was false and threatened to sue the company."

"On what grounds?" I'm sure my face looked as unimpressed as my voice sounded.

"When I asked him that, he said *'These grounds!'* and then just walked away. So I'm not sure." Winny was frowning like he was still trying to navigate what Todd could have meant.

I let my head fall into my hands and followed it with a groan of defeat, "So, everyone here thinks I'm sleeping with a relative."

"What's important is that we know the truth." Winny just nodded to himself, swiping a carrot stick into the hummus he held close and crunched on it thoughtfully. It felt obvious to me that that was actually *not* the most important part of everything that had transpired.

"So, what does this mean?" I looked up at my boss and prepared myself for the fatal blow of being let go. Instead, he lifted up a finger for me to hold on and hopped up to yell for Jess out his office door.

"Hey P," she murmured, sitting down next to me looking equally as confused.

"Oh god," I looked from her to Winny then back to her. "What is it?"

"Well," Winny looked at Jess then back at me, "Jess, well–"

"You can't fire her!" I stood up without my own permission. An accusatory finger flung dangerously close to the hummus Winny had once again picked up and clutched to his chest. "This has nothing to do with her. Just because we're friends doesn't mean anything. If that's the issue then we're not friends. I don't even know her!" I sounded deranged and a chance look at Jess told me she was grateful for what I was trying to do, if not marginally afraid.

"Fiddle-faddle, Poppy!" Winny's eyes looked like they were about to fall out of his head. "Please sit down, neither of you are losing your jobs! Heavens."

"Oh." I dropped back into my seat unceremoniously and Jess reached over to grab my hand.

"Thanks anyway, P." She squeezed my hand and I squeezed hers back.

"I've called you both in for a couple reasons. Firstly, Poppy, I asked Jess to come in as I thought you might find comfort in having a friend nearby."

"Oh," I said for the second time in as many minutes and quietly wanted to die.

"There are a few things you should know about Todd's behavior on account of his false beliefs around your private life."

My head dropped into my hands again and I wanted to melt off my chair but Winny, undeterred as usual, pressed on. "He said that he was going to expose you both as the 'trichophobes you are.'"

Jess's expression was one that almost had me peeing my pants. Especially when she added with the perfect amount of hesitancy, "I'm positive he doesn't know what that means?"

I nodded vigorously, positive of that too, and then I was struck with a thought that twisted my stomach worse than the spaghetti: what if he'd gone out to the news outlets? I hadn't seen anything, but I hadn't really been looking at the news either.

"So," Winny went on, oblivious to the way I was slowly losing my mind, "as you can imagine he's caused some unrest in the office and that's brought me to my second reason for having you both here. I've decided to postpone the Say No To The January Blues party until February. I let the rest of the staff know in this morning's meeting but you two were the only ones not there so I wanted to let you know discreetly now."

Ah, yes. We'd been under my desk.

All I could think, besides the fact that this could already be circulating in global news, was that Winston had absolutely no idea how to appropriately read the room. I could hear that internal voice inside my head rising to a dangerously high pitch that spoke to mental breakdowns and spontaneously changing one's legal name to something rebelliously otherworldly like Gwendelyn or Fantasia.

The faces of Aspen and his brother and their bandmates flashed through my mind and I was certain I was on the precipice of losing it completely.

'It', more than likely, being my dignity.

Winny gave Jess and I the rest of the day off on account of emotional distress caused by another member of staff and that was how we found ourselves down the street in the back table of a little cafe that Jess came to for lunch sometimes.

"I know the circumstances are less than ideal," Jess said, taking a sip from a coffee that was placed in front of her in something better resembling a small bowl rather than a mug, "but I'm glad to finally get to do this with you."

There was no maliciousness in her tone. Honestly, there was nothing but pure, unbridled delight and it just made me feel even more like an asshole. Jess and I had always gotten on like a house on fire since my first day at work. She'd sat with me for our entire lunch break that first day in the office kitchen and even valiantly defended me against Todd who'd had his sights set on bringing me as close to the brink of constant food regurgitation as possible from day dot.

In the office? You would actually look at the pair of us and think we probably had our own two person book club and drank wine together on Thursday nights but in actuality, we waved farewell at the front of our office building at 5:30 PM and left whatever budding friendship we might've had right at work.

I knew it was me. I was the reason and it was because the thought of putting down roots anywhere terrified me beyond any reasonable comprehension to anyone outside my own mind.

"Jess…" I started, determined on putting together some sort

of explanation but she stopped me there.

"No, please." She put her bowl-mug down and gave me one of her genuine smiles I was familiar with. "You don't owe me a single thing. You're a private person, there's nothing wrong with that."

"I am," I nodded, grateful for the out she was providing me.

I wasn't quite sure if it was the realization I had with Aspen the night before or knowing that she defended me to the paparazzi outfront of our building. Maybe it was the realization that I had been ready to defend her to Winny at any cost, even without fully realizing that it was something I would do before the moment arrived, but I found myself not wanting the out she was giving me.

"I, uh, move a lot."

"Oh, that's fun!" She grinned, leaning back in her seat.

"You know, not really." I realized the words were truer than I thought. "It's actually exhausting. But it makes it hard for me to make friends." That was *sort of* the truth.

Jess's eyes softened with the kind of understanding that I wasn't sure she actually grasped, but it was comforting to know that she was trying for my benefit.

You know what? I have no idea if she did or didn't grasp what I was saying because I didn't know Jess at all, and that made me infinitely sadder than I'd been when we started our conversation.

"That makes sense. My boys travel back and forth between me and my ex, then sometimes with their grandparents, then back to me. It's been a really unpredictable routine, actually, for the last year or so. We can't seem to nail down the best way to raise them together." She found something on the table in front of us worth picking at and kept her eyes lasered in on it as she kept speaking, "Anyway, that's not the point. Well, actually, it kind of is. There's a group of five or six kids on my street and they're the best group of kids. Just really…*nice*. You know? But the twins–"

"*Twins?!*" I pretty much yell the word right at her. I had fallen right into the clutches of Jess's story. I knew she had two boys, but I didn't realize they were twins.

She laughed and it was this beautiful, proud, joyful sound. "Aiden and Leo." She was glowing as she said their names. "They're seven. I can't believe I never told you they were twins!"

"Identical?" I was in awe.

She nodded, "It has been my biggest struggle and also my greatest source of endless entertainment. They're *very* identical."

"Jess, holy *jeepers*. You're my hero."

She blushed bright pink and it made me want to introduce her to Leah right on the spot. "Thank you, but I really just meant to say, I sort of understand what you mean. The boys have never wanted to make friends with the kids on our street because they're too upset about the idea of missing out on things that they would just prefer to be set apart all together. One of the little girls had a party and invited them but they were with their dad that weekend and couldn't make it. It only happened once, but I think they could see what the pattern would look like, and decided to stop hanging out with them."

"That's heartbreaking," I said, meaning it. I could feel how much my face had fallen. "Surely that doesn't matter, they would all still be able to hang out when they're with you?"

"That's what I said, but they don't see it that way," she shrugged, like this was something she had tried to broach with them and had yet to get through. "Anyway, sorry that was a very long walk for a very short drink."

"I feel like I know you, like, thirty percent more in the last five minutes than I have learned the whole time I've known you."

"Me too!" This time, she shouted the words at me and we both dissolved into a fit of unrestrained laughter when the entire cafe went pin-drop silent at the outburst.

It was another thirty minutes before we got up to go, our coffees had long been drunk and Jess now followed both Leah and Natalie on Instagram. We'd parted ways with an actual hug and tentative plans for wine at my house soon as our next after work activity and a promise to see one another tomorrow.

A free day wasn't something I'd had in a long while.

Days off during the week were not at all like free days on the weekend when you tried to cram all your resting into a measly forty eight hours and half of that time was dedicated to cleaning out fish tanks and wiping down the outside of the fridge.

So, I took the opportunity to wander the city. I bought myself a coffee from four different places I'd never been to before and decided not to dress myself down on how I only had a quarter of each. I made a point to enjoy my own company and refused to let any thoughts in from the part of myself that usually creeped out when I was alone. The part that reminded me of *why* I was so alone. Alive and alone when I shouldn't have been, when I had been the person to put someone I loved in a situation they shouldn't have ever been in yet in some cruel twist of fate I was the one who had walked away.

It might have been selfish but I didn't want to think about any of it. For once I wanted to remain in this lighter side of myself, the one reserved for company. I spent the entire day marveling at the realization that I might have just solidified the first adult friendship that I'd ever made with another woman that wasn't Leah and I was feeling a little…nutty about it. *Proud.* Like I was finally grasping the concept of what it meant to be 'high on life'. I even went so far as to berate myself a little at all the times I'd taken the side of a cynical heart whenever I'd seen a bumper sticker or a shirt on a stranger sharing that exact sentiment.

I hadn't realized that I'd essentially spent the whole day walking around with four cold coffees that it was already dark by the time I headed to the closest train station and straight onto a waiting train.

The look on my face was a goofy version of happiness as I began planning all the ways I would tell Leah about Jess. How she'd probably want to fly in ASAP to meet the person behind the choking bell. How I would tell Aspen and how his face would light up because even without knowing, he'd *know* the importance of this moment for me.

It had been nice while it lasted, but I should have known better than to think it *would* last because It was at that moment that I looked up to see the man across from me reading a magazine. The exact magazine happened to be *Rolling Stone* with *Lady Luck* right on front.

My eyes zoned in on the man just to the right of Wyatt, who had his hat on backwards and a cheeky smirk on his face. His green eyes danced with the sort of mischief I'd had the pleasure of seeing up close.

The fear and panic that had only just begun to descend into

my stomach when I'd been sitting in Winny's office sparked back to life with vengeance. Todd and his super massive big flapping mouth hadn't been shy about sharing factually incorrect news with our entire floor and I'd been silly enough to leave him unmonitored in an easy-to-approach location by the nosy men with big cameras during our sidewalk confrontation. People who would have asked him questions he would have had absolutely no problems answering.

The echo of my fear ping ponged around every nerve ending in my body in the least enjoyable way possible, reverberating with every step I took during the walk from the station to my house.

I wasn't sure, but I might have also been muttering to myself which would have sent anyone with any modicum of sense running in any direction away from me. That's why I released a blood curdling scream when I walked right up to my house and came face to face with a broad, yet not immediately familiar, man sitting on the steps leading up to my house.

"Poompaloompa, *ow*." Aspen clutched the sides of his head in a very dramatic way and I just stared at him for a whole three seconds. Half because my eyes had been tethered to the toes of my boots while I walked and now they struggled to adjust to the outline of him loitering on my lightless porch, and also because I was relieved and shocked all over again that this man was, in a very real way, *mine* in some capacity. At least right now.

"I come bearing the gift of food?" He said it like a question, like he was unsure if he should be sitting on the steps of my house.

I was overwhelmed. The door I had sealed shut was rattling, determined to break free of all its locks. Jess's face and the way she had hugged me goodbye. The way I missed Leah and wanted her there at coffee with us and then there was him. Solid, safe and *good*. This man who's career I was certain was going to come to a crashing end because of me but also wanting to be told it would be okay by no one else but the very man who's career I might be responsible for ending.

That was the driving force that made me launch myself right at him. His solid form had suddenly become the only *right* thing I'd ever wrapped my arms around and when his arms held me back it was like I'd never taken a deep breath before and if I had, it had never been this easy.

# 18

## January 29th

**Poppy**

"He offered you *hummus*?" Aspen's face was this mix of confusion and, what I would classify as, misplaced awe.

"You're focusing entirely on the wrong part of the story." I pinched the bridge of my nose while I paced. I had been pacing since we walked into my living room and Ap sat on the couch with his take out food on his lap.

"You're right, just…can we circle back?"

"Yes, we can. But this is important, Aspen." I stopped in front of him but I found myself completely unable to meet his gaze.

It was then that he seemed to realize that there was in fact far more to this explanation than Winston's hummus.

"Poppy." He reached out, but I stepped back away from him because the truth was, this situation could be really bad and there was no doubt that it was my fault.

I wasn't looking at Aspen so I didn't see the flicker of concerned hurt that I knew would have flashed across his face. It didn't matter though, I felt what it did to him in the shift of the air around us.

"The thing is," I started again, keeping my eyes on my hands which were twisting in front of me. "I should have known that he was going to tell people about the whole cousin thing. We left him right there on the sidewalk. He even had his phone out when we left. I wasn't thinking straight but *now…*" I took a deep breath, knowing it was taking far too long to tell him what had happened in my day. Mainly because it might be the thing that removed him from my life. Something that in all honesty should have already happened.

"Poppy, you're kind of making my chest hurt with the suspense." Aspen's tone was joking but I knew that he was on edge because of my poor delivery.

I sat down next to him, still not meeting his eyes. My voice was small and my heart was galloping, "Todd told the whole office about the cousin thing. And the paparazzi stopped my friend Jess outside of the office to ask her questions about me and so I think that he probably would have spoken to them too."

The feeling swimming around in my stomach was dread because as I said it outloud it was becoming more real that this was the sort of thing that would snowball, not just for Aspen, but his whole band. One member getting bad press would turn into an opportunity for things to be written about the other members too.

"Aspen, I'm so sorry. I think–"

"He did," Aspen cut me off and I finally looked up at him. His face was this calm mask of understanding but his eyes were…they were *twinkling*. Like, they actually had a sheen that I would have probably placed as the result of tears of laughter. He was clearly trying not to laugh and I was obviously trying not to cry and one of us was missing something very important.

"Dax had a great time announcing to everyone that if I was sleeping with our cousin, it was news to him. The biggest flaw in the story was that we don't actually have any cousins."

"You what?" I had reverted into a toddler, unable to have one single thought and follow it to completion.

"Todd did speak to the paparazzi, but because I'd told Jane straight away she was on high alert for news of the impending stories so when they popped up today to be printed tomorrow she was all over it. God, I love that woman."

He paused for a second, like thinking of the right path in his mental fork in the road to go down before he kept talking. "Plus, our entire family tree is all over the internet and… no cousins. No one would believe the articles regardless. If stories do get out, which I'm sure there will be, it won't mean anything and they'll die as fast as they were written." Aspen fell back into my couch, the once large-looking piece of furniture now looked entirely too small for any respectable living room. "Anyway, Jane called Allie, 'cause none of us were answering our phones, and Allie called Dax and you know everyone always answers for Allie. She was all 'Did you know Aspen was sleeping with your cousin?!'" He rolled his eyes as if to say, *she knows we have no freaking cousins.*

"I've been thinking about how I can get her back. I was thinking maybe brownies with salt, not sugar–"

He stopped talking the moment he saw my face which was, as you could imagine, a weird mixture of *'what the fuck?'* and '*what the* actual *fuck is going on?!*'.

"*Aspen*, how are you so *calm?*" I was trying, and failing, to keep my cool.

"Because, *Penelope*, this sort of thing happens all the time and that's why we have people in place to make sure stuff doesn't get too far where it could cause any real damage. But this isn't that sort of *stuff*. The world will not end if someone thinks you're my cousin, which they won't. The next article they'd read would probably be about how eerie it is that Dax and I don't have a bigger family and how that somehow is a direct juxtaposition on the state of our careers. People write the *darndest–*"

"You're not taking this seriously, Aspen. This isn't some small thing, this could ruin–"

"I *am* taking it seriously." His face changed a little, showing the side of him that didn't freely give beautiful smiles.

"No you're *not*. This—"

"I know, Poppy. I get it. Todd scared you and that's made you scared for me. I'm not going to get sappy here because I know this is a serious discussion but you being scared means you care and…well, I'm pretty fucking stoked about that." The side of his mouth tugged up and he shrugged like he couldn't help himself. "But that's beside the point. I know what it's like to be scared about the press and scandals. I have seen how stories get spun out of control, I *know* how vicious the media can be. That is not going to happen here. It's one guy who apparently neighs at everyone in your office building. They're going to think he's insane."

His face softened a little as he looked at me, and then he said a little more quietly, "I'm okay, Poppy."

"They wrote about that? The neighing?" I asked, momentarily taken off guard.

"Yeah, just this morning, and something about a toilet brush," he said, trying not to laugh.

I opened my mouth to reply but thought better of it. I shook my head and got the conversation back on track because it was and *wasn't* the point, "Don't you think that it's a sign that this," I waved between us, "is not a good idea?"

"*This?*" he waved between us, "is an *awesome* idea. But *you*," he pointed a finger gun right at me, "are determined to believe otherwise."

"I'm still leaving." It was a last ditch effort. I wasn't determined to believe otherwise. I wholeheartedly believed… *wise.*

I saw the way Aspen's throat worked on a swallow and how his mouth quirked at the side. It looked forced now that I knew what a real smile looked like and the way even the smallest of them transformed his entire face.

"I know."

"This is an omen," I tried again, going so far as to get up off the couch and take two big steps away from him. When I turned back to face him, he'd stood as well and set down the bag of food.

"Omens can be good." He took a step towards me, his face now completely serious.

"I'll hurt you, Aspen. This can't end well," I whispered between us, desperate for him to leave as much as I was for him to stay and knowing full well that was the very last of the strength I had reserved to push him away.

"Then hurt me." He took that last step towards me until there was no space between us at all.

I was done for. So absolutely *done* for.

Would it matter, I wondered, if even knowing this was likely the very thing that would send me to hell had my previous transgressions not done the trick, that I tried? If I was at the big, flaming gates of hell and said to Lucifer himself, '*Hey, big Lu! Well, I tried!*'. Would he believe me and turn me away? Or would he say the very words I repeated to myself day in and day out…'*Maybe. But not hard enough*'.

Aspen's hands were rough and warm when he touched me. One reaching around to hold the back of my neck and the other settling on my lower back. I was putty in his hands. I was someone who'd never been awake before this very moment. I was clothed and very much wished to be completely naked, to say to him '*You can look everywhere, not just my shoulder blades. You can touch me everywhere*'.

His lips had barely touched mine, both my hands in tight fists at the front of his sweatshirt already so lost at the mere *thought* of him that I didn't care what noises were coming out of my mouth. Didn't care that I could feel the flush that I was sure covered my whole body spread up from where my stomach was in knots, making my neck redden and my cheeks tingle. How I could feel it moving down, settling between my legs with a pulsing ache I was sixty percent sure could absolutely kill me if left unattended.

Aspen's kiss turned harder. More desperate. Using the hand he had pressed on my lower back to press me flush with him, he'd just slipped his tongue into my mouth when my phone started to go off.

And I mean it was *going. Off.*

I'd put it on the loudest volume thinking that if Ap called about something with Todd I didn't want to miss it. That entire thought process backfired on me so severely that I shoved him from me in shock. He didn't move an inch but I managed to propel myself back from him with such ferocity that I was going to have to think about what I would do with the dent that now resided in the drywall behind me thanks to my elbow.

"That's my phone," I croaked, like it was some revelation that he hadn't been totally aware of.

"Are you okay?" He made a point of leaning around me to stare directly at my elbow-hole in the wall and pressed his lips into a tight line.

"I should answer my phone." I was losing all my brain cells and for the second time today, I wanted to perish immediately.

"While you do that, I'll put us some dinner." He plucked the bag of food off the coffee table and pressed a kiss to my temple. He didn't say a single thing but I felt his smile nonetheless and it made every part of my body turn a little more into jello.

My phone rang out for another second before I dove for it. Really, I shouldn't have answered the device under any circumstance. I had a flaming hot Cheeto of a rock star divvying up take out between my single plate and single bowl in my half unpacked kitchen and I was answering FaceTime from…I hadn't even checked it before answering but I really, *really* should have.

Leah had filled her lungs with enough air to sustain a deep sea free dive and was thus able to get right to the reason for her phone call.

"Before you say a single thing I just want you to know that I get why you don't date, and even though I'm confident your isolation is the reason you have so many fewer wrinkles than I do, I have held out hope that something was going to happen to remind you that you're a real life woman who deserves to have great sex with hot men. I am *confident* that Aspen is said 'hot men'. Or man. He's your hot man."

"I…" Oh my *fucking God.* "I have lots of great sex." All the noise from the kitchen went completely silent.

"Oh?" Her eyebrows hit her hairline. "Pray tell, Penelope, when was the last time you had an orgasm because of a real life penis?"

"Definitely in the recent past. Leah, *please–*" I whisper-shouted at my best friend but it was no use. Not only did she know it was a lie, but my house echoed worse than the Grinch's cave lair and to make it even better, my phone was still on full volume and wouldn't go down no matter how violently I pressed the button.

"*Errrrrr,*" she screamed the noise into the microphone of her phone, pressing her mouth to it so closely that all I could see was one perfectly groomed eyebrow. "You've had sex with like two people and your dry spell has lasted five years."

"Four people," I mumbled on reflex and hated myself immediately for participating the tiniest bit in this conversation that I was completely aware was being overheard right now.

"Three and a half," she tutted in mock seriousness. "We agreed that Henry Lexington didn't count as a full point."

I wanted to scream into a pillow. I wanted to be swallowed by a black hole. I wanted to change my name to something obscure like Nebraska and live as a recluse in the Swiss Alps.

"And also," she said on the back of another deep breath.

"Leah, *wait–*"

"No, this is important and I knew you'd try and stop me."

"You can say anything you want later, but right *now–*" I was getting hot and cold flashes.

"No, I won't be silenced, Poppy. Do you know how many

photos are going around of you guys out front of your office? You guys look *incredible* together. Like, I am talking a perfect fucking *match.*"

"Thank you, but you need to stop talking, like right now." I was trying to tap the call end button, but my fingers were so sweaty that the grip on my phone was less than ideal and no matter how many times I tapped the big red circle with the 'x' in it, her big pretty face was still on my phone screen.

It was too late though, Aspen was standing in the doorway from the kitchen to the living room with the biggest – and I mean it was *absolutely behemoth* – shit eating grin on his face holding one bowl and one plate, both piled monstrously high with food.

He kept his eyes on me the whole time, taking measured steps until he was sitting right beside me and then he did the unthinkable. He leaned into the camera frame and without dropping his smile even the smallest bit delivered a cool, calm and collected, "Hey, Leah."

Well, that shut her up real fast.

What neither of us were prepared for was the scream that followed her 'caught with her pants down' expression.

My phone went flying from my sweaty grip and the food Aspen had been carrying dropped the last inch to the coffee table with a clatter.

Everyone was silent. The only noise coming from Nat's water pump in the kitchen.

"Poppy?" Leah's muffled voice came from somewhere behind the couch but I was too mortified to move, even when she started chanting my full name to the tune of Three Blind Mice.

Aspen was the one to make the first move. Reaching down

the back of the couch, he retrieved my phone and faced Leah front on even though I knew he was a little nervous given her last two responses to seeing his face.

"Please don't scream again. If we're going to be friends you should know that it scares me every time you do."

"I've done it twice," she countered and I could visualize the single raised eyebrow she favored as her visual examination point.

"And it was equally as frightening the second time." Ap placed my phone against a rogue pile of books so that Leah was facing the pair of us before he picked up the bowl of food and placed it in my lap.

"Poppy," he said before shoveling the first mouthful of food into his mouth, "was just starting to tell me about Winston and his hummus."

"Fuck the hummus," Leah said, her own bowl of food materializing out of thin air, "have you heard about the choking bell?"

"I have not!" Aspen's genuine enthusiasm sent a pang through my heart and my hand on reflex reached up to grip my shirt right about the traitorous organ.

My eyes volleyed back and forth between the two of them and I was momentarily floored with the notion that these were my people. At least for right now, they were both completely mine and a splinter of the weight I carried around with me shifted, making breathing a little easier.

"Poppy!" Leah shouted like she'd said my name more than once. "Is she there?"

"Mm," Aspen said, looking right at me with something that looked a whole lot like what I was feeling and leaned in to kiss my jaw, the spot erupting in goosebumps. "She's here."

"Poppy, tell Aspen about the choking bell. Aspen, this is what we're getting for Christmas so when you get yours you still have to act surprised. That's a must do with Poppy and presents, even if you know what they are."

"Roger that." Ap saluted the phone before giving me a wink.

Leah was done waiting for me to start and launched into the story of the choking bell herself. I watched Aspen nod along like it was the most incredible story in the whole world.

I did something dangerous, then: I let myself see – really *see* – how he fit into my world. Even when I was certain he couldn't, that I couldn't fit into his. That I might even be the person who *ruined* his world, I could see it.

The thing that terrified me the most was that it almost felt like this was the feeling I'd been running towards, that all my searching had been for this exact moment whether I felt like I deserved it or not. And because I'd already done one dangerous thing this evening I decided to do another.

I let myself imagine what it would be like to unpack all the boxes I had still taped shut. To revel in the relief of how it would feel to stop running, of the blinding joy I felt at the possibility of staying still.

# 19

# February 3rd

**Aspen**

"I can't do it!" Poppy yelled from the top of the rock climbing wall.

"Yes, you can," I told her for the fifth time from my position on the ground acting as her belayer.

"No, I can't. This was an awful idea!" she bellowed, smooshing herself closer to the wall.

"You just finished climbing the whole way up verbalizing an essay on how this was the best date you'd ever been on." I knew she could hear the smile in my voice. I was in a particularly good mood because when I'd picked her up and told her this was a date right from the get go she didn't fight me on it. Poppy merely looked at me with her big, amber eyes and released a sigh with a small smile before nodding her head and whispering, "Okay."

"I lied. I'm a big fat liar. I'm going to be stuck up here forever."

"No, you won't–"

"Tell Leah I love her," she yelled again.

"Poppy–"

"And look after Natalie, the password to her instagram is her name backwards, four exclamation points and the numbers zero, two, one, four." By the time she finished speaking her voice had trailed off into a little whimper.

If this place had been packed, I'm sure we would have drawn a crowd, but I'd called ahead and booked the place out for the afternoon so it was just Poppy, me and my security guy Jason who was hanging by the front door trying not to laugh. I came here often enough that the owner knew who I was and trusted us both to climb safely, so he was tucked up and away in his office on the second floor. I made a note to send him a couple tickets for the first show of our tour as a thank you. I'd called last minute and it was only because he was a real, honest to Zeppelin legend that we'd been able to book the place out on a Saturday afternoon.

Jason released what had to be the start of a chuckle and I shot him a glare that had him promptly leaving the center to stand out front.

"Poppy," I started again, "I need you to take three big, deep breaths. Can you do that?"

"I don't know," she squeaked.

"One," I took a deep breath and watched as she did the same. "Two."

She did it again and I saw a small amount of tension leave her body.

"And three...I thought you were having fun?" I asked in all seriousness because I was sure I hadn't picked this wrong.

"I was." She sounded at least thirty percent calmer.

"And now?"

"I didn't realize how high I'd come." Her voice was muffled on account of her mouth being pressed almost directly to the wall. "It's way too high and everything's moving and if I open my eyes I'll pass out."

"Okay, but you know this rope I'm holding onto?"

Poppy nodded her head jerkily without actually looking at me.

"Well, that means that I control whether you fall or not. You don't have to climb down, you can let go and I'll drop you slowly."

"I'm heavy," she cried.

"Sure you are, and I'm also a star fish that lives under a large boulder." The tone of my voice said it all and my heart tripped over itself at the small giggle she released.

"I love Patrick," she said, still talking directly to the wall. "He's my favorite."

"Another thing we have in common." I grinned even though she couldn't see. "Remember when I said it was all about trust?"

Poppy was silent for a bit before her muffled reply came, "Yeah?"

"Well that's what we're doing, we're getting right of that pesky little 'but' because you're going to learn to trust me."

"I didn't think you were being *literal*." She was yelling again.

"Literal is the best approach. Now, do you trust me?"

"In *theory*…"

"Poppy, if you let go of the wall, all you're going to do is swing back. I've got you." I watched her knuckles go white with the grip she had on the wall and just when I thought I'd have to get a ladder, trying my best not to be disheartened by this date going to shit, she spoke.

"Okay," she said quietly and I was half convinced I imagined it.

"Okay?" The question was mainly fueled by my own shock.

"Okay, I'm going to let go now, are you ready?"

Her voice shook with her nerves and all of a sudden this seemed a lot bigger than just letting her down slowly to the ground.

I knew she found it hard to lean on people. To let people look after her. I'd gleaned as much when she was incoherent on my couch, gripping her stomach and asking if she could do anything to help me look after her. She'd fallen back asleep before I had to deign that with a reply.

"I'm ready."

And then she let go. It was accompanied by an ear piercing scream, *but*…she let go and then her scream dissolved into laughter. This huge, incredible laughter that had to have come straight from her soul. I half expected all the lights around us to implode, unable to contain the energy that burst into the room. She paired that world changing sound with an expression that lit up her entire face in a blinding show of happiness and it did something to me.

It did *everything* to me and I couldn't help but begin to compile a list of ways that I could hear that sound all over again, every day for the rest of my life. There were lyrics and melodies and drum beats that had never existed before but now did, just for her.

She was bright eyed and rosy cheeked and then she was right in front of me.

Poppy's helmet had gone a little wonky from the way she'd pancaked herself to the wall. She peered up at looking like the world's biggest goofball. I knew I was staring, but it wasn't my fault. She was beautiful.

"Hey," she said, still beaming up at me.

"Hey," my voice was a rasp and my mouth was dry and all I wanted to do was kiss her.

"You had me." She reached out and looped a finger through my own harness. It wasn't a question, or a tentative statement. It was three little words that she spoke clear as day with not a single ounce of doubt.

"I did." I was still staring at her, trying to slow my own heart, to slow down my emotions and calm down but she was still looking at me in that way and I wasn't sure I could remember *not* feeling like this. Like any time before Poppy was just simply missing her until I met her.

Lifting up onto her tiptoes she slid her arms up my chest and around my shoulders pulling me down to her until she could press her lips to mine.

I snapped back into myself and reached for her, sliding my arms around her waist and then standing back up to my full height and bringing her with me so her feet were dangling in the air.

She laughed into our kiss and the feel of it drove me wild. I wanted to hear it again. To feel her laugh against my skin over and over until it was all I knew.

Poppy pulled back, her cheeks flushed and helmet still crooked, looking the happiest I'd seen her. She kissed me again gently and then spoke softly with her lips against my ear, "I want to do it again."

I'd seen Poppy almost every single day of the last week. We'd gone back and forth on meeting at her house for dinner and then deriving a very skilled and watertight plan of getting her up and into my penthouse even though new photos of us together and alone surfaced on the internet daily.

It was the Friday night before our wall climbing date, something I still hadn't told her the details about even though she'd pleaded a great number of times.

She'd been pulling a pasta bake she'd made out of the oven by the time I got home from the studio. The elevator doors opened to the lights on and dimmed, casting the living room into a warm glow where she'd already put two glasses of what looked like wine on the coffee table and lit a candle I was pretty sure I'd owned for like two years and hadn't lit once.

I could hear her around the corner in the kitchen and walking into her pulling the dish out of the oven, an episode of what sounded like *Queen Charlotte* playing from her laptop. She'd seen me right away and her face had lit up in an easy upward tug of her full lips. Those looks of genuine happiness were coming easier and easier from her.

I knew I was breaking down her walls. That whatever those 'rules' she'd mentioned that we'd broken were losing their grip on her. I'd half wanted her not to notice me right away, so that I could see her moving around, bringing so many of my wishes to life just by standing right where she was.

"I hope you like pasta bake!" she beamed, taking off the oven mitts and pausing her show.

What Poppy didn't know was that I was a die hard *Bridgerton* fan, and nothing made me cry like a baby quite like the final episode of *Queen Charlotte*, so I was familiar with the episode she had paused; right when Charlotte and George were about to dance together at the ball for their son. I walked over to her laptop and pressed play. *'You and me,'* George said, and then the instrumental music started.

I reached for Poppy and she came to me easily. I held one of her hands in mine against my chest and felt her other hand wrapped around my back, gripping my shirt.

We moved in slow circles and when Poppy looked up at me with a small, happy smile on her face, I moved down to kiss her knowing I had everything I'd ever wanted right then and there.

# 20

# February 5th

## Poppy

"Tell me again!" Leah squealed. We were FaceTiming while folding our laundry.

"Let the people note this will be the fourth time I've told this story." I rolled my eyes but it was all for show.

Something in me felt *lighter*. It happened gradually over the last week and I was struggling to recognize this version of myself.

"You're lucky that I love you so much that I'm willing to look over the fact that I'm hearing all this juicy goodness *months* after it actually happened. All I ask is for you to tell me your sexual escapades over and over again whenever I ask no matter the time of day."

"It hasn't been months," I counter, folding a sweater that wasn't mine. "Hey, this is yours!" I held it up to her.

"You're joking, I have been looking for that for *days*." Leah had pulled the phone right to her face.

"Want me to mail it?" I set it off to the side.

"Nah, I'll grab it when I come to visit next." She kissed the camera of her phone and put it back down. "Now, please tell me again like this is the first time you're saying it."

"Leah–"

"*Please,* Poppy? I haven't had sex in so long my lady bits are pretty much filing me for divorce." She pouted, a facial expression that would now forever have me recalling Leah's 'dry spell'. Just for reference, it had been *maybe* a month since she'd seen any action.

I took a deep breath, "I have something to tell you."

She dropped the clothes she was folding, eyes widening comically, "What is it? Are you

okay?"

"Aspen picked me up from work a couple weeks ago."

"I saw the photos, but do go on." She gave me a half hearted glare and I glared back,

having not so soon forgotten how she aired my sexual history with vigor on loudspeaker while Aspen had been in the other room.

"I ended up having food poisoning and he took care of me for a while on the weekend."

"I'm swooning!" The back of Leah's hand shot to her brow and she disappeared from view.

"I threw up on myself so he bathed me."

"He bathed you?" She sounded overjoyed.

"He had to undress me and hold me upright in the shower and I was so incoherent I'm pretty sure I was speaking Klingon and he didn't even look. He just kept his eyes on my shoulder blades."

"Your shoulder blades?" Now she sounded in awe, regardless of this not being the first time she'd heard the story.

"You're just repeating everything I'm saying."

"Because the words coming out of your mouth are rocking my world." Leah popped back up into view with her own beaming grin.

"On another note, I think I'm going to make a real effort with Jess."

"The founder of the choking bell?"

"The very same."

"I have a wonderful feeling about her. I want to meet her," Leah said with an air of finality.

I wanted them to meet too, Jess and I had been spending more time together throughout the last week, not just because of the leaps and bounds we'd made on the friendship side of things, but because Winny had the capital idea of volun-telling us that we would be the soul organizers of the Say No To The January Blues party that was now supposed to be at the end of February.

We'd been permitted an hour every day to sit down and plan. It was far too much time for what needed to be done, but Jess and I had made the cafe just outside our building into our official meeting place and most of the time we spent there had been used to get to know one another more. We'd even tentatively put down this Thursday as our Wine Night because her boys would be with their dad.

"Speaking of me coming to visit," Leah said as a segway. She'd just taken a deep breath when my phone started to buzz with another incoming call. It was Aspen.

"Leah, Aspen's calling," I said, and because I was on Face-Time, I could see the way my own face lit up.

"Already ditching me for boys," she heaved a sigh that had

absolutely no substance. She was just as happy as I was. "I'm so happy for you, Pen."

I knew if she'd been here she'd have wrapped me in one of her hugs that had acted like glue to all my cracks for so many years.

"Godspeed, sissy," she said as her farewell before stopping a second and doing her best to hold meaningful eye contact with me through the phone. "Hey, I really like seeing you like this."

"Like what?" I asked her even when I already knew the answer.

"Happy." With a little wave she ended the call and I picked up Aspen's incoming one.

"Hello?" I held the phone to my year, already smiling like an imbecile.

"I'm desperately sad and lonely, will you come have dinner with me?" His voice was muffled and it sounded like he was either talking directly into a pillow or he was super far away from his phone.

"Can we get take out from that Mexican place near your building? The one that's always playing Jamaican music?"

"Poppy, no one has ever said anything so perfectly perfect to me in all my twenty eight years of life."

"I'll order an Uber," I laughed, putting my folded laundry away and the unfolded stuff back in the basket to, let's be honest, never find its way out of there again until it was time to wear the articles in question.

"No need you sweet, sweet lady. I'm out front."

"Of where?"

"I can't be sure, but it looks like a huge boot."

"You're outside the house of the old lady that lives in a

shoe?"

"I wouldn't say you're *old*, but–"

"You better watch your tone or I'll steal all your queso and hide your favorite apron."

"Now you're just being mean." I would bet my next paycheck he was pouting.

"I can't believe you drove here before I said yes," I said, pulling a sweater on and making my way downstairs.

"Call it quiet optimism. Oh, and pack a bag, I refuse to return you to your humble abode after our meal. It kills me a little every time." After a second he added, "If you want." Another second, "I'll take the couch if that's what you're worried about."

"I wasn't worried," I said, not meaning to make him freak out but I had been too stunned to speak. Stunned silly, actually.

Silly with oodles of excitement that I was trying really hard not to scream in delight. I'd taken the stairs two at a time back to my room and had already finished backing a bag by the time he'd spoken about the couch nonsense and my reply was accompanied with the solid click of my deadbolt.

Aspen still had the phone to his ear when I slipped into the car and for the first time I didn't let myself think about any of the repercussions when he leaned over the console and kissed me. And I mean, he *kissed* me. Like it had been years instead of hours since he'd last done it. Like, if that was the last kiss we ever had, he'd gone out with a bang.

"Hey," he smiled against my lips.

The sigh that left my body took with it all worries as I let myself fall into him, to kiss him again and with everything he made me feel, "Hey."

Aspen had parked his car and grabbed the bag of take out food from my lap before I'd realized he'd pulled the keys from the ignition. He was up shoving corn chips into his mouth before my shout of baffled displeasure had finished leaving my mouth.

"You're eating my corn chips!" I shouted at my lap while trying to get the seat belt to unclick.

He had replied with something but his mouth was so full of *my* chips that I didn't understand what he said.

In my haste to get out of the car, my phone dropped from my lap and disappeared under the seat, so far that I couldn't even remotely figure out where it had gone.

Aspen's laugh was bouncing around the basement garage in unbridled glee while I rolled my eyes and crouched down next to the car, sticking my head into the footwell to try and see where my phone had gone. It was only after I'd spotted the device, reached in and grabbed it did I notice out of the corner of my eye all the stickers that littered the underside of the dash.

"Asp–" I tried to say his name because my heart had started to beat too fast and I was half convinced I was seeing things.

Half the stickers have been peeled off, the ones closer to the part of the dash you might be able to see from the seat. The outlines of old glue still remained, an ode to a time and place long come to pass, to a whole separate life entirely. But further underneath, I could see them. The once white bubble stickers in shapes of unicorns and rainbows and flowers all yellowed with age.

"Aspen," I said his name again, but I wasn't sure any noise was coming from my mouth.

I remembered putting those stickers there.

I'd been small enough to sit in this very footwell, seven maybe. Casimir had stopped at his work because he'd forgotten his wallet and needed to grab it on our way to do something, I couldn't really remember. He'd just gotten me these stickers and I had been in an awful mood all day because I loved them so much and I hadn't been able to think of a special enough place to put them.

Somewhere that I felt was deserving of them.

But then I'd thought about how much my brother deserved my fancy new stickers. I climbed into the front, pushed the seat all the way back and started to decorate his car. Something *he* loved, with my stickers, something *I* loved.

Looking back now, there had been a moment of shock on his face when he opened the driver side door to see me, mid sticker-sticking, and anger had crossed his face. No doubt thinking that not a single thing in his life could be just his. It had to be covered in stickers, or hold little ballerina slippers or sparkle in some capacity. I hadn't seen it then though, I'd simply held a sticker out for him to pick where it would go and just like that, his face had softened. He'd walked around to my side of the car, opened the door and sat right on the ground next to me.

*"You wanted to put your special stickers on my car?"*

*"You said it was our car, Cassy." I still held my little finger out to him, sticker and all. "So, these are our stickers too."*

*I would give anything now to know just a single thought that went through his head.*

*He plucked the sticker from me and placed it front and center*

*on the glove box before leaning in to give me a kiss on the cheek
and saying, "Thank you for sharing them with me."*

The memory was so painfully vivid. It had thrown open
that door in my mind where I kept it along with everything
else that had to do with Casimir.

I was crying. A full, snotty, hiccuping mess. I'd even go so
far as to say I was beside myself, half there in Aspen's garage
and half with my brother, all those years ago.

"I got you," Ap said into my hair, hauling me up and into
his chest. "You're okay, I've got you."

He just kept saying it over and over again. He didn't know
why or what was happening, but he didn't need to. I knew
with certainty that he'd always be there, just like this, knowing
or not.

"I'm here," he murmured into the hair on the top of my
head, "I'm right here."

I wasn't sure if it was being safe in that very knowledge,
that I was being held up by hands that I knew wouldn't let
me go no matter if all the jagged pieces of the grief I couldn't
even express cut him as they exploded from me, but I knew
for sure that I surprised us both with what came next.

When the crying had eventually subsided and my breathing
returned to normal, I looked up at Ap who had nothing but
helpless concern on his face and gave him a watery smile.
Tears filling my eyes again and paving hot tracks down my
face. I reached out and put my shaking hand on the top of his
car, looking at it like I could see Casimir's hand there instead
of mine.

"This was his car." I looked back to Aspen who was looking
between me and my hand and then back to me before his face
softened out in complete understanding.

"Your brother?" His voice was soft, but encompassing a hint of the awe that I knew was written all over my face.

I just nodded and gently pulled him back down to the ground where he followed me without hesitation. I pointed to the stickers that he had probably never noticed and watched as he reached out to trace what was left of them reverently.

"Those are my stickers, Ap," my voice cracked but I was still smiling. Caught in this weird limbo of heartbreak and happiness.

Aspen turned his attention back to me, reaching out to wipe the tears from my cheeks and then using the sleeve of his sweatshirt to wipe my nose which made me laugh and hiccup some form of the word, 'ew'.

He got up and came back with our take-out bag, resuming his previous position. Reaching into the bag he pulled out my corn chips, stopping only to give me a pointed look with a small eye roll, single-handedly making the moment that much easier to bear. He pulled out the queso dip next and dipped not one, not two, but three single chips. He handed one to me, kept one for himself and put another in the foot well of his car.

Aspen reached for my hand to cheers my chip and then the one he'd placed in the car, "To Casimir, and his car's safe return home."

He had no idea what he'd just done. Such simple words and he'd unpacked everything I'd always kept close to my heart about home, and that feeling you got when you were there. Of just *knowing*. Like he knew how it felt too. That it wasn't the house you lived in in the city you were born in, or the share house you paid too much rent for with your friends in your first lease after college. It was knowing that you could be anywhere in the world with the people that were on the other side of those doors and feel whole, simply from being safe in the knowledge that they were there with you.

I couldn't do anything except nod my head, tapping my chip to Aspen's and then to the one he'd set aside for my brother, feeling more complete in that moment than I had in the last thirteen years.

# 21

## February 5th

### Poppy

I thought I'd be borderline catatonic after Aspen and I had sat in his cold basement, eating our Mexican food with my brother's car, but I wasn't. He hadn't treated my breakdown as a plague. He hadn't tried to say anything other than reassure me he was there and then he'd sat down and eaten with me like it had been perfectly okay for me to be both sad and happy.

Like it was okay that I was sitting in my grief almost thirteen years on from its moment of inception but also laughing at the way he had managed to smear guacamole onto his forehead and regardless of my detailed description and even *pointing* where it was, he hadn't been able to wipe it away.

It felt as though, until that moment, I hadn't realized that I could have both.

Aspen hadn't treated me like I was something in need of fixing. He'd just treated me like 'Poppy'. The same as he had at the bar, then on the hike and every day after. During all our phone calls and messages dates. Always the same.

He had retreated into himself a little since we'd made our way up to his apartment and I desperately wanted to know what was running through his head because whatever it was, it had taken him somewhere else. It wasn't so much that I thought I could help, or that it was even anything he might want my help with, but I wanted to sit in whatever troubled him *with* him, like he'd done for me.

If he could feel my blatant staring at his face while he watched the movie I picked but hadn't watched a single moment of, he didn't say anything about it. He didn't even look at me while all I did was catalog his features over and over again like he was all the answers to everything I'd ever be asked from this day forward and I needed to know it all.

One of his hands rested on the top of my legs which were draped over his lap, his thumb moving in a gentle path up and down.

I took a deep breath and moved before I could over think the entire situation. I grabbed the remote from where it lay discarded between us and paused the movie. Ap didn't look at me, didn't even seem to realize that anything had changed until I pulled my legs from his hold and made my way onto his lap, straddling him.

When I finally brought my eyes to his, he was already looking at me. Clarity coming back into his forest green gaze, his hands settling on my hips.

I didn't really need to say anything, not as I reached up to take off his hat, pushing my fingers through the thick, soft strands of his dark brown hair. So dark that in the dim light of his living room it looked black.

Aspen was striking. He was both beautiful and handsome all at the same time.

My fingers grazed the roughened edge of his jaw, a shadow of his stubble making itself known and I couldn't stop my smile from growing.

"What?" he said, the corner of his mouth pulling upward a fraction while he watched me watch him.

"You're very handsome, Aspen Killian," I whispered the simple fact into the space between us.

His features slipped into something serious and I watched, transfixed, as his throat worked on a swallow.

My own breath caught when he gripped my waist tighter and when I braved a glance back at his eyes, they were on my lips.

"I want to kiss you," he said, eyes unmoving.

"Okay," I nodded, really putting my self control to the test by not squirming in his lap.

He said those words, but he didn't move.

"But?" I prompted, my hands had settled onto his biceps and it was an actual effort to keep my grip on him soft.

"There are no 'buts' for me, Poppy." And I knew exactly what he meant. "Are there any for you?" His eyes were all seeing. Breaking down every wall I'd put up between us, making me want everything from him. Trusting me to trust him, to be able to navigate it all together, whatever 'it' was. No matter the fall out of the decisions we made.

"No," I said, and I meant it. Right then, I meant it more than I'd meant anything. "No 'buts'."

And then he kissed me.

Aspen's hands were in my hair, they were rough and soft, tugging and caressing all at the same time. His teeth grazed and then pulled at my bottom lip before he let go and we both looked at each other.

"Woah," I said, blinked at him like I was seeing him for the first time. My bottom lip tingled from the lingering sting of his bite.

"Woah good? Or woah bad?" His eyes were bright and his mouth already curving upwards.

"Good," I nodded. "Very good."

"I told you I could seduce the shit out of you." He was leaning back in, arms wrapping around my back and pulling me close to him. His hands were warm in the path they carved out, gliding over my shirt, but every single point of contact was lighting me up and I wondered how he'd react if I just spontaneously combusted.

"Never doubted you for a second." I crashed my mouth back to his, no longer wanting to be timid or careful. Only wanting every part of him pressed to every part of me.

I pulled back abruptly, "Wait, just to clarify, we are going to have sex right now, right?"

His smile was blinding. It was wide and carefree and existed solely for me, "Yes, Poppy. We're absolutely going to be having sex. Imminently."

I nodded in whole hearted agreement, "Okay. *Good.*"

Even if I'd wanted to get another word in, there was no space for it.

Aspen was incredibly thorough in the way he kissed me, just like the times before. His hand reached up to hold the side of my face, his thumb sliding along my jaw to angle it. Kissing me slowly, in ways that lingered and sent pulsing waves of heat through my body, starting at the base of my throat and pounding outward. The languid, lazy way his mouth moved made my body respond to him in a way I hadn't even known it could.

With the gentle roll of my hips against him, urged on by the way his hands gripped me, the way he helped me move, it was going to be the very thing that made me go insane.

I pulled back, however reluctantly, to tell him as much, that I needed *more* but he dragged his mouth down to my jaw. To the place behind my ear, to my neck and my collarbones and I realized if I had lived all the days of my life without being touched like this, by this man, it wouldn't have been a life I much wanted at all.

"Aspen." I was perhaps the most impressive woman alive to still be able to speak under my current circumstance.

"Mm?" He reached for my shirt and pulled it up and over my head, leaving me in front of him in my best bra (thank God for laundry day and leaving my best if not arguably most uncomfortable bra to the end of my rotation).

I knew what he'd see the moment the shirt came off and I steadied myself for it. For whatever was going to happen, the questions. He'd seen the scar before but he hadn't said a thing about it.

This felt different now and I realized if he asked, I'd tell him. I'd tell him anything he wanted to know.

His eyes moved from my face to the scar of the bullet wound on my left shoulder. I saw the way his throat worked, the way his jaw flexed, but nothing happened the way I had thought it would. I should have known that.

Nothing with Aspen had ever played out the way I thought it would.

His thumb moved across the scar, causing me to shiver before he pressed a kiss to it once then leaned his forehead on my shoulder like another puzzle piece of me had slid into place for him.

Like those pieces were things worth collecting. He made me *believe* they were.

I let my hands move into his hair and pressed a kiss of my own to the top of his head.

"You said imminently." I could have just run through the finish line of a marathon for the way I practically panted the words.

"Poppy," Aspen was talking to the place where his hands touched the skin of my waist.

I looked down, just to see what he was seeing and was almost rendered unconscious by the sight of his hands splayed over my rib cage. "You're in no way allowed to rush me in this moment." He stood up in one fluid motion, doing wonders for my self-esteem. His mouth didn't leave my skin, walking the memorized path all the way to his bedroom.

He set me on his bed with a gentleness that no one had ever shown me, not even myself and, with a quick look up at me for quiet permission, unbuttoned my jeans. He tugged them off along with my underwear in one fell swoop. The entire visual was wildly impressive.

I reached up to unclasp my bra and then I was just there, completely and totally naked. Aspen's eyes unabashedly roamed over me. His appraisal was slow and unhurried and only when he finally looked back up to my eyes did he speak, "I think this is the best moment of my entire life." He delivered the words in a quiet reverence that made me immediately laugh.

"You're such a dork!" I reached for a pillow behind me and threw it right at his head.

When it dropped to the floor he was grinning at me in complete and total satisfaction. I knew my expression matched his own as I moved to kneel on the bed in front of him and reached for his shirt.

"My turn," I whispered. I took my time undressing him, making sure I cataloged every part of his body. Reveling in the way the muscles on his back, his arms, his stomach tightened at the slightest brush of my fingertips. Infatuated with the goosebumps that erupted along his thighs when I pulled his own jeans down his legs.

Then it all came to a crashing halt.

I couldn't breathe. Breath wouldn't enter my lungs and my eyelids were paralyzed.

"Poppy?" he whispered.

"Holy Toledo," I blurted. "That's—" I was, in fact, staring right at his penis.

"You have to know, my ego will never, ever, recover from this." He was beaming at me so big his eyes crinkled and his dimples had nowhere to hide. I wanted to flick his nose.

"No, Aspen, I've never–" My mouth was completely dry.

"Had sex?"

I gave him a look that could have wilted flowers, "I've had sex."

"I know, three and a half times." He wagged his eyebrows at me and I shoved his chest lightly.

"I've never had sex with anything remotely close to your… caliber." I couldn't look away from it. It was actually staring me down.

"Caliber?"

"As far as I'm concerned that's a weapon. I'm not sure I'll…that it'll…" I couldn't get the word 'fit' out because that would mean potentially a. Not having sex with Aspen and b. Reinforcing just how likely the reality that I'd regrown my own hymen actually was.

He didn't say anything for a while and I was still…well, I was still staring at his *weapon.*

"Poppy," Ap spoke softly, only the barest hint of amusement still tracing his words, "do you trust me?"

"Yes," I said, right to his penis. "I trust you."

He pinched my chin to tilt my face up so I could see the exact way his face looked when he spoke again.

He looked ravenous.

"Then it'll fit." He ducked down, capturing my lips with his.

He moved into me, urging me back up his bed until he was above me, and all I could focus on was how I had imagined what it would feel like to have his skin against mine a hundred different ways, but it hadn't measured up to the reality of it all.

I saw us from outside of my own body. Saw the way his hand glided up my thigh, the way he looked at me from above, how my mouth opened in a silent moan. It did something to me. Made me wildly, insanely needy for him in a matter of seconds. More than I had been before, if that was even possible. It inflated my confidence beyond measure and I didn't even recognize myself when I reached between our bodies and took him in my hand.

"Oh my holy *fuck,*" Ap's breath hitched and his hips gave an involuntary thrust, "Poppy."

My name on his lips, in that very moment, was like being picked first. Like winning gold in the Olympics. I was getting a Nobel Prize. Being handed an Oscar. Like waking up every morning for the rest of my life and the first thing I get to see are eyes of brilliant forest green.

"Yes?" My voice was husky and I was morphing into a butterfly. I could feel it.

"Your hand is cold." His eyes were half lidded with lust but they still glinted with amusement and I knew that sex with Aspen would never be anything but fun and easy and comfortable. Because *Aspen* was all those things.

He made absolutely everything better.

I pulled my hands up and breathed into them, rubbing my palms together, "Better?" I raised an eyebrow at him, letting my hands travel down the length of his chest, feeling the dips and hollows of the muscles beneath his warm golden skin until he was in my hand again.

"Uh-huh." Aspen's mouth had gone slack, eyes almost closing. He swallowed once, twice, "Thank you."

I had no idea who I became when Aspen's lips found mine again, when I continued to touch him and capture his sounds in my mouth, desperate to keep every single one of them forever.

"Poppy," Aspen said into the crook of my neck, "I just need to see something." He spoke the words against my neck, continuing his descent until he pulled himself from my grip and a small, displeased whimper left me. I felt the curve of his mouth on the skin of my stomach, leaving a trail of nips and kisses on his way down.

"What are you doing?" That was my voice, but also not. It was the voice of someone who was currently way more turned on than I'd ever been in my whole entire life.

Aspen looked up at me, eyes dark and hair falling in front of them, "I want to taste you."

"You do?" I squeaked.

He nodded, still moving down, "I've thought about it more than you could comprehend."

"You have?" *Holy cow.*

"A lot," he confirmed, settling down between my legs. *Ohmygod.*

I had little to no warning before his mouth was on me. Licking and tasting and devouring me until I wasn't *me* anymore. I was light as fairy dust. I'd completed my metamorphosis and had become a butterfly that was the only one its kind.

My hand reached down to thread into his hair while the other gripped the sheets beneath me.

Aspen splayed a hand across my stomach and locked the other around my thigh, keeping me still when my back was determined to bow off the bed. Every movement he made was a match striking, a flame igniting. I didn't think I could keep existing when I heard him groan in pleasure of his own and I opened my eyes to find his shadowed gaze already looking up at me. It was picture frames falling from walls and houses crumbling and planets colliding as everything I'd ever thought I'd known collapsed so that room could be made just for him.

His name was the only thing I knew. Over and over again. Shudder after mind altering shudder I knew nothing but the feel of his mouth on me. Nothing but his hands keeping me anchored to the bed instead of letting me disappear straight through it.

"That was the sexiest thing I've ever seen," he spoke against my skin. "And I'm positive I've never loved my name as much as I love it right now." He settled himself back against me, my thighs shaking and vision blurred and fingers still tangled in his hair.

"Poppy," he said into the skin of my neck, as he dragged his mouth along my jaw, his hands roaming my body. My stomach, my breasts. "Poppy. *Poppy,*" his voice cracked and I lifted my eyes to meet his. He kissed the corner of my mouth and said, "I think I knew you before I met you."

I couldn't speak. I had no idea what he was doing to me but I never wanted him to stop.

Ap gently pulled my wrists from him one at a time and guided them away from their happy place around his neck and in his hair. "I try to remember everything before you and all I can think of is how much I missed you until you showed up." He pulled my arms up above my head and firmly held both wrists in one hand. His other hand tracked back down the length of my body along with his eyes, like he was unconvinced this wasn't just a dream.

"I have wanted you *everywhere.* All the time. I've dreamed about this, did you know that?"

I just shook my head.

"How you'd sound, how you'd taste, how you'd *feel.*" He kissed me and I could taste myself on his tongue. The feel of him everywhere except where I was most desperate for him made me whimper, pushing me to my own absolute breaking point. "Aspen, *please.*"

That's what did it, I could see his restraint break but then he moved to get off me and I hadn't anticipated that at all.

"Wh–where are you going?" I hooked my legs around his waist to keep him against me, frowning up at him.

"Condom?" His voice was raspy and his eye were hooded like battling through the fog of

lust that covered us both was maybe the hardest thing he'd ever done.

"It's okay," I shook my head. "I'm on the pill and I…you'd be the first person I've done this with."

He knew exactly what I meant and if I thought he was ravenous before, he was vibrating with it now.

"Me too." He nodded, his grip on my wrists tightening again. "Are you sure?"

"*Yes.* Aspen, plea–"

The words died on my tongue as he lined himself up with my entrance and pushed into me slowly. *Completely.* A hand coming to my leg, hiking it higher up on his hip as he pressed in and in and *in.*

"Are you…is this…*Fuck.*" His jaw was clenched, every muscle in his body taught as we both watched the way he moved into me, until there was no space left between us.

"Poppy?" he gasped, dragging his eyes up to settle on my face.

I'd never in my entire life felt so perfectly, excruciatingly full. I was convinced that what was happening between us was altering the chemistry of my brain forever. How could anyone ever be the same after this?

"We're having sex." *Real profound, Poppy.*

"Mostly, yeah," Aspen said, his body still tense even as his face softened, the side of his mouth twitching upward.

"Ap," I whispered, wanting to reach for him but his grip on my wrists was absolute. "*More.*"

"You want more?" he rasped, grip tightening as he lifted my leg higher, eyes frantically trying to read my face. To make sure I meant what I said.

"I want everything." And *God* did I mean it.

There's no other way to explain the way Aspen felt but extraordinary. Mind bendingly, body meltingly, marvelous.

He moved in strong, even strokes. His lips were always on my skin, sometimes murmuring things I couldn't hear, and sometimes saying things I could.

"You're not real, Poppy. How are you *real?*" He released my wrists and moved his hand down to my waist. Broad and strong and beautiful.

"Aspen," I gasped, and he knew what I meant, knew he could feel the way my body was tightening around him. "I'm..."

Losing my mind?

Not sure of my own name?

Inspired by your athleticism?

All the above.

"Fuck. *Poppy.*" It was all he had time to say before I was exploding around him into tiny fragments of every incredible feeling that ever existed. Until he came back into focus and greeted me with the start of a smile that was lazy and satisfied and *happy*. A reflection of what I knew was on my own face.

I reached for him, just as he rolled us onto our sides. I couldn't even open my eyes fully but I tried, desperate to remember him, just like this, for the rest of my life.

"Well, we'll certainly be doing that again." He sunk his fingers into my hair, capturing my mouth in a smiling kiss and taking every note of laughter that tumbled along after it for himself.

As if they could have ever belonged to anyone else but him.

# 22

## February 9th

**Aspen**

Poppy had been soft and warm in my arms. I'd felt her fall to pieces around me twice more after that first time, and I cataloged every sound she had made. Every spot she liked to be touched. *How* she liked to be touched. It was my name on her tongue over and over.

That's all I was thinking about.

How this woman who'd been in my arms wanted me in the very same way I wanted her. It was *all* I could think about while I held her to me, a new rhythm filtering into my head and tapping along the surface of her skin while she ran her fingers through my hair.

Those were all the things running through my mind through every interview I had. It wasn't that I didn't like talking about the band. I loved telling people about the new album, the new tour, sharing dates for the first time and seeing our fans go absolutely insane about the upcoming shows and reading their theories on the theme of our next record. Taking photos with as many people as I could and signing so many autographs my hand started to cramp.

The fans weren't the problem. It was that I was terrified that I'd say the wrong thing. Blurt an important date wrong, release a secret I'd forgotten was a secret.

My phone rang showing Dax's name and I picked up on the first ring, "Yo."

"How's it going?" He had stayed home with the rest of the guys. None of us coped particularly well with the press stuff which sounded kind of stupid considering we were a bunch of kids that actively chased this life. But we just wanted to play music, that was all the motivation we needed. When all of us going to anything media related could be avoided they usually just volunteered me. "Just happy to be home. If I was there with you right now I actually think I'd cry. Thank you for going, by the way."

"Well, we can't have a crying rock star."

"Crying would be bad for my image." If you could hear someone wagging their eyebrows, that's exactly how Dax sounded.

Not a second later I heard Allie yell from somewhere next to him, "We just watched Spider-Man 2 and he cried!"

"Which Spider-Man?" I held the phone between my shoulder and ear while I got into the back of my waiting SUV and buckled in.

"The one with Andrew Garfield." Dax sounded distraught just recounting the actors name.

"Oh, he's my favorite. Was it that scene? With Gwen?"

"Yeah." His voice was thick with emotion. "Look, I gotta go. Thanks again, Ap. Love you."

"Alright, hi to Allie for me. Love you guys."

"How's your brother?" Jane asked from the seat next to me.

"Crying." I shrugged, giving her a big grin.

"That sounds about right. Alright, you have two interviews tomorrow, a free day on Sunday, then two more Monday and then we'll fly you home the day after."

"I can't just leave on Monday?" My heart sank.

"The second one is the *Late Late Show* so I figured you'd want to crash and I'd get you home early the next morning." Jane was already putting her phone to her ear letting the hotel know we were on our way.

The group chat we had as a band that usually went dormant when we were all in the same place had suddenly sprung back to life.

**Rip:**
Aspen, we miss you

**Rip:**
Aspen, come back

**Me:**
You assholes wouldn't miss me if you just came to these WORK events like you're supposed to

**Luke:**
Pls, we all know ud be the only 1 not having a mental breakdown

**Dax:**
You looked sexy in that interview last night.

**Angus:**

So sexy, Ap.

**Me:**

Fuck off

**Me:**

But thank you.

**Rip:**

Did your girlfriend see you on TV like
the famous rock star you are?

**Angus:**

Oh my god, did she?

**Dax:**

That article that just went up about you guys
was cute

**Luke:**

Your names sound so nice together, Ap

**Luke:**

When do we get to meet her? Why are you
keeping her from us?

**Angus:**

Why are you keeping her from us??

**Luke:**

I just said that…

**Angus:**
I was emphasizing your point. Will you
bring her to family night?

**Aspen:**
I'm going to mute this chat.

**Rip:**
So you can call your girlfriend?

**Angus:**
GIRLFRIEND!

**Angus:**
What's your couple name?

**Dax:**
Paspen?

**Luke:**
Popspen?

**Rip:**
Aspoppy?

**Angus:**
Aspenelope?

*Aspen has left the chat*

*Angus added Aspen to the chat*
*Aspen has left the chat*
*Dax added Aspen to the chat*

As soon as the door to my room closed behind me, my phone started to ring. The irritation I had at myself knowing I'd pick it up when all I really wanted to do was hurl it out the window sent a flare of anger through me until I realized it was Poppy.

She'd called me Tuesday evening after I flew out and told me all about how she and Jess had been asked (forced) to do the coordinating for their office party to help with morale on account of Todd, who apparently started coming to work again but stopped harassing Poppy in the kitchen. She'd talked the entire time which had been sort of amusing because it had been totally *not* like her. I knew it was because she was trying to help me take my mind off the trip.

When Jane had called to confirm all the details for this press trip which I'd completely forgotten about on the night before, Poppy had been dozing on and off in my arms. I'd only just begun my mission of trying to wake her up for a fourth time because keeping my hands to myself now was probably going to be borderline impossible. I'd gotten off the phone and saw the little frown that had scrunched her brow because I knew she heard me tell Jane how excited I was and that I couldn't wait, when Poppy knew for a fact that couldn't have been farther from the truth.

"What I'm specifically after is your opinion on the color combination of magenta, dark brown and mustard yellow," she said as her greeting.

"I'm struggling to visualize it without getting this really

horrified look on my face."

"So you see the dilemma Jess and I are facing."

"I'm actually wishing I could unsee it entirely," I said while pulling a pillow under my head from where I landed in the middle of the bed.

"Well, too bad. You're in this with me now. You were all 'trust me, Poppy. Let's do that fun thing that adults do again and again and again.'"

Somewhere in the background of her phone call I heard someone, I assumed Jess, say, "Poppy, that was not at all discreet."

The rumbling laughter that she pulled out of me at her attempt at mimicking my voice even shocked me, "Okay, point taken. Let me see, it can't be that bad."

She was mumbling something about how it *was* that bad while she swapped our regular phone call into a FaceTime and…that's when I saw it. Poppy had taped three different colored balloons together and stuck them to the wall in what looked like a kitchen.

"Oh, wow." I could see my face, which meant she could see my face. I did my best to control my facial expression.

"You look constipated." She sounded wildly amused.

"Constipated with pride at what you've achieved here with your limited resources?"

"That was very smooth." She flipped the phone back around and the moment I saw her I just wanted to reach through the screen and pull her to me.

"Hey," I said, feeling like I could breathe properly for the first time all day.

"Hey," she said back, a little grin on her face. "How's your trip?"

"About how you'd expect."

"So you really are excited and having the best time ever?"

"You're a brat, you know that?"

"I am merely repeating your own words back to you." She walked out of the kitchen and now sat in what looked like a little cubical.

"You're working late," I said, trying to change the topic.

She gave me one of those looks that made me want to hide under the covers of my bed and never come out, but relented.

"The party's on Monday so this is it as far as time frames to set up and Winny wanted us to wait until everyone had left." And because it was Poppy she didn't even wait a whole second before she asked, "Why do you do things you don't want to do?"

I'd known she would ask me that question again. Knew that the lack of answer I gave the first time she asked on our hike would eat at her until she built up to ask again.

"Poppy –"

"No, I know. It's definitely none of my business it's just... you did it when I asked you about the singing too, I just..it makes me sad. I know the press stuff is something you *have* to do. But...you doing it on your own because everyone else likes it as little as you do? That doesn't make sense to me.."

"I'd love to sing for you," I said, and I meant it too.

"Ap, you know that's not what I mean." She frowned a little harder.

I was tired from the day, yes, but also tired of lying all the time. *All the fucking time.* I didn't want that with Poppy, I wanted her to know me for the person I was, not the person that I tried to be for everyone else. When I thought about it that way, telling her the truth was exceptionally easy. "They think I like it. Love it, actually. Because I told them I did."

"Why?" Her frown morphed from something sad to something confused.

"I wanted to help out. I was stressed about them being stressed. I thought, what if one of them went without me and something happened to them that I could have stopped? A freak accident, maybe an unhinged fan. What if something happened because I didn't want to go? So, right at the start when the band was just taking off I told everyone I actually loved doing press and I'd do it all when everyone else could get out of it."

I had never felt more seen as I did when Poppy's face softened and it was as if I'd become a little bit clearer to see in her eyes.

"Aspen." Her voice was quiet and full to the brim with all the thoughts that must have been swirling around in her head. It was the closest I'd come to telling anyone about my past and, actually, it was a relief. It was a fucking *relief*.

"Well, I wish I was there with you." That was all she said on the matter. She didn't push me, just sat with me without even knowing fully what my reality was.

A reality that maybe who I had been, maybe the way I had decided to cope with things, wasn't working for me anymore.

I knew nothing at that moment except the fact that there'd never been anything that made me want to break free of the shackles I'd put on myself over the last decade. That I'd become who I was because I'd been the cause of something awful once, and I felt like I owed it to the people in my life to never be that again.

But I hadn't accounted for Poppy.

Now there was her, this person in my life that made me

want things for myself when I never had before. I'd never cared to want anything more than to play music with my friends and do everything I could to keep the people I loved safe. By doing everything I could to make sure that I was there for them.

I was happy to be second. *Needed* to come second. But I wasn't the only one now that would be impacted by the ghosts of my past and if I wanted to keep Poppy, I knew I'd have to learn to let them go.

"Poppy?" I said.

"Yes?" She looked at me like she wanted to reach through our phones too.

I decided that she made me brave enough to do that, to want this for myself. "When I think about coming home, I don't picture my apartment."

She looked like I'd reached right into her chest and held her beating heart in the palm of my hand. "What do you picture?" she asked, sounding devastatingly vulnerable.

"I picture you," I whispered.

# 23

# February 11th

**Poppy**

Jess and I hadn't been able to have our wine night on Thursday. So, instead, she asked if I wanted to go over for dinner on Sunday with her and her boys and after a quick pep-talk from Leah, I did it.

Turned out her kids were the actual best and we all sat together and played board games after dinner. When monopoly got too heated between the twins they went off for an hour to put together a choreographed routine to a song Jess had picked by Taylor Swift.

They then came back and performed their routine for us. We laughed so much that Jess had to crawl to the bathroom, all the while yelling "I'm peeing! I'm peeing!" and I caught the wine that shot out of my nose in the palm of my hand.

I'd left with a permanent look of contented happiness on my face and called Aspen on the way home to tell him all about it. He told me about his day off and that he had tried meditating and when that didn't work he spent pretty much the whole day in the gym because he was filled with all this restless energy and no drum kit.

"No drum kit, or girlfriend." He said it so casually that it took me a second to realize that it was the first time he had, in fact, said it.

The reality was that I could only see one way out of this, and it wasn't a fairy tale ending. It would mean getting hurt, *Aspen* getting hurt, because of me. But I'd compromised with myself, hadn't I? That I'd give into him even though I hadn't really had a choice. Everything about falling for Aspen Smith was as inevitable as me leaving.

It was wrong to take everything he was willing to give me while I could, but I did it anyway.

"Okay," I said, my heart thrashing in my ears.

"Okay?" He said the word in a way that I knew, without a shadow of a doubt he was smiling so big his dimples would be on full display.

"Yeah, no 'buts' right?" If I hadn't been sitting on a train right at that moment I think I probably would have screamed in delight. Shoving the debilitating guilt behind that door in my mind that was now bursting at the seams and trying to reassure myself that he knew what he was getting into.

Aspen knew that I was leaving and he wanted to do this with me anyway.

"Will you come to our Fun Friday Family Fiesta night next week? Everyone's been wanting to meet you for a while and I've held them off as long as I could."

"I have no idea what that means but the alliteration could have convinced me all on its own."

"That was Allie," he laughed.

"They know who I am?" Why did that make me nervous?

"Well, sort of. They know that I have a friend who is a girl. The only person I've actually spoken about you to is Allie because she told me to pretty much go and find you after that first time we met. Everyone else has been scouring the internet for every picture and article they could find."

*"Aspen!"* I whisper shouted and felt my blood pressure rise a fraction. I'd been actively *not* looking at the news but Leah had promised to let me know if anything alarming came up. So far it was a lot of speculation and photos of me coming and going from work. Aspen coming and going from his apartment, and one unflattering photo of Aspen driving his Jeep into the underground parking of his building with me in the front seat and his hand covering my entire face.

"What do you think?"

"I think Allie and I will get on swimmingly," I said, getting off the train at my station and starting the walk home.

"So you'll come?" He sounded so hopeful, it made me hopeful too.

"I'll come."

"I think this is a hit," Jess said, waving at two of our coworkers that walked into the Say No To The January Blues party.

"Jess, they're the first people to arrive." I forced my mouth into something that looked sort of pleasant and waved too, even though I felt about as comfortable as one might feel if they'd discovered an ants nest in their underwear. If there was one thing I would have been confident that I *wouldn't* do in my life, it was help to organize an office party.

"Yes, but they came. To me that's an instant success."

"Here's to hoping your optimism rubs off on me."

"Oh, speaking of rubbing, my cat has changed your blue sweater into a white sweater because I didn't realize you left it on the couch and she's absolutely demolished it with fur. Like, I didn't even know it was your sweater because it was so white." She cringed while telling me, not even making eye contact just staring directly at my boobs.

"Consider it a gift from me to your cat." I could actively feel my esophagus closing at the thought of that amount of cat hair.

"Are you sure?" She looked at me from under her dark rimmed glasses.

"Desperately."

"Ladies!" Winny said with the sort of enthusiasm you had to wonder where he got the energy to possess it.

"Winston! Welcome to the party!" Jess matched his enthusiasm completely.

"You guys have done a fantastic job, and I see you got the balloons I ordered!" He

pointed right at the cluster of balloons that consisted of colors no one in their right mind would ever look at and think 'yes, that works. That really, really works'.

"It just works, doesn't it?" Winny said, reaching forward to give Jess a weird side hug that she half accepted and flushed into a serious shade of magenta. It must have been written all over my face because she reached out to subtly pinch my side.

"Hey!" I yelled, swatting her hand away and unintentionally gaining all of Winny's attention. "Hey *hey!*" I said, trying to cover my outburst and wanting to die a little at the way I sang those words out. "That…is a true statement. Thank you for the balloons."

"You're very welcome, Poppy. I think the rest of the office is really moving past the whole," he leaned in very close and all I could smell was peanut butter, "cousin thing."

Jess and I both looked at the two people who had arrived before Winny. Her face said 'I worked on a cheese board for a whole hour and the two people that came to this stinker of a party are dairy free'. My face said something that contained a few more cuss words and my smile was more of a wobbly showing of my teeth. "Thanks, Winny."

I clung to Jess for the rest of the evening and when Winny volunteered me to start a round of acapella karaoke, Jess, bless her literal soul, jumped up so fast her chair clattered to the ground before she announced, reluctantly, that she would actually like to go first. And second. *And third.*

Jess sang the entire evening and Winny had sat with impeccable posture, clapping along to every song she sang like it was the concert of a lifetime. The man had hearts in his eyes. When it was just us after Winny and the two other dairy free cheese board neglectors had left, I pulled her into the biggest, most grateful hug.

"Jess, I'm indebted to you."

"I will cash it in in the form of another Sunday night dinner, but you bring that cousin of yours." She hugged me back just as hard.

"Deal," I laughed knowing that Aspen would have the time of his life watching her boys perform. He'd probably get up with them.

I wish I'd realized earlier that that was going to be my last easy moment for a while; I would have held onto it a little longer.

# 24

# February 14th

**Aspen**

It was like the universe was demanding balance and I was just the closest person to provide the cause and effect.

Everything had been fine on the way to the airport. Jovial, even.

I mean, sure it was a little wild on the roads, but I'd driven in heavy snow before. I was no stranger to the defensive maneuvers you needed to master, especially considering how lackluster the Taurus was (said with nothing but love), but it didn't really seem *that* bad.

Turns out, it was actually *that* bad and we had been in the midst of a blizzard. Jane kept on talking about how our driver, Garrett, was super human for getting us to the airport in one piece only to not blink an eye and drive us all the way back to the hotel when they canceled all the flights for the rest of the day. I think Jane just really liked Garrett.

Jason, my security guy, had sat up the front while Jane and I were in the back and I should have known, really, considering the way he held firm to the assist grip like his life depended on it.

"You okay, bud?" I did my best to hide all the amusement from my voice but it was impossible.

"I quit," he said, sounding like he was trying not to hyper-ventilate.

"You can't quit, Jason. You're the only security we've had that's managed not to get the slip," Jane said, a little smile on her face while her fingers moved at the speed of light across the screen of her phone. I wasn't entirely sure what she was doing seeing as no one had service because of the storm.

"That's not true." I sounded like a toddler but it took incredible skill to out maneuver one's security and I couldn't let her take that from me.

"I follow you to that bar and sit outside. I'm literally always with you, even when you don't see me. Please shut up now so I can concentrate on not dying," Jason groaned and I sat there feeling like I'd just been told my mom was in the row behind me at the movie theater the first time I took a girl on a date.

"What? Even Poppy's house?"

"Yes," he squeaked.

"I can't believe this." I didn't really mean to say it out loud.

"Believe it, Aspen," Jane said, her tone half chiding and half amused.

"I mean, I'm impressed, Jase. I've never once seen you."

"Thank you." The man sounded like he was about to shit himself.

We were back at the hotel and every time I tried to call Poppy the line dropped or crackled or just didn't connect at all. For my last attempt I'd been standing on a chair and half of my face was immersed into the curtains trying to keep the line. My messages were also refusing to send which was just the cherry on top of this incredibly awesome press trip.

That wasn't totally fair. It had been great, really. The response was exactly what we'd hoped for. More, even.

The double upside? We'd pretty much finished the album. There were a few drum tracks that we needed to rerecord. There was nothing wrong with the originals but after listening to what was supposed to be the final versions of the tracks, there were a couple songs that I wanted to tweak and I'd been buzzing all week to get behind a drum kit.

I wasn't entirely sure how it happened but I'd sent Poppy a message that I knew wouldn't get through until the storm passed and then, shockingly, fell asleep. I didn't even remember closing my eyes before I woke up with my fingers tapping and this insatiable itch to get to the studio.

For a long time, drumming was the only thing that had never lost its spark for me. I craved it consistently. Just doing it, getting better at it, finding new ways to record sounds I wanted to create and new things I could do while playing live that would blow the ever living minds off our fans. That hadn't changed, but now I felt that passion and want and *need* for something else.

*Someone* else.

Look, I wasn't one to make that big of a deal of Valentine's Day, but if I had been home I would have probably baked something in the shape of a heart and hand delivered it to Poppy. I didn't know if she loved the holiday particularly, but I picture the way she would have looked at it and then at me with her classic, unrestrained grin and launched herself at me. I could feel her body beneath my hands, feel her pressed against me and, holy *fuck*, did I miss her.

That first bit was a lie, I fucking *loved* Valentine's Day. I was now actively in a relationship on this very day for the first time in a very long time and I'd purposely played it casual over the last week when Poppy and I spoke.

I'd been very proud of the fact that I hadn't brought it up once. A task that had been like swimming against the current of my own mind. So, I knew the bouquet of roses that were due to land on Poppy's door step any minute now would not be something she expected but I hoped it would be something that might earn me one of those smiles she'd come to give me freely and I'd come to crave hopelessly. The second most exciting part was I knew for sure she wouldn't anticipate the bouquet of fish food canisters I had organized for Nat.

There had been no word from her at all, during the storm yesterday or since I'd woken up. Which usually I wouldn't have thought about twice. She probably ended up doing something with Leah through FaceTime and then fell asleep while still on the call. I'd seen it happen before and both their faces had been smooshed to their phones. I'd screenshotted the visual of Leah before I had ended the call on Poppy's end and when she woke up to see it she laughed so hard she fell off the bed.

I was practically bouncing in my seat with excitement to hear from her now though. And usually I was patient. Okay, *sometimes* I was patient.

This was not one of those times.

**Me:**

Happy Valentine's Day Poompaloompa x

I sent off the message just before shutting off my phone and settling into my seat on the jet. Thankfully, the storm had passed and the roads had been cleared by the time Jane knocked on my door. I'd been up for hours when her wake up call had come in at 5 AM.

I was desperate to get home. Back to the band.

Back to Poppy.

When the plane landed I checked my phone, vibrating with fucking excitement at the very idea of what sort of message she'd have sent through, what she might think of Nats Valentines day present, but…nothing. There was nothing.

I watched the screen of my phone the entire drive to the studio, waiting for her three dots to show up but a message from her never came.

I knew the storm had come through Blazewood too, though nowhere near as bad, so it was still possible that she had no service on her phone. Or, she was at work probably learning something increasingly random like facts on emus from a zoology seminar that was specific to flightless birds. Poppy was relatively diligent about replying, but when she got stuck into something that fascinated her, she got lost in it.

I pocketed my phone and moved my mind from one obsession to the other.

My brother came for me in a bear hug that the rest of the guys piled.

"Is everyone's feet off the ground?" Luke's muffled shout came from somewhere behind me and was answered with a swarm of equally muffled confirmations.

"He's not budging," Dax said, his mouth closest to my face. I could feel his body shaking with laughter more than I could hear it.

"Ap this is by far your best pile yet," Angus said from where he clung to my waist. "But I'm letting go because I'm looking right at your crotch."

"Lucky you." I was laughing and the more I laughed the harder it was to stay standing, before any of them could jump off I went down and almost pissed my pants at the sound that came out of Luke from taking the brunt of my fall.

"It was like," Rip wheezed, "*a yodeling donkey!*"

That was all it took before we were off again, laughing so hard no sound was coming out of anyone's mouth except for Luke and his never ending yodeling-donkey noises.

"I leave you guys for like, two seconds," Adrian said, coming back into the room with the biggest coffee cup I'd ever seen and just like always, the ability to bring us back on track and focus on what we were there to do.

"You're up, Ap." He extended his hand to help me up and gave me a one armed hug. "Nice to have you back, our little drummer boy." He ruffled my hair.

"Thanks, band-daddy." I blew him a kiss and he held up the middle finger of his free hand.

"Alright, boys get up." Adrian sat down and rubbed his hands together. "Let's finish this album."

I took off my shirt and dropped it on the couch that Rip had settled into before setting my phone on the coffee table just in front of it, zoning out completely and letting myself find that place I could exist in forever. Where it was just me and the drum kit in front of me and the singular focus that was to be the backbone of the song. To pave the road for all the other parts of the song to drive on, to get from where it all started to where it ended.

That's how I'd been the entire day until we were done with the very last song. The album was done. It was *done.*

I took the headphone off, feeling the thrum of excitement watching the boys celebrate and hug and pile on top of one another until something got Rip's attention on the coffee table, a howling Luke still clinging to his back. Rip leaned forward and picked up my phone and I watched as he looked from it to me. With what had to be the most mischievous, cheekiest and shit-stirring grin I'd ever seen on his face he brought the phone up to his ear and I saw his mouth say the words, "Aspen's phone, this is Rip speaking."

"I didn't do anything! I swear!" Rip's hands were up in front of him in full surrender mode and my phone was now face down across the room.

"He threw your phone across the room." Angus said, looking down and focused completely on the guitar in his hands, still playing the baseline for the song I'd been drumming to without the guitar plugged into an amp.

"There was a woman," Rip's face was the perfect picture of fear. "She asked me to hold on a second and then she *screamed.*" His eyes were now looking at the phone and he was pointing at it like it was possessed. "Aspen, she screamed *right into the phone!* Who *does* that?"

I looked from Rip to Dax who was actively trying not to laugh and take our friends' clear terror seriously, sparing only a second to grab and pull on my shirt. I didn't need to check the screen before I put the phone to my ear.

"Leah?" I felt the frown on my brow start to form. Leah hadn't called me before but we did swap numbers the night of our FaceTime dinner at Poppy's. She said it was in case of emergency but Poppy was sure it was because she liked walking around knowing she had the number of a famous person in her phone for the first time in her life. Apparently, it was a bucket list item.

"You mean to say you *know* that woman?!" Rip sounded genuinely affronted.

"Aspen, this is Leah McDonaugh, Poppy's best friend. Did I just speak to Rip Reynolds?" Leah was audibly hyperventilating.

"I know who you are Leah, and I mean, technically you screamed at him, but yes, that was him." Now *I* was trying to be sympathetic to Leah's mental breakdown without laughing.

"This might be the best day of my whole life," she said, sounding like her eyes were full of stars and she might just be clutching her heart.

"Leah," I said, trying to get her back on track.

"What?" She still sounded out of breath.

"Is everything okay?" As soon as I asked the question my stomach dropped and I had no idea why.

"Oh, yeah I just wanted to see how Poppy was today? She usually goes pretty quiet over the next couple of days and I know things can get dark for her. I know I'm being nosy but she's never wanted me around for it and I always worry about her."

"Poppy?" Everything she said immediately confused me.

"Well, yeah?   I just assumed you'd be with her today considering…everything."

"Everything? What's everything?" I could hear the element of mild hysteria creeping into my voice and felt the stares of five pairs of eyes on my back.

"Aspen…you mean she didn't tell you?"  Leah sounded devastated.  "She's always been way too private about her grief. Right from when we were kids."

"Leah." My voice was sharper than I intended it to be. "Why are you calling me asking if Poppy is okay?"

"Today's the fourteenth of February." She delivered it like it should have been this light-at-the-end-of-the-tunnel kind of answer.

"I don't know what that means, Leah." There was no doubt about the panic in my voice now.

"It's her brother's birthday today."

"I—" I didn't have anything to say. I was trying to work out why she hadn't told me that. This huge part of herself that she was still figuring out how to navigate. Why she hadn't trusted me enough to be there for her through it.

"Sometimes she won't talk to me for a week except for random messages here and there so I know she's alive. She falls into these…I don't really know what else to call them but endless emotional pits? And she's always forced herself to brave it alone."

I nodded even though Leah couldn't see me, nodded in a little understanding of all the 'why's' racing through my mind before replying, "Not anymore."

"No," her voice was thoughtful and grateful all at once, "I don't think so either."

I hung up without saying goodbye, turning around to see

my brother already standing there, my hat and jacket in his outstretched hands. His face was set into an expression of worry. His mouth a slash across his face and brows drawn down.

Dax knew what it was like to love someone who was hurting. He didn't have to say a single thing for me to know that he got it, in however broad a sense it might be, he still got it.

"Ap," he called out and I turned just in time to catch the keys to his car before I was out the door.

I will say something for Wyatt's car, it was very fast.

He'd bought the Porsche a year ago as a present to himself for literally no reason and now constantly referred to it as his 'bestie'. It had absolutely nothing on the Taurus but I promised myself I'd never say another bad thing about it. It got me to Poppy in a very timely manner.

I was standing out front of her house, the flowers that were delivered this morning already wilted from the cold with Nat's canister bouquet right next to it.

Poppy didn't have a car, but I knew she was home.

I knocked on the door, "Poppy?"

There was no answer. Not the first, the second or the tenth time I called her. No matter which version of her name I used, there was nothing but silence on the other end.

"Fuck it," I said, walking around the side of her house to where the first of the downstairs windows began. The first one didn't budge, but the second one did and though I was stoked about a way to get to her I would need to explain at some point the importance of locking all the windows and doors when you lived alone.

Poppy's house was dark and quiet. The bubbling of Nat's tank made the space feel homey even amid the still packed boxes and pale walls.

"Poppy?" I called out again, but didn't hear a single thing back. Walking over to Nat, I bent down to her level. "Hey Queenie," I said, pressing the pad of my index finger to her tank lightly before giving her a bit of food.

This might have been the most stalkerish thing I'd ever done but I would think about that later and use this very moment as an example in my 'for' points on locking all points of entry. Right now though, I made my way up the stairs towards Poppy's bedroom.

She was where I thought she would be.

I only hesitated for a second before I stepped into her bedroom, my chest going tight and heavy all at once, filled with a breath I'd been holding for way too long. Like my lungs had forgotten how to work entirely from the moment Leah called me to this very second.

Poppy didn't move, but I knew she knew I was there.

I didn't know what to do.

I wanted to do everything, *anything*, and I had no fucking idea where to start.

Toeing off my sneakers I walked to the end of her bed and stood there for a second, watching the rapid way her chest rose and fell.

I lay down facing her, my heart clenching and breaking a little at every detail I took in; her swollen eyes, the dampness of her pillow. The salty tear tracks that had dried on her cheeks and the new once being made by the rivulets still falling.

Poppy opened her eyes then, bloodshot with moisture clumping her eyelashes together and I'd realized I'd do anything, *anything*, to stop her from feeling the need to carry her pain all on her own. Of thinking that she had to sit in it by herself.

Her lips were cracked and dry like all the water in her body had made an escape, her voice husky like she'd used it all up.

"It's my brother's birthday today." Her eyes were sad and her face was drawn.

She took another breath before she spoke again and I didn't expect the next words that came out of her mouth, "I killed him."

Poppy's first line of defense was to push people away. She'd done it to me more times than I could count. I'd had to actively chip away at the armor she'd practically sewn into her own skin.

"You don't believe me?" she asked, her voice almost angry, like she was reaching for anything to feel other than what she already was. I knew what that was like, because I'd done it too.

"No." I didn't need to think about it. I knew the woman in front of me. I knew her mind and her heart and her soul because she'd let me close enough to see them all.

Her chest hadn't stopped its rapid rise and fall. I could see it building, whatever it was she needed to do to be able to tell this story that she'd kept so close she'd forgotten what it was like to live without it. That was another thing I knew, because I'd done the same thing with my own.

I didn't particularly care if the reason she was telling me was because she hoped it would scare me away. If she was hoping I'd look at her and see a monster, someone who deserved to suffer all on their own. It just mattered to me that she told me.

She took a final deep breath and started, "I was raised by my older brother."

# 25

# February 14th

**Poppy**

"I was raised by my older brother," I started talking and didn't let myself stop. "He was quite a bit older than me when I was born. I was a surprise for the entire family after my parents thought Casimir was their one and only miracle baby. He was fourteen when I came along.

My mom, she died giving birth to me. My parents both traveled a lot for work so she missed a lot of appointments so all these things that could have been avoided, weren't. That's what I was told, anyway. After she died, my dad had to work more. Longer hours, a second job. He traveled more and more and then one day, he just didn't come home. He's actually still alive, but after my mom…anyway, he has a new family now. I'm not sure where he is."

Aspen just lay there listening to every word, barely breathing, his eyes never leaving mine, determined to live this with me.

"Eventually it was just the two of us." I swallowed, letting myself drop Aspen's gaze. I focused on the rise and fall of his chest and let myself be pulled into the memory.

"It was my sixteenth birthday. We'd been planning it for a long time. We went back and forth on a party. Doing something with some of my friends, maybe just Leah, but in the end I decided I just wanted it to be the two of us. He had started to work more to pay for school. He wanted to do more for himself – more for us – than to be a mechanic in someone else's shop. He wanted to be a mechanic in his *own* shop. So, he started studying while working and his classes were at night so we hadn't really been spending as much time together over the last six months he was alive. I missed him." I clutched at my shirt, wishing I could stifle the ache where it ricocheted off every broken piece of my heart.

"I'd picked a take out menu from our little pile in the kitchen and ordered right at 6 PM so that it would just be arriving when he got home." I felt a smile tug at my lips for the briefest second at the memory before it fell away.

"But he was late. They were understaffed and I knew he usually had to work through his lunch. They had a last minute drive in and he was there so he stayed to help out. He said he tried to call me, but I never heard the phone ring. I must have been in the shower maybe, I guess. I was *so mad.*" My voice broke and it took me a second but I pushed on. I still felt Aspen's eyes on me even though I couldn't meet them.

"He tried and *tried* to speak to me when he got home, he explained everything through the door but I closed myself in my room. I wouldn't even *look* at him. He stood outside my bedroom door for over an hour. We had no locks but he had this rule that if you weren't invited in, you weren't allowed in. So he just *stood* there. Apologizing over and over and over again." I felt the tears as they fell down my face and did nothing to stop them. They were hot and angry and full of the hatred I felt for myself every single fucking day.

"It was like this light bulb lit up in his head and he said he knew what would fix it, what always fixed it. There was a place seven blocks from our apartment that made this frozen custard I was obsessed with. I used to say it was the best in the world even though I'd never been out of the country. Cas had worked a full day, including overtime. He hadn't even changed out of his work coveralls because he'd been standing at my door and then dashed out the house to make up for the fact that he was bending over backwards for us and had been a little late to my birthday plans." I couldn't even say the words out loud properly. They fell from my mouth in a strangled whisper and when I finally looked back up at Aspen, my vision blurred from the tears that had continued to fall. I knew that he could see the shame I felt, that I carried with me every single day. Refused to let go of because of what I'd caused.

Aspen reached for me across the bed, leaving his hand halfway between us, his own eyes glittering with the sheen of unshed tears, but I didn't take it.

I didn't reach back for him, for his embrace that I knew would help to soothe all the wounds that had never really healed and forced myself to tell him the rest of the story.

"He'd only been gone for ten minutes, that was all. It took ten minutes for my stupid sixteen year old tears to go from hurt and angry to ones of guilt and shame. I ran out after him, not even bothering to lock the door."

I closed my eyes, reliving it all in my own head as I finally told Aspen the truth of who I was.

What I'd done.

*"Casimir!" I yelled his name while I ran, not stopping until eventually his jacket clad form came into view just a block away from the dessert shop. "Cas!" I could barely see him, my vision blurred and chest heaving from the six blocks I'd run, pushing my legs to move as fast as they could. I collided with him at full speed, wrapping my arms around him, sobbing into his chest.*

*"I'm sorry," I cried, voice muffled by his coat, immediately enveloped in his grease and tobacco scent that I would know anywhere. "I'm sorry, I'm sorry."*

*His hand came up to rest against the back of my head. I could still feel the ghost of it.*

*His voice soft and calm, "Penny, hey—"*

*"I'm such a bitch, a huge bitch."*

*"You're not a bitch. Also, don't say bitch."*

*"I am."*

*"Pen—"*

*"I am." I cried harder.*

*"Okay, fine. You are." There was only humor in his voice and I scowled into his now tear stained jacket, pinching his side.*

*He'd been too focused on me, on my tears. On trying to stop them from falling and keeping me calm that neither of us had seen the three men that approached us.*

*"Well, isn't this sweet."*

*As long as I lived, I'd never forget the sound of that voice. Like rusted nails.*

*My stomach dropped out of my body right when Casimir pushed me behind him. I could see the eyes of the two men behind the one holding the gun. I knew what that look meant. What people like them thought of when they looked at sixteen year old girls.*

*There wasn't a version of me, in any other version of reality that wouldn't know the intent behind their eyes. The first guy came close enough that Casimir tried to go for the gun.*

*In the struggle it went off, going right through Cas's heart before lodging itself in my shoulder.*

*There was a moment of silence before a scream involuntarily ripped from my throat, and my brother stumbled back. I didn't register the pain lancing through my own body; my entire purpose became catching him.*

*A sound of shock escaped him as he stumbled back into me, his weight too much to hold as I fell back with him, his body crushing mine.*

*My hands were frantic before they settled on the wound in the middle of his chest.*

*"HELP!" My throat had burned with that scream. "Somebody, Some– HELP!"*

*"Pen-" Cas blinked up at me rapidly, like he was trying to clear his vision, to clear his eyes. "Penelope."*

*"I'm here, you're okay, help is coming," I sobbed while I kept my hands on his chest. Desperate to stop the blood from leaving his body.*

*"Penny, I—" Blood trickled out the side of his mouth and I knew another scream ripped from me. I could hear it then, the sound of my soul fracturing.*

*"Don't go." I pushed harder on the wound in his chest, my hands covered in red and trembling. "Don't leave me, don't you dare leave me. Please, please."*

*"It's okay." His words were weak, but when I looked at him again his eyes were on me, clear and focused. "It's okay," he said again, and I could see the goodbye in his eyes. See the love on his face.*

*Then I watched as it faded from his body.*

*His life, his soul, his love for me. It was there one moment, and then it was gone the next.*

*I woke up in the hospital with faces looking at me that belonged to people I didn't know speaking words I couldn't understand but knowing in my heart one undeniable truth; my brother was gone and for the first time in my entire life I was all alone in the world.*

"So, you see," I rasped, lifting my heavy, swollen lids to find that Aspen was now right in front of me, tears streaming down his own beautiful face. "Hurting you is inevitable. And I refuse," my voice broke, "*refuse* to do that to you."

Aspen's hands shook as he moved into me, one sliding beneath my waist and the other around the back of my neck. I couldn't stop myself from leaning into his touch. I couldn't stop myself for hating how I did it, even as I'd just ripped myself apart to show him *why*—

"Poppy," his voice was quiet. A reflection of the pain I felt. "Poppy, you were sixteen."

I didn't know what to do, so I just shook my head. I shook it over and over refusing to hear what he was saying, but he held me firm, bringing his forehead to mine. "It wasn't your fault, do you hear me?"

*No,* I shook my head. *You don't understand.*

I didn't have to speak for him to know what I was saying.

"You were a *child*, Penelope. It was not your fault," he said again. He said it again and again and *again*. Until I was clinging to Aspen like he was the only solid ground I could find. Until the gentle repetition of his words against my temple, broken only by the gentle kisses he placed there, started to break their way through the walls I had rebuilt in his absence.

I'd been told those things before, many times, but never like this. Like I might believe them.

Aspen was silent for a long time before he spoke again, "I didn't have a lot of friends growing up. I was insanely attached to my brother and my parents weren't around a lot, it was sort of like they had kids to just tick it off on this list of things you did in life. Once we were there and old enough to manage on our own they...it was like having two old roommates."

I huffed a laugh despite everything and leaned into him more, reveling in the feel of the vibrations of his voice and the beat of his heart beneath my cheek.

"I had a panic attack on my first day of school, and this girl, Trixie, calmed me down. She was my only friend and I wouldn't even call her that, really. She lived on the same street as us so she was the only other person at my school that I ever really spoke to and when I started driving to school, sometimes I would give her rides. I'd always have to drive past her house and if she was there, I'd ask if she wanted a lift."

"That's a very Ap thing to do," I whispered, more to myself than to him.

His only answer was a soft kiss to my head.

"When Dax moved to college I fell into this intense sort of depression. I'd never been without him and I didn't want to bother him with calls or visits because he was at college, you know? But I started sleeping through the day, missing school...that sort of thing. Days would just blur into one another and I didn't have the energy to do anything.

"My phone buzzing woke me up one time and it was Trixie, which was weird because she never called me. I didn't know what the time was or the day but I looked right at my phone and watched as it rang out. She texted after asking if I was free, and I said no." Aspen's voice had gotten progressively more strained and I realized what he was doing.

A story for a story.

"It turned out to be a Saturday night and her mom forgot to pick her up from her job across town. She was calling to see if I could give her a lift, I found out after."

"After what?" I whispered back, my heart in my throat as he pulled me into his secret the way I'd pulled him into mine.

"She was walking along the highway making her way home. A drunk driver had passed out at the wheel and she was—"

*Oh my God.* "Aspen–" I moved away from him to look at him, the tears in my eyes now a reflection of his.

"Dax came home the next weekend, took one look at me and turned around and walked out." Aspen sniffed and wiped at his face, "I thought he hated me, thought he knew what I did and what I caused."

He shook his head, "It turned out my school had called him after Trixie. My parents hadn't been taking their calls, and so they called Dax and told them about the change in my behavior. The drop in my grades. As soon as he saw me I think he knew how bad I was." Aspen looked down at where my hand lay over his heart, and his hand lay over mine. "He moved home that afternoon, walked right back into my room and said, 'So, how about we start that band?'" Aspen laughed, wiping at his eyes again.

"I promised myself that I'd never do anything like that again. That I would make sure I picked up the damn phone when someone I cared about called. That I would do anything and everything I could to make sure the people I loved were safe. That Dax's sacrifice to move back home would be worth it, that when I was needed I would show up. I'd be that person between them and danger, no matter what. That I would always, *always,* put them first before myself, no matter the cost."

I stared at him and felt the shift in my body as the whole picture of who he was clicked into place. It felt like I was meeting him all over again for the first time. I wanted to say back to him the very things he'd said to me, that I'd shook my head at and refused to believe.

*You were a child.*

*It was not your fault.*

He looked at me the same way and I knew why he'd told me his story too.

Sharing the hardest parts of myself had always been easiest to do in the quiet darkness, but. I don't think that was the case for Aspen. I knew that Aspen didn't like the quiet, he didn't like the dark, but he'd done it anyway for me. To show me that he was like me. Living a life that had grown around grief.

"I've realized, though," Ap said, his eyes cleared now of the story he'd shared, and completely focused on me, "that what I've been doing, how I've been living, might not be working for me anymore. That I've got to learn to be a little selfish, to put what I want first."

I could feel the way his heart sped up beneath my palm, "How's that going?"

The side of his mouth quirked up, "You tell me?"

I heard what he was saying in the same way I had when he'd made me his chicken soup. Seeing through the words he said to the ones he hadn't.

*I'm letting go of my ghost, so I can hold onto you.*

*Hold onto me, Poppy.*

My bottom lip trembled as I nodded my head, "Pretty good."

He reached out to swipe a final falling tear, "Yeah?"

I nodded again. "Yeah," I said, knowing he'd hear the hidden words there too.

*I am.*

I felt it as I melted into the kiss he pressed into my lips. From days of being apart, from the relief at knowing I had all of Aspen right there before me and he had all of me.

*I am.*

I thought it over and over again as he peeled the clothes off my body, leaving a lingering kiss to my scar. While I peeled all his clothes off too.

*I am.*

I chanted it in my own head as he whispered more secrets just for us two into my skin and pulled his name from my lips. Pushing into me, again and again, until there was no way of knowing where his soul started and where mine ended, only that there were two of them where there used to be just one.

*I am.*

Aspen held me in the quiet of my bedroom. The blankets tangled up in our legs and the

steady sound of his breath the focus of all my attention. Neither of us slept and just when the sun began to rise it occurred to me that I hadn't actually let him inside my house.

"Ap?"

"Mm?" he hummed from where he was nestled against my

neck.

"How did you get into my house?"

Aspen pulled back, his hair mussed and expression lazy, "Your window. That reminds me, we'll be having a discussion on locking all points of entry as a person who lives on their own."

I ignored him in favor of the first part of his sentence, "You mean, like Edward Cullen?" I was laughing already at my own personal joke. Of being totally in love with that fictional character right beside Leah, though she was also partial to Team Jacob.

"I have no idea why you're laughing," he said, his face so serious it only made me laugh more. Aspen gestured down the length of his body, "This is the skin of a killer, Poppy."

That sent me so far into a laughing spiral I started to laugh *backwards*. My body was only able to make noise when trying to drag air into my lungs instead of out and then Aspen finally broke character, trying to mouth something through his wheezing laughter that looked like 'yodeling donkey' but I couldn't be sure.

I was sure, though, that I don't think I'd ever felt like this before. Maybe once, but it was different. This feeling I had now was new and old. Like the way wine only gets better with time, that's what this feeling was like. It was a hand holding mine in a crowded place. A seat saved at a table just for me. It was making me soup when I was sick and leaving the house just to feed my goldfish.

It made me want to run nowhere else but straight towards it.

# 26

# March 1st

**Poppy**

The day after Aspen stayed over, it was sort of like I'd never seen clearly before. Like my prescription had been wrong for years and I just learned to live with seeing things with fuzzy edges.

The two weeks that followed when I saw him with my brand new eyes, and he could see me with his, were this blur of incomparable happiness. I found myself feeling guilty from time to time before I pulled myself back into it.

*You knew what you were getting yourself into.*

That had become my mantra. That and, well, it seemed Aspen's name had also become a mantra of sorts. One that I said out loud rather than in my own head.

Was this what it was like to date someone? Because it was fucking *fun*.

Aspen had been working long days and late nights, filled with finalizing all the songs for the new album, some he even shared with me. One he let me FaceTime Leah so she could hear it too. As you might have suspected, she excused herself off frame and screamed in terrified happiness.

Now that the album was done, it was time to start on the tour prep. Named after their new album, the *Salvation Tour* was going to be their biggest yet. Every arena they were playing was the biggest the cities had to offer, more dates than before had been added to every city and they were going to be on the road for longer than ever before. They were doing photo shoots to prepare for their new tour merch and actually started to practice for their shows. It was so incredibly exciting to be able to watch the way the band worked up close. It made total sense to me that they were as successful as they were.

The mini press tour Ap had done was to announce the sale dates for their tour which officially started in June, but *Lady Luck* had always done things a little different and loved to play a stream of shows in their home city of Blazewood. Those would all be done at the start of April so the boys were completely immersed in set lists and rehearsals.

I asked him about it and he gave me one of his dimpled sunshine smiles when he replied, "We owe it all to this city. It only seems right that they get their very own pre-tour tour."

And that's literally what they did. There were a bunch of venues in the city and I learned that Allie's best friend Savannah managed them all.

Actually, that's not true. That was my best guess.

"She's a big-wig," Aspen said one of our many evenings together. He was in the kitchen making blueberry sourdough bagels he'd started to prepare earlier in the week and I was sitting at the island counter chopping up strawberries for the homemade jam he was going to make with them.

I saw a video online of this lady who had made her own bagels, all I said was 'yum'. I may have groaned it gutturally, sure, but it was still only a single word. Next thing I knew, I arrived at his penthouse thinking he'd still be with the band to find him shirtless in the kitchen wearing one of his many random aprons, this one said *Check Out My Bakers Dozen*', with flour on his nose.

"Ap, that doesn't actually tell me anything." I rolled my eyes, putting all the strawberries I'd already chopped into a bowl and getting more.

"Yes it does, sweet Poppy. It means she's a *big*-wig."

"Okay, but what are you saying? Am I meant to take it literally? Like, she has big hair?"

"I guess you could, but that's not what I mean in this instance."

"What's her job title?"

"B-"

"If you say 'big-wig', so help me I'll spank you with a spatula."

He gave me the goofiest eyebrow raise, "Hey now, don't threaten me with a good time."

I did my very best at following through on my threat. It resulted in flour on almost every part of my body and the vigorous christening of his kitchen floor.

The paparazzi were still outside my work, but they pretty much just left me alone except for a picture here and there. No one had followed me home from what I knew and I hadn't seen any photos of my house online. I knew I probably had Jane to thank for whatever she had managed to do. And I would thank her profusely if I ever go to meet her.

Sometimes I'd get to Aspen's place and he wouldn't be there.

It never really bothered me though and it never felt weird to be there without him. Walking into Ap's apartment was like being surrounded by the very essence of him. On those nights, I would cook something or order in enough for him to eat if he was hungry when he got back, shower and then read on his couch. Sometimes I'd fall asleep there and wake up to the gentle rhythm of his fingers combing through my hair, and sometimes I'd make it to his bed and be woken up by his lips on me. My throat. My stomach. Between my legs.

Then there were the nights when we were at my place. He'd come over early enough for us to have an evening together and we fell into that version of our routine.

In one of the posts that went up on Nat's instagram about her new bedazzled tank, Aspen's elbow was in it and that post now had over two thousand comments requesting (demanding) a face reveal of me and 'the guy with the hot elbow'.

"You do have hot elbows," I said, scrolling through the comments while Ap rested his chin on my shoulder.

"Mm." I felt the rumble of his chest against my back and it made my entire body shiver. "Your compliments are so erotic, love."

We'd ended up christening the floor of *my* kitchen that evening.

It was the end of the week now and I was exhausted. Todd now left me alone at work, but he stared at me unblinkingly whenever we crossed paths in the office. I won't admit it to anyone else, but at the start of the week when he stared for way too long I flipped him off.

I didn't say a word, just held up both my middle fingers in what felt like the most impressive power move I'd ever made and got into the elevator. The doors closed before he gathered himself enough to try and get in with me.

I wanted to wait up for Aspen, but the week had caught up with me and my eyes were sealed shut with the heaviness of sleep before I even registered my head hitting the pillow. I was cocooned in his bed when I came to from the mattress dipping behind me. It only felt like it had been minutes, but the digital clock next to his bed read 2 AM.

"I didn't mean to wake you up," he whispered, smelling like minty toothpaste and his woodsy body wash. His body was still hot from his shower when he pulled me against him and kissed the very back of my neck.

My sigh was a tangible thing.

"I've decided I'm taking you out on a date, Poppy." He sounded so awake and resolved, like he'd been thinking this for a while. I turned in his arms to face him, stealing a kiss before I spoke.

"What about Fiesta Night?" My sleepy mumbles against his chest were barely coherent.

"That will come after. I'm warming you up first."

"People will see you." I tucked myself in closer to him and he wrapped his arms around me, settling his chin on the top of my head.

"I have a plan, don't worry."

"Alright," I said around a yawn. I wondered if maybe he'd gotten us a table at that restaurant *Clover* his sister-in-law mentioned to him a few times. I'd heard only the best things about it but it was fine dining and I'd never done fine dining a day in my life. The idea that I might not know the right spoon to use gave me a little heartburn and I tried to make a mental note to watch a YouTube video on how to eat at a fine dining restaurant.

"So, that's a yes?" Aspen's question roused me awake again. I was pretty sure I had started to dream about spoons.

"That's a yes." I placed a kiss to the base of his throat. He might have said something else, but I'd already fallen back into a dreamless sleep where there were no spoons at all, only the smell of freshly cooked bagels and jam and violets.

# 27

# March 3rd

**Poppy**

I opened the door to Aspen already striding in. He was the epitome of a man on a mission and he was also wearing… overalls?

Linen overalls. They looked like a bigger version of a pair I'd seen Jess wear.

"Aspen, what –"

"It will all make sense." He waved away my confused concern with a flourishing hand before he tacked on a reassuring, "And I'm wearing two sets of thermals."

He turned on his heels to face me from the middle of my kitchen, "There are a couple things we need to do first." He walked up to me and, contradictory to his firm strides, he held my face gently between his hands and kissed me, "Hey."

I wrapped my arms around him and just as I was going to say hey back, to complete the circle of our usual greeting, my hand came across…drumsticks?

"Um," I pulled back and took them with me, holding them out between us. "Can't separate the man from his craft, huh?"

"I know you're being silly, sweet Poppy, but no. You cannot. I realized I didn't have any here. Can I, uh, put them near Nat? Just in case."

"You want to leave a pair of drumsticks here?" I was trying not to swallow my own tongue.

He gave me a double take, "I mean, yeah? But not if you don't–"

"No, I— Yes, of course." I set them right next to Nat's tank and took a photo of the pair together.

"I'm thinking the caption for this one will be *'Dad's going to teach me how to play the drums'.*" I was too busy laughing to myself while I typed it out that I didn't register right away that Aspen hadn't laughed too.

He just looked dazed and I couldn't figure out if I'd said something right or wrong.

"Sorry, that was a bad joke." I started to delete the words, but then Aspen was there, taking my phone.

"No, I just…what about a family photo?" I saw his throat move as he swallowed.

"You want to post a photo of me, you and Nat on her Instagram?"

"That would be correct."

"But they've never seen my face before. They don't even know my name. They'd see *your* face."

Was I excited or horrified by his suggestion? Maybe both. Excited for sure on the whole 'family photo' suggestion. And horrified because that was over two hundred and fifty thousand people seeing my face.

"First time for everything." Aspen could see the horror on

my face and I knew this just amused him to no end.

"There are people in the world that think I'm your cousin, though."

"Oh, well that's easily rectified." Aspen pulled out his phone, held it out in front of us and looked down at me. It all happened so fast because one second he was looking down at me like he'd won something important then he was kissing me until my knees began to wobble.

"Done!"

"What?" I was still trying to remember my own name.

He just held his phone out to me.

It was a photo of him grinning down at me and me with a small smile looking back up at him, one I didn't even realize I'd been wearing. He swiped over to the second photo and my breath caught in my throat. He was kissing me. And yes, I'd experienced it in real life, but it was a whole other thing to see it in photographic evidence.

*We looked good together.*

The thought was small and fleeting and completely over-shadowed when I noticed the caption.

"Aspen!" I grabbed his phone, pulling it closer to my face until the words were blurry like somehow that would make any difference.

He'd written, '*Managed to get @queen.nat.the.first's mom to eat my bagels. What a woman. #definitelynotmycousin #ihavenocousins #poompaloompa #sweetpoppy*'.

"You didn't," I gasped in mock outrage. It was just for show, to see that twinkle in his eye that flickered anytime he did anything mischievous. I was actually trying very hard not to laugh, to maintain my serious disposition.

"Oh, yes I did." He grinned, pulling me back into him. "Now, about that date."

We did not, in fact, do to *Clover.*

"Aspen, you cannot be serious about this," I whisper shouted while I walk-ran next to him, trying to keep up with his long strides. He held one of my hands and the other was trying desperately to keep the bright purple wig with a bob cut from flying off my head.

"I am absolutely serious." He walked with the confidence of a man who's wig was staying where it was supposed to. He'd explained his date idea to me in detail. I, of course, decided to humor him. Fully expecting the towel to be thrown in once he got a look at me in his chosen getup.

I was wearing the aforementioned purple wig paired with an oversized sweater that had in extremely large font across the front, 'my grandmother knitted this' and a pair of those jean-leggings in a light acid wash color paired with my black boots. It was all topped off with a pair of thick, black rimmed glasses that reminded me of Jess.

Aspen…well, he was another story entirely. He was wearing the aforementioned linen overalls. He'd paired them with his regular black boots but added a jacket that someone had clearly painted on the back of saying 'honk if you're horny'.

"Where did you even find these clothes?!" I was still whisper-yelling while intermittently laughing every time a car drove past us and honked.

"The thrift store near my apartment." His voice was so full

of pride I knew I'd never be able to get rid of a single thing I was wearing. Ever.

The best part of this entire date-mission was his face. Aspen was wearing a blond wig styled into a long, curly mullet, with big aviator sunglasses and a handlebar mustache.

He had no reservations at all when he pushed open the glass door to the ax throwing establishment called *'Let's Get Axey'* that resided in a town an hour out of Blazewood and dragged me right up to the help desk.

He turned to me and quickly threw over his shoulder, "Your name is Darla, by the way."

"What's your name?" How had we not covered this before embarking on this exercise?

"The reservation is under Cletus." He was peering at me over the top of his glasses.

I suddenly got the full body image of what it was he looked like and a laugh erupted out of my mouth, pushing past my clamped lips, making me splutter.

"You've got to be kidding me…" I clamped a hand over my mouth to try and stifle the way my body was desperate to release all the pent up laughter.

"Poppy, if you make me laugh, my mustache *will* come off," he spoke quickly before turning back to the receptionist guy who looked about fourteen and frightened for his life.

"We've got a reservation under Cletus." Aspen delivered it with a southern drawl that had also not been in any of his verbal briefing notes.

I gave up and pressed my face into the back of his musty, thrift store pervy jacket, the laughter wracking my body in silent tremors.

"Last name, sir?" The kid's voice trembled as his eyes darted from us to the computer, unsure where he should be actively looking.

"You mean there's more than one Cletus with a reservation here today?" Aspen dropped his accent entirely and the same noise from the other night that he'd referred to as a 'yodeling donkey' launched out of me and assaulted the air. That's all it took for Aspen to break character. He clutched the edge of the reception desk in a white knuckled grip while he tried to keep it together.

We eventually let the poor boy know that there was no last name on our booking, and he showed us to our ax throwing cage. The longer he was with us, the more troubled his face became. It wasn't until he'd left after explaining to us what we were supposed to be doing with the *rubber* axes and how they lodged into the special bullseye made out of rubber pegs did Ap and I actually turn to face one another.

That was when I realized that Aspen's handlebar mustache was hanging half off his face.

My face hurt from smiling and my arm hurt from throwing but I'd never laughed so much in my life. It had been both the best and most challenging experience. The best because Aspen turned it into a game of who could do the most bizarre leadup to their throw, and the most challenging because none of my axes lodged into the bullseye and stayed there.

And no one noticed him. Not a single person.

Sure, lots of people looked our way, but no one said a single thing. Not even the older couple who we asked to take a few photos of us, one of which was now the background of my phone; Aspen sticking his tongue out at the camera and me, looking up at him like I was determined to remember him just like that with my own two eyes.

We'd stopped for ice cream and decided to walk a little though it was still freezing outside, even at the start of March. It was also a very poor choice of food for maintaining our body heat but I wasn't complaining, and neither was he.

Aspen's hand around mine was anchoring. An anchor to the moment we were in, to everything I had felt through the entire day we'd spent together. I'd been staring at our joined hands when he stopped abruptly and turned to face me. His brows were furrowed and his eyes were focused on my mouth like maybe I'd be able to say whatever it was he was thinking for him.

"You're my best friend, Poppy." It was like he'd weighed each word for its importance before he spoke it out loud and then he finally looked up at me. His eyes flickering through different shades of green, all reflecting off the trees that surrounded us.

That's when it hit me.

Right then and there like a bolt of lightning striking me directly in the chest. Like an obscure fact that you just *knew*, without remembering when you'd absorbed the information. It was like I'd never known anything as completely as I did just then.

I didn't know how people didn't *know*. How you could look at someone and not immediately feel that overwhelming, earth shattering, breathtaking shift to the very foundations of who you were and not know that it was love. And I loved him. *God,* did I love him.

"You're mine too," I said, feeling the truth of it in every part of my body. "This was the best day, Ap."

"Not bad for a real first date, huh?" He leaned in to kiss me, forever imprinting the memory of today to the flavor of his mint choc-chip ice cream.

I shook my head, kissing him back, "Not bad at all."

# March 8th

**Aspen**

"This was the absolute wrong thing to bring." Poppy looked from the tray of carrots and hummus in her hands up to me with horror on her face. "How did you let me bring this?"

"Poppy, trust me, they will love it." I knew she could see the amusement in my eyes. She'd talked about how her boss, Winny, always gave people hummus and carrot sticks as a snack in high stress meetings and it was weird but sort of nice. For some reason, that inspired her to do the same.

"You're laughing at me." She pointed between my eyes.

"I'm not." I shook my head.

"You are, I can see it. That's it, Aspen, we need to –" and it was that exact moment that the front door opened.

Allie greeted us with a mildly insane look on her face that I assumed was meant to be not at all threatening and probably warm and welcoming.

I shot her a look of my own that I hoped said *'What's wrong with your face? Please, for the love of God, fix it'*. She rolled her eyes and stepped back to let us into her house. Dax was right behind her, an arm sliding into place like a band across her chest. Mainly (I was certain) to stop her from pouncing on Poppy.

It didn't work.

Allie gripped Poppy by the shoulders and pulled her into a squeezing hug.

I managed to grab the tray of food from between them and my heart started thudding at double time as I watched her slowly wrap her hands around Allie. Tentative and unsure and first, and then she really hugged her back.

"It's so, so nice to have you here, Poppy," Allie said, pulling back and looking over her shoulder to my brother who nodded his agreement.

"We've heard a *lot* about you," he said, and Poppy's face went white.

"*Wyatt!*" Allie hissed at her husband.

"Okay, that was a lie. Aspen has been annoyingly tight-lipped about your existence and so, please prepare for what will likely be a very inquisitive evening." He grinned at her before giving her a hug of his own.

"I can handle inquisitiveness," Poppy said with a lift of her eyebrows before turning back to Allie. "Thank you for having me. I brought carrot sticks and hummus. I have no other excuse except that I've been super nervous for Fun Friday Family Fiesta night that I blacked out when deciding on my contribution."

"Sweet *maple bacon!*" Allie's face lit up. "It sounds even better when someone else says it!" She looked at my brother,

"See! I told you it would catch on."

He just rolled his eyes and led Allie back down the hallway to the living room where the classical music was already playing. He called out over his shoulder, "Come back when you're ready!"

"I thought that was the name of the evening?" Poppy asked while taking off her coat.

"It is, but besides me, Allie and Sav are the only ones that use it. They're trying to get it to catch on so you probably just made her whole week."

"One point for Poppy then," she said, rubbing her hands together.

I couldn't help but tip my head back in shocked laughter.

"What?" She raised an eyebrow at me and I just shook my head.

"Nothing," I said, taking off my own coat and hanging it next to hers. "Just that I think you guys will get on great."

Everyone started on their best behavior and I dare say it had something to do with Savannah threatening their balls with some sort of painful repercussion. The good behavior lasted about an hour before everyone returned to their normal selves. Poppy sat right next to me in the spot that had always been empty, a glass of wine in her hand and a look on her face that said she wanted to be nowhere else but where she was.

She was talking to Rip about how she and I first met and he was in tears at the part where she asked me if it was a felony to have come up to me.

"God, I hope you said yes." He looked at me with hope in his eyes.

"I didn't say yes, you dick." I pushed him back onto the

couch with a hand on his face.

Allie brought out the grazing board, Poppy's hummus and carrot sticks included, and when it was finally time for charades, the girls had the audacity to try and change the teams to girls versus boys versus boys.

"No fucking way!" I set my beer down on the table. "The one time I finally have a partner and you try to take her from me." I grabbed Poppy and pulled her closer to me.

"I'm confused," she whispered.

"Don't worry, Poompaloompa, I've got this," I whispered back.

"Did he just call her…*Poompaloompa*?" Luke whispered to Angus sounding befuddled and I did my best to ignore them both in favor of the more important matter at hand.

"No, I'm putting my foot down. Poppy and I are on the same team and everyone else stays in their couples."

"Luke and I are not a couple," Rip said, earning a somewhat hurt look from Luke.

"You may as well be," Sav mumbled and the rest of us sort of shrugged our agreement.

"Fine," Allie conceded, looking a little sad, but her puppy dog eyes would not work on me this time.

"Fix your face, Alice Smith, I'm not falling for it." I pointed right at her and she just leaned further into it.

"Oh, this is a good one," Sav said.

"Nope." I held my ground.

"You sure?" Allie asked, a final attempt, a mischievous little grin growing on her face.

"I have never been more sure of anything pertaining to Fiesta Night. Get the fresh deck out, we're going to win the shit out of this."

"Ap, what are we agreeing to?" Poppy sounded a little frightened.

"The new deck?" Luke guffawed. "We've been saving it for like a year."

"Ap's right," Allie said, her face now back to normal if not a little proud. "It's time for the new deck."

Poppy and I were winning.

*We were winning...*kind of.

It was down to the wire. Dax and Allie had eleven points and so did we. Sav and Angus were on eight and Luke and Rip were on three.

"You're not interpreting any of my movements properly," Luke said, sitting down in defeat after Rip guessed his attempt at a rocket ship was 'someone texting'.

"I am, you just suck," Rip said back, equally as unimpressed.

Allie was up and, in all honesty, it was a valiant effort. Dax thought she was doing hopscotch, Allie was in fact trying to portray someone walking through the house with mud on their shoes."

"Close, babe," Dax said, pulling his wife down onto his lap and kissing her on the cheek.

"This is it," Sav said, rubbing her hands together in delight. "If Ap and Poppy get this one, they win. If not, we have a draw for winners this time around."

"You ready?" I asked Poppy, who had settled into this game like a champ. Her game face was on and she hadn't shied

278

away at all when the game was announced. She simply stated that it was something her and her brother used to do.

"Oh, does he live close?" Dax asked, not knowing any better because I hadn't said anything. Poppy's hand gripped mine a little tighter but that was all. Her voice was strong and even when she answered him. "No, no. He–Casimir died when I was sixteen."

"Oh, I'm sorry, Poppy. I didn't –"

"No, it's okay. Really." She gave him a smile that made her words feel true.

I leaned over and placed a kiss behind her ear which she leaned into. My silent support for this incredible woman.

"Wait, sorry, you said your brother's name was Casimir?" Dax had this look on his face that was a mix of shock and disbelief.

"Yeah, not super common I know." She nodded and it was something completely other to see her so at ease talking about this part of her life that had caused her pain for so long. "Penelope and Casimir. We were quite the pair." She laughed and so did my brother.

"Hey, you know what's wild?" I chimed in, "He actually owned the Taurus."

That little nugget was met with a chorus of baffled '*Woah's!*' and one very exuberant "No fucking way!" From Savannah.

"Yeah, Poppy saw something that confirmed it and I asked Jane to help pull up the old records of the car. Last person to own it before Wyatt was Casimir Hart."

"I thought the car was yours now?" Poppy asked, leaning into me.

"It is, but it's still in Wyatt's name. Never had a reason to change it."

Everyone had moved on easily from what was by default a heavy conversation but Dax got up and left the room for a bit, not coming back for a good ten minutes. When he did though, he was back to himself and I just played it off as being unprepared to learn about Poppy's loss.

Her experience in this game turned out to be invaluable. She looked at me with determination in her eyes, "Oh, I was born ready."

She got up and took the 'stage'. It was just the middle of the living room with the coffee table pushed off to the side, but it was a stage for all intents and purposes now.

Poppy picked up a card and the moment she read whatever was on the other side her face lit up like a fucking Christmas tree.

She slapped the card down on the coffee table and held up one finger to me.

"One word," I said, and she nodded.

Poppy didn't break eye contact as she tucked her arms close to her sides, stuck her hands out and started fluttering them like her life depended on it while jumping up and down in a squiggly sort of way. She looked like…like…

I stood up and pointed right at her, "NATALIE!"

She nodded with a big grin on her face and did the motion that told me to keep going, but that I was on the right track.

"MATING CALL!" I was yelling. I was yelling so loud but I couldn't help it.

"How the fuck is he getting that from–" Angus started.

"*Shut up!*" Savannah hissed at her boyfriend.

Poppy made the same motion to keep going and I knew it with certainty. "GOLDFISH!"

"YES!" She yelled back. Laughing with her head tipped back

before jumping into my arms and wrapping her legs around my waist.

"That was the weirdest thing I have ever witnessed," Rip said, staring at us like we'd lost our minds.

And maybe we had, I didn't really care. I just knew without a shadow of a doubt that I was madly in love with Penelope Elizabeth Hart and there wasn't a damn thing I could do about it.

# 29

# March 10th

## Poppy

Waking up on Saturday was like being dipped in honey.

The warmth of Aspen's body wrapped around mine kept pulling me back under and I could only assume the same for him. Every time I swam to the surface of our honey pool of sleep and into consciousness he was breathing evenly. Mouth slightly lax and face absent of any traces of worry.

He was so completely peaceful.

On one of our many nights together at his place, when we'd both been half pulled into the fog of sleep, he mumbled that he now finally 'got' the allure of sleep.

"What do you mean?" His question had woken me up enough to be determined to get my answer.

"It was too loud in here," he lifted up one of his strong, broad hands and pointed right at his temple. "I hated it. Every time I closed my eyes it was a constant stream of; did I do enough today for the band? Or, did I miss any calls? Or, was I everything everyone needed?"

"But it's not like that anymore." My response was a statement because I knew it was true. I could see it with my own eyes.

"No." He opened his eyes and looked right at me.

I was completely captivated by his bright green eyes. With no trees around us for them to reflect in their color I could see them clearly. They had a dark ring of green on the edges that got lighter the closer the color got to his pupils and they were nothing less than absolutely beautiful.

He kissed me before speaking again, "No, it's not like that anymore."

We spent the day in bed, some of it quietly memorizing one another's bodies. Some of it *loudly* memorizing one another's bodies and all of it with this inescapable happiness that moved through every moment. Like a vein right from the heart. Happiness was an undeniable part of what was between us. It was this thing we were both acutely aware of and instead of tiptoeing around it, we dove straight in. Covered ourselves with it completely. Reminded one another of it consistently in touches and looks and laughter.

That was how every day with him had been since we'd met. Bright and full of color. Like moving into the sunshine and, little by little, removing the layers of clothing you'd put on to keep away the cold. Feeling your fingers tingle as they started to defrost.

It was uncomfortable at first. I had wanted to pull away from the burn, from the unfamiliar sensation, but now the thought of eventually having to put my layers back on and go inside was almost too much to bear.

It was now Sunday night and Aspen drove us back to my house. We both shuffled in out of the cold, both yelling out greetings to Natalie.

I jumped into the shower and Ap made us a couple of teas. I was drying off and getting dressed, listening to how he was playing out a drum beat with the sticks he'd left here on the kitchen counter while he waited for the tea to steep.

We passed each other on the stairs with a kiss while he went up to shower and I got out some cookies for us to share.

Without even realizing it we had started to live life *together*.

There were so many routines that had just formed. Naturally and all on their own. It made my heart pang while I sat at the kitchen counter and waited for Aspen to come back down stairs.

He pressed a kiss to my temple just as he took his seat beside me.

One of the best things about Aspen was the silence we could sit in together. It was this comfortable safety blanket.

The same night he told me his secret about sleep, he'd also shared that he had never been a fan of the quiet, but when we were together he could stay in it forever. That had felt pivotal to me. Another secret he had let me in on, just like I continued to let him in on mine whenever one made itself known.

I wish that we would have had enough time for me to share them all with him.

"You know," I said quietly while we sat with Nat and drank our tea. I could feel him looking at me but kept my eyes on the bubbles from the water filter in the fish tank as I spoke. "Sometimes I'll let myself imagine what it would be like to have you forever."

I reached for a cookie as something to do but just held it in my hand and kept talking. "I imagine game nights with your friends and family, but maybe Leah is there too sometimes and she screams every time she sees everyone. Maybe Jess too. I picture my clothes next to yours in your closet and a bigger tank for Natalie. Going to that Mexican place near your house so often they know our names and all the different people we would become on all the different dates we would go on."

Aspen reached across to tuck some hair behind my ear, "We can have all of those things." He sounded so sure. So certain it broke my heart a little bit.

"I don't see how." I put the cookie down, my sweet tooth gone.

"Those are the things our lives would be full of anyway, my love."

I looked at him then, my heart aching with every beat, "Aspen, come on. That's not funny."

He just frowned at me, "Why can't we?" We were standing on two opposite ends of a river and both just waiting for the other to jump in and swim to their side.

"Aspen, I'm—" I frowned back. "I'm leaving? April fifth, I told you when we met."

"When we met, sure, but things have changed since then." His frown was made up of all the things that I knew would break my heart.

I'd already begun to hurt him and it killed me.

He was right and wrong. Not just 'things' but *everything*. Absolutely everything had changed and now it was all careening around my head without any order or sense. That door to the part of my mind I had closed off had been ripped off its hinges the night we exchanged secrets in the dark quiet of my room. I had meant everything I'd said to him, meant everything I'd felt but it had never crossed my mind that I would stay.

Never crossed my mind because the possibility of it wasn't something I could conceptualize. This version of myself I was with Aspen was not the real version. Who didn't hide the darkest parts of herself from the world, who let her sadness coexist with her happiness.

This person who'd been forgiven for everything that she'd done. Who'd forgiven herself.

No, none of that was real, and I didn't see how it ever could be when the only person who could fix it all, who'd always fixed it all, had been gone for almost as long as I'd had him.

I knew that no matter how much I loved Aspen, I would still hurt him and it was better to control when it happened than to have no say in it at all. It was the only way I could manage the damage inflicted.

"Aspen," I said it again more firmly, refusing to think about what I was about to do in more detail than the surface level. More than the simple truth I'd always known; I was leaving. He *knew* I was leaving. *He knew I was leaving.*

I said the words I knew would hurt him and refused to acknowledge the way my voice shook. "I'm leaving. I was never going to stay. I…I thought you understood that. Right from the beginning. *Aspen,*" my voice hitched, now barely more than a whisper. "I was honest with you right from the start. I was never going to stay."

The words were bitter. They tasted foul on my tongue as I took that version of myself I'd been with Ap and led her back into me. Right into that room in my mind where she stood and watched while I fixed the hinges of the door that he'd helped me blow right off. The moment it was sealed shut I could feel that part of me banging on the other side. Scraping and scratching at that door, her throat being ripped apart by pleas not to do this. That version of myself who had only started to get her color back. Skin golden from the sun that was Aspen, fingers warm and tingly from being in his orbit.

I knew once the memory of it all faded, when the color from her skin paled with each passing day and the feeling in her hands dissipated that it would be easier to look back on the decisions I'd made and feel fondness instead of devastating loss.

Ap looked like he'd been winded, but I also knew that Aspen Smith had been putting the people he loved before himself for as long as he could remember. I was sure there was a special place in hell for people like me. Who knew the secrets of the people they loved and used them *against*, instead of *for*.

So, I knew that there would be no other option for him but to nod his head. To tell me that he understood and that it was okay.

That night when we went to bed and Aspen hovered above me before sliding into me, slowly, deeply, I didn't think about the ways that it was different than before. How every touch of his lingered longer than normal, just like mine. How he held me tighter, closer. Watched the way our bodies met with fierce determination, like he was making sure he'd never forget it.

He held me close and only when I felt his breathing even out did I let myself cry and hold him tighter, knowing with world fracturing certainty that we had just said goodbye to one another.

It had been the only right way forward, and I knew It had to be right because it was painful.

In the moments of my life when I had been sure nothing could be worse than it was. When I was positive there was no room left to hurt the people I loved, the thing I remember most was unfathomable pain.

It was physical at the time, in part. But I'd learned the day I turned sixteen that pain manifested itself in many different ways, and the worst of which was the way no one could see. Lacerations on your soul, your mind.

Your heart.

It had been selfish of me to give into Ap, but it was always going to be okay because it was never meant to be forever. That's why this momentary happiness, this joy and freedom, had been okay. But when I felt like that, it meant there was a very long way to fall and I always seemed to soften my own landing with the people closest to me. Leaving them to take the brunt of the fall.

If I kept on moving then I'd never be in one place long enough to make a mark. You might know I'd been there but like everything, with time, the traces of me would fade away and it would have been like I'd never been there at all.

So, I told myself I needed to go. To keep moving because I was looking for something important and refused to admit that maybe what I'd been looking for, I'd already found.

# 30

## March 11th

**Ap:**
You wanna come over tonight?

**Poppy:**
Hey, I don't think I can make it.

**Poppy:**
Rain check? x

**Ap:**
Okay, rain check x

# 31

## March 14th

**Aspen**

"Aspen?" Dax came into focus right in front of me. I'd been looking at him the whole time but I hadn't been in the room. Hadn't really been there with the band working through one of our many remaining rehearsals.

"Sorry," I said, taking my hat off and running my hand through my hair before putting it back and rubbing my eyes. "Sorry."

"You said that already, but I'm not sure what I'm supposed to be accepting your apology over?"

"Probably for having his head in a sex crazed cloud instead of in the rehearsal like he's supposed to be," Rip contributed unhelpfully with a stupidly happy expression on his face and a wag of his eyebrows.

I pointed at him with a lackluster expression on my face, "Stop thinking about my dick."

Rip's expression dropped and he lifted his hands before

dropping them in defeat.

We'd been here all day but only started to actually play in the last hour or so. Up

until then we'd mostly been finalizing our discussion from the last session where we'd decided to scrap the original set list and start again. Though we'd been rehearsing for the *Salvation Tour* since February it didn't mean as much now that we'd shifted our approach.

The way we played our live shows had always been with the same goal: be able to give our fans the experience of listening to our recorded album live, yes, but also to make it a whole new experience.

It was exactly what I needed to pour myself into because if I didn't, I would focus on how I was watching as Poppy pulled away from me day after day. I would focus on how she had gone from being someone who I'd had all of and face the reality that that was changing.

And I had.

I had every single part of her and it had been the single best thing I'd ever experienced. Being trusted by someone like that? Being *loved* by someone like that?

She hadn't said the words to me but I didn't need to hear them. She didn't need to hear them either to know I felt the same. I felt it in the way she looked at me when she thought I wouldn't notice. The way her head tilted to the side when she was listening to what I was saying, absorbing every single word like each one spoken was a revelation. A secret of the universe that she wanted to covet.

I knew she loved me in the way she fit herself into my side, as close as possible while we were watching an episode of *Friends* on her couch, in the photos on my phone that I began collecting. Of her sitting at my kitchen island helping me bake, of her on the balcony of my apartment, hands on the railings and face raised towards the sun. Her, rumpled from sleep wearing one of my shirts and messy bun hanging off to the side with a small but mischievous look on her face and the photo after of her that very next moment, running straight for me, her smile big and her eyes bright.

It was in every single photo that told the story of us. This story that had only just fucking started and somehow I'd convinced myself would never end.

"Aspen?" Dax called my name again. He hadn't moved from where he was in front of me, and I'd been looking through him again.

"Sorry, just tired." I waved him off and all he did was frown deeper. It wasn't a lie, I was tired. I hadn't been sleeping and after getting used to the longer hours of rest with Poppy beside me, the soft and gentle curves of her beneath my hands, my return to my previous way of living had been…well, it had been fucked.

"Maybe we should call it —" he started but I cut him off.

"No. *No*." My voice was louder than intended, catching the attention of the other guys, but calling it early meant going home. To my apartment that had learned what it was like to host a life better than the one I'd been living and now in the absence of it I found myself completely unwilling to face that reality. "Let's keep going."

Dax stared at me for a while longer and only after putting every single ounce of energy I had into convincing him through the expression on my face did he nod. The moment he turned away, I dropped my smile, picked up my drum sticks and fell into the comfort of putting them to use.

That's how it went on.

Day after day.

Night after night.

I would wake up and head straight for my drum kit. If it was a day that something else was on for the band like doing stuff with our label, or meeting with our tour manager, or flying across the country to do more press, or approving designs for the new tour merch, then I did that instead. But, I always came home to sit right behind my drum kit.

I couldn't remember when I'd practiced this much. Maybe when I was first learning. I knew I had been borderline obsessive before but I knew I was particularly bad when I woke up with blisters on my hands. It was tough to keep playing like that, tougher than the time I'd dislocated two of my fingers on tour a couple years ago when Angus and I were throwing a ball back and forth during the day before a show. I had been distressed to the point of throwing up at the idea of not being able to play the show that night, of letting down the fans and the band.

I'd asked the doctor to wrap them in a way so that I could still play. He'd advised against it of course and it took twice as long for them to return to normal, but I'd done it.

I'd put everyone else first, just like I always did.

I'd tried being selfish, putting what I wanted first. Chasing after it with both hands but it hadn't done me any real good in the end.

I put the people I loved before myself and that's why instead of picking up my phone to call Poppy, I picked up my drumsticks and started to play again.

# 32

# March 17th

**Aspen**

**Me:**
Poppy?

**Poppy:**
Yeah?

**Me:**
I miss you.

**Poppy:**
I miss you too.

# 33

# March 18th

**Aspen**

The new routine I'd settled into was like a familiar balm on an open wound. We rearranged the set list *again* and added another date to what we'd dubbed the '*Salvation Pre-Tour Tour: City of Blazewood*'. It had sold out in minutes.

We were now doing four nights, all of them had a day in between and the first date was April fifth.

That felt painfully poetic to me.

I'd decided somewhere in the last week – fuck me, *longer* than a week – that I hadn't seen Poppy that this old version of myself felt about as good as the sleep routine I'd reverted back to.

It didn't *fit* anymore. It was like wearing clothes that were too tight. I couldn't breathe right in them. This ghost of mine I'd let go of and forced back to my side looked at me with pity. With a very obvious sense of displeasure at being chained back to me the same way I'd chained myself back to it. So, I turned off my phone.

*I turned off my fucking phone.*

I would have thrown the thing right off the balcony if I hadn't actually needed it for whenever I needed to call someone. Mainly the pizza joint across the street for delivery.

I turned off my phone and I didn't go to Fiesta Night.

What was the point? Actually, that's not true. Or fair. I loved Fiesta Night, but I hadn't wanted to walk in and carry the weight of all the people I loved until I buckled beneath it all. I hadn't wanted to sit down and stare at the spot Poppy had once been. I knew they would worry and that was never my intention, so I had turned my phone on to let Dax know I wasn't going and then I turned it back off.

My brother was a smart man, who'd married an even smarter woman who was best friends with an equally smart woman and the rest of them would catch on eventually. I knew that they'd figure out something had happened with Poppy. I'm sure they'd be confused and wouldn't be able to understand *why*.

*Why?*

I hadn't had the mental capacity to try and explain it to them, at least I let myself put it off until tomorrow.

There was only one real explanation for the 'why' that they'd ask, and it started long before I started losing Poppy.

I'd just wiped the sweat from my eyes when I heard the knock at my door. I couldn't tell you if that was the first time they'd knocked or the twentieth. My heart immediately started hammering because there were only a small number of people it could have been and I'd immediately let myself hope for one in particular.

I opened the door drenched in sweat, still holding my drumsticks and came face to face with my brother.

"Dax?" I stepped back and let him in.

He was on his own which was the first indication that something was amiss. Where he went, Allie went and vice versa (unless you count Allie and Savannah's weekly wine and Italian night which was strictly no boys allowed - I'd tried).

I turned to find him standing in my living room, one hand rubbing the back of his neck the other clutching something.

An envelope.

"What's up?" I stepped closer to him on instinct. Immediately wanting to help him, to make sure he was okay. Not because of some fucked up idea that by doing that I'd make up for not being there for someone when I should have been. For being unable to pull myself out of the pit of loneliness I'd fallen into, but because he was my brother and I loved him.

He held the hand out to me that was clutching the envelope. Now that I could see it clearly, it had a business logo on the top left that I'd never seen before and the paper had yellowed with time. Black marks dotted the sides like someone had gripped it with hands covered in grease.

It wasn't those things that all but stopped my heart.

My drumsticks clattered to the tiled floor beneath me.

No, it was none of those things. Rather it was the writing on the front. Written in neat, clear letters.

Penelope,
Happy 16th Birthday
Love, Casimir

# 34

## March 20th

**Aspen**

**Me:**
Poppy?

# 35

# March 24th

**Aspen**

I realized it had nothing to do with putting Poppy first that stopped me from driving to her house. From banging on her front door and telling her no.

No, I don't *accept* that you have to leave.

I accept it a whole fucking zero percent because I know for a fact that everything you need is here. With me. I knew it in every bone in my body. In every thought in my head. Knew it as confidently as I knew the drum pattern for a new song we'd only begun to write.

It just *was*.

I didn't go to her because no matter how much I wanted her to stay, no matter how much I wanted to keep her with me, it would mean nothing if she didn't want to stay for herself too.

I knew she was it for me. Knew it the first time I saw her, probably. I knew now too that it had nothing to do with letting go of my own ghosts.

Poppy had to come back to me all on her own.

I *needed* her to come back to me all on her own, otherwise there would always be a part of her wishing she'd kept on running.

# 36

## March 30th

### Poppy

I had been ignoring all the calls from Leah to the best of my ability. I had successfully managed to not talk to my best friend for a total of twenty days.

That's two followed by a zero, and in doing so I'd broken one of my three golden rules. There was a list, a really fucking *long* list, of rules that lived under the 'Poppy's Life Rules' title, but speaking to Leah no less than three times a week had been one I'd never broken.

My phone was ringing in my hand and I was terrified to pick it up. It was 6 AM and I was sitting on the floor of my bedroom, slowly packing up my stuff in boxes and making detailed notes on the sides of all of them. I picked up the call.

Leah's face came into view. As usual, she was so close to the camera I mainly just saw her nose. It occurred to me that for a millennial she had really no idea how to use a phone.

"Sissy?! What," she screamed and it made me jump, "the

*actual* flaming motherfucking *fuck* is wrong with you?!"

*I deserved that.*

"Do you have *any* idea how worried I've been? What the hell is wrong with you, Penelope?"

*I deserved that too.*

"You think that just because you found this perfect man, with that perfect face and brain and heart and ass that you can suddenly forget about your *best fucking friend?*"

And that's when I started crying.

I hadn't cried since I was sixteen. Right up until Aspen, and now? Well it was like my tear ducts woke up from the world's longest hibernation and were working overtime in a real big F U to the layer of dust they no doubt had to make their way through to start operating correctly.

"Wh— I—" Leah's whole face came into view when she pulled back the phone and looked at me like I was an alien. Looked at me like the world was ending and all she had to hold it together was craft glue and painters tape.

"I didn't mean it!" she yelled. And now she was crying. Big, huge tears that tracked her mascara down her face. "I didn't mean it, but you fell off the face of the earth and I thought you had *died*, Penelope. You scared me really fucking bad." Her voice got higher and higher as she spoke and it wasn't funny but a little bubble of laughter mixed in between my sobs sputtered out of me.

"I need you." It was all I managed to get out.

The moment the words hit Leah's ears she stopped crying. Just...*stopped*, just like that. Wiped her face and gave me one, solid nod. That one movement flipped a switch in my brain, catapulting me back to a different time in my life. A time when I was younger, made of glass with fissures running through every part of me. My arm was looped into the arm of a sixteen year old Leah's. She was talking a million miles an hour about something I couldn't recall, but I did remember the way she held onto me tightly as she had started to do. Clutching me to her like maybe she was scared something might snatch me away right there in broad daylight.

We had been in the sun but I hadn't felt its warmth, I'd merely wondered how it could still shine when my whole entire world had been ripped apart.  No single part of it remaining whole.

Except for Leah.

I remember her looking over at me, her sentence stopping halfway through its existence. I was looking right at her and watched her face change. Like this mask slid into place and then she nodded at me. Just once.

Just one solemn nod and I could see it now for what it was. It was this silent acknowledgment that she'd made for the both of us that she'd carry my weight right along with her own until I could learn to bear it myself again.

And it had been *heavy.* It had been so heavy it was crushing me beneath it and I hadn't realized then like I realized right now that yes, I lost my brother, but Leah had lost her best friend.

That I changed in order to figure out what navigating life was without Casimir, but she had changed too. She'd had to learn how to navigate life with enough will to live not for just one soul, but for two.

Leah had had other friends besides me, but day after day, night after night, she'd been *right there.*

That was all I thought about while I waited through all the hours of the day. Until evening came and my doorbell rang and I flung myself into the arms of my best friend and told her truthfully, *honestly*, for the first time in my life the very thing I should have said at sixteen.

"Thank you."

Leah and I lay on my couch, my feet near her head and her head near my feet. It was the same way we'd always settled into any couch, made infinitely better by the way we rubbed each other's feet.

I told her everything.

It had been frighteningly difficult to push past this bizarre notion that I'd somehow managed to shield this woman from the most fragile and broken parts of myself for the last twelve years when in reality she'd been there, woven basket in hand picking up the shards as they dropped. Pieces of myself I had disregarded and deemed to have no value while she picked them up, held it up to the light and thought *'yes, you'll do just fine'*.

"I love him," I told her, feeling the pressure behind my eyes increase again. "I love him and I'm terrified I'll hurt him."

"Do you think it's fair to make this decision for the both of you?" she asked plainly.

"No," I said honestly, "but I've done it anyway."

"You'll regret it, Poppy." Her words were sad and resigned, like she knew even as she tried that I couldn't be swayed in this.

"I know." She'd find no argument from me.

"You'll live the rest of your life regretting it," she said.

"I know," I said. "But I already know how to live like that."

Leah sat up, legs tucked to her chest where she sat on the other end of the couch, me on the other side, her mirror image.

It was dark outside but the room around us was bright, and I owed it to her to share this secret where there was nowhere for it to hide. "I'll never forgive myself, Leah. I can't." I shook my head. "I don't know *how*. I tried. I've tried. With Aspen, *I tried*." I swiped at the tears furiously as they fell, sick of their constant presence. "I'll never be able to forgive myself," I repeated, knowing with my whole heart that was the real reason. I couldn't forgive my sixteen year old self, for how I'd failed the one person who had never failed me. I'd never be able to love Aspen like he deserved. There would always be this shadow, this dark cloud that would follow us and eventually, it would completely overtake every bit of sunshine that he was made of.

"You're punishing him too, you know." Her words hit a pain point, one I'd thought of and conveniently ignored.

"Maybe, for now," I nodded, "But with time, he'll forget me."

"I think you underestimate how much that man loves you."

We were at an impasse. I think I might've underestimated how much he loved me too, but it didn't change the truth of it all.

She stared at me and I stared at her and then there was that nod again, the one that I'd always thought meant 'I don't know what to say. I don't know how to help you.' but really had always meant 'I've got you, do you hear me? *I've got you*.'

"Alright. I'll get the wine, you call Jess." Leah was up and in the kitchen between one blink and the next, just like that.

Shifting gears like she always had.

I picked up my phone, my heart panging as I scrolled past Aspen where he sat right at the very top and tapped Jess's name.

"Poppy?"

"Aspen and I broke up and Leah is here and would you like to come over?" The words tripped on one another as they all but fell out of my mouth.

"I'm malfunctioning. I have the boys, Poppy –"

"Leah, she's got the boys!" I called out to her in the kitchen.

"Then we're going over there!" Leah called back.

"We're coming over, see you in twenty?" I asked.

"I'll make a cheese board."

# 37

## April 3rd

### Poppy

Winny had tried to organize a surprise farewell for me and it all panned out in a way that seemed almost fitting to the way that I felt.

I'd managed to walk into the staff kitchen (the same one Todd had tainted with his overbearing cologne) just in time for Jess and Winny to sing "Surprise!" and then to see one of the brown colored balloons unstick from the wall and slowly flutter to the floor.

"This is…" I was smiling, or at least trying to smile.

"Average at best?" Jess supplied helpfully.

"Jessica!" Winny admonished from his spot beside her. What caught me off guard was the fact that instead of rolling her eyes and walking over to me, she rolled her eyes and gave the man a kiss. *Right on the mouth.*

Winny went beet red, Jess's whole face was practically twinkling in a manic sort of delight and I was gaping like a bigmouth buffalo fish.

"I've missed something crucial here." I was waving my hand between the two of them, and set my gaze right on Jess. "*Jessica?*" I quirked an eyebrow and all she did was walk over and throw her arms around me. I hugged her back without question. It was the same way she'd greeted Leah and I when we rocked up and her house.

Leah had six bottles of wine in her hands all of which she'd packed in her luggage before flying in.

Jess had hugged me, pulled back and held my face between her hands. "The boys have put together a small performance for you in hopes it might cheer you up."

With that, she sent me into the living room where Leo and Aiden were wearing pots on their heads and matching pajamas. I was still close enough to the front door to overhear what Leah said though.

"She loves you, so I do too."

"Words from my own mouth. I Ubered another four bottles of wine too, they're in the kitchen."

I turned in time to see the two women hugging and wondered if maybe we'd all been friends before, in another life.

"Also I'm a big fan of the choking bell concept," Leah was breathless in her awe, still hugging Jess tight.

"That means a lot to me, thank you." Jess replied with her face pressed against Leah's chest. Their height difference was polarizing.

Mostly, I think it was Leah and Jess who were one soul split into two because Leah needed to excuse herself halfway through the boys routine, walking pigeon legged to the lavatory screaming something about how she'd already started peeing.

Leah had to leave Sunday night but we now had a three way chat she'd called '*Sistaz*'.

Jess pulled back and looked at Winny who'd busied himself taking photos of the cheeseboard she'd had put together with copious amounts of pride.

"You didn't say a single thing on Saturday," I grumbled to her with a pout.

"It didn't feel like the right time to tell you I was in love with our boss."

"A younger man, huh?" I waggled my eyebrows at her and tried desperately to shove the sadness that sprouted at her words down deep into my body and just be happy for her. Like, deep down into my feet somewhere.

"I know," she said, looking at him again where he was still snapping photos but from a different angle. "He's a good man and he loves the boys. And I think he might love me too."

"Oh, he loves you," Winny said without an ounce of hesitation, not even moving his attention away from his phone. Jess turned back to me with a crimson blush creeping up her neck.

I lost control of my features then, unable to help the way my mind reached down into my feet and pulled up image after image of Aspen. Unable to ignore the feel of his unanswered text that was burning a hole in my heart.

"Oh, Poppy." Jess wrapped her hands around my waist, squeezed tight. When I looked up again, Winny had left the little kitchen.

"I'm so happy for you, Jess." I wrapped my hands around her and hoped she knew I meant every word.

"You really have to go?" She asked, her face pretty firmly

pressed into my boobs. She hadn't asked me that question yet. Her questions and comments all through Saturday had been fiercely non-invasive and I loved her for it. All she did was nod during the moments I was steadfast in my resolve and hold my hand in the moments when that resolve had crumbled a little.

I just nodded, because I didn't want to, but it was the only thing I knew how to do.

# 38

# April 5th

**Poppy**

I'd descended into this state of pure movement and no thoughts. There wasn't a single thought in my head except for just a narration of the things I was doing. A step by step monotone recount of the things I did, as I did them.

Wake up.

Shower.

Make sure Nat's travel tank was secure.

Make sure the lock on the back of the U-Haul was secure.

Force myself to eat something.

Message Leah.

Message Jess.

That's all I could do, just one thing after the other, knowing the steps because it was pure muscle memory. I'd done it all more times than I could count.

The last couple of days had been a blur. I'd finished packing up my stuff, most of the boxes I'd never unpacked at all still left me wondering what was even in them. I'd been tempted to leave everything behind. The things I would unpack when I got to my new apartment and would look at only to remember Aspen.

But I wanted to remember him. I wanted to never forget him for as long as I lived. This man who had settled into my bones, who deserved so much more than to be loved by someone like me.

So I kept everything, made sure to spend extra care keeping safe the things I knew would hurt the most to unpack and lugged everything out to the U-Haul I'd parked in my drive. My next door neighbor was a burly man I'd only ever seen twice. Once because he had accidentally gotten my mail and once because I'd accidentally gotten his. He helped me move my couch, my coffee table and my mattress.

When he asked me how I managed to get them into the house and even up the stairs in the first place I said, "It's surprising what you can achieve when you're not afraid of getting a hernia."

He'd looked at me like I'd responded in the form of interpretive dance. I decided there was no love lost there on account of the fact I'd made no effort to get to know him at all in the year I'd been there.

Have you ever woken up with that feeling of dread right in the very center of your body? Like you knew without a shadow of a doubt that something was wrong. Very, *very* wrong, and you didn't know what or why or how to fix it?

I was covered in that feeling.

It clogged my pores and coated every part of my body like invisible tar. The worst part was, I knew why. I knew *what*. I even knew what would fix it.

I sat there in the middle of my empty house and let myself think of him. Of strong hands and green eyes. Dimples and trail walk narrations. Of being able to see my whole life in one person.

I sat there, holding the hand of the version of myself I'd been with him and meant it when I whispered the words 'I'm sorry'. But there was no other way I could protect him but leave.

I stood up, swiped the tears from my cheeks and wrenched open the front door to find probably the last person I'd ever thought would be on my porch.

Wyatt Maddox Smith.

I stood in my empty living room now, standing across from the front man of the biggest rock band in the entire world.

His black hair was shaggy and flicked off to the side. Like he'd pushed it up and back and it had just slowly fallen back down. He was dressed the way I'd always seen him dressed; a leather jacket, though this one seemed to be a little more lax on the buckles, a pair of black skinny jeans and, ah, converse. I sort of thought he always just wore those black Doc Martens with the harness across the front.

The only thing that had changed in the years the world had watched him from afar was his rings. Wyatt used to wear all these silver rings on both hands. Now, he only wore one, and it sat on his left hand.

If you're wondering if I'm cataloging everything he was wearing in order to not think about the fact that Aspen's brother was in my living room, then you'd be correct.

My heart was fucking *galloping*. "Is–" I cleared my throat, "Is he okay?"

"Mm," Wyatt hummed contemplative, sliding his hands into the pockets of his jacket. "Define 'okay'." He didn't say the words like he'd wanted them to hurt me, but they did anyway.

I was exhausted. Just so fucking tired. I walked over to the wall where my T.V. had been and slumped against it.

I hadn't really expected Wyatt to follow me, but he did. He released a weary sigh that spoke volumes. More than any words could.

"I'm sorry," I whispered to him, too tired to do more than that. "Believe it or not, I'm doing this so I *don't* hurt him."

I braved a look at Wyatt and he sat looking straight ahead, his head resting back against the wall and legs splayed out in front of him, hand still in his jacket pockets. I'd wager a bet this guy just always looked cool.

I stared a little longer than I should have, probably. But I could see a bit of Aspen in his side profile. The slope of his nose and the height of his cheekbones. I looked away quickly, wiping the tears that had escaped in their silent journey down my face quickly. But Wyatt wasn't stupid, he saw.

"My brother," his voice was deep and thoughtful and I stared straight ahead where Natalie sat on the floor near the front door and did my best to listen to each word he said, "he's always been secretive. I think that *he* thinks I'm completely unaware of his...certain way of coping with things, but I know. Maybe I didn't realize it at first, but I eventually figured it out."

He took a deep breath, pushed his hair back from his face and kept going. "I will be the first to admit I could have done more to help him. Done more that made him feel like he didn't need to keep doing things for everybody else the way he started doing.

"I don't know if he told you about Trixie –"

"He did." My voice cracked and I cleared it.

He just nodded and kept talking, "When I came home I didn't even recognise him. He'd lost so much weight and his eyes were sunken into his face. I was looking at my brother but I had no idea *who* I was looking at. I was furious at my parents for not noticing, but that wasn't fair. They had never noticed much. Good people," Wyatt said, looking at me, "just, absent."

"Ap said it was like living with two old roommates."

Wyatt huffed a laugh, "Yeah, that's pretty accurate." He pulled a hand out to rub at the back of his neck before he kept talking, "All that to say, I kept a pretty close eye on him after that. So, when he started to change, to become this version of himself I hadn't seen since we were kids, I noticed." He looked back to me for a beat and I knew what he was saying; *that's where you came in.*

"There were times I wish I'd done better. Not called him as much even though I knew he'd answer. Not asked him to go and do something just so I knew he was getting out of the house. Put him up for press events just to get him out of his routine. I even pulled him into doing this half marathon with me one time even though he hates running. Even though *I* hate running." I couldn't help but smile at that. Mainly thinking about how Aspen would throw his head back in howling laughter, too. At the pair of them grinning and bearing it, all while cursing one another out on the inside.

"I think I got really close to losing him at one point in my life, and I'm haunted by the face of this seventeen year old boy looking back at me with…with these *lifeless* eyes. Every day. Every single day I see him. I wish I could go back and see the things I missed, say the things I thought of too late. Protect him a little better than what I did. But, I can't. I can only help him now, and I'd do anything for my brother. So, I guess that's why I'm here."

"You're going to ask me to stay?" I kept my eyes on my shoes, because I wasn't sure I'd be able to say no.

"No," Wyatt said, pulling out an envelope that was folded in half from his pocket, "I don't think he'd want me to do that. But I do want to try and help you heal."

Wyatt handed me the envelope and I just looked at it hovering between us.

"Take it," he said. With a final look at his face I reached for the envelope and unfolded it.

My whole, entire world just stopped. Everything, *everything,* it all just stopped.

"I was eighteen when I bought my first car," Wyatt spoke to me softly and I could feel his eyes on my face. "It was the start of my senior year of high school and I saved up enough over the summer to buy something. Not particularly fancy or safe, but I saw it in the lot and pointed right at it, 'That one' I said."

I saw Wyatt hold his finger out in front of him from my peripheral vision, but I was still looking at the envelope in my hands.

"This guy had bought it cheap for his car lot from the other side of the country. There was something about being shown the wrong photos and he got something he didn't want so he wanted to get rid of it fast. It still had a bunch of stuff in it and so he gave it to me for cheaper than what he'd had it listed. I loved that car. It was my ticket to freedom. Aspen's too."

I didn't expect it, but Wyatt turned to face me, cross legged and hands out of his pockets folded in his lap.

I tore my eyes from the letter and looked at him. His face blurring in my vision, then clearing, then blurring again.

"I didn't mind the stuff. There were some clothes in the back, a whole cardboard box of pine and vanilla air fresheners in the boot."

Wyatt stopped on account of the sob that escaped my throat. I hadn't meant it too, I was determined to hear every word out of his mouth but I could see it all. Everything he was describing. He waited a second more before he kept talking.

"The most peculiar thing that I found though," he pointed at my hands, "was that letter."

I looked back down at my hands to see the envelope with Casimir's old mechanics logo in the top left. I could make out his fingerprints imprinted in grease stains on the edges and his handwriting in the very middle of it all, looking right back at me after thirteen whole years of not being able to see it. Not being able to recall it.

"He died on my birthday," I told Wyatt. I hadn't thought about him yet today. I always tried not to, but I wanted to tell someone. Because at that moment, there wasn't just one person who knew my brother in my house, there were two.

"When's your birthday?" he asked.

"Today."

I felt my eyes on the envelope as Wyatt stood up. "I'm sorry I read it before you, Poppy. I didn't ever think I'd meet the person who it was intended for, but I'd also never managed to throw it away. I guess I felt like I understood a lot of what he said. How he felt about you is how I feel about Aspen."

I just nodded, the letter getting heavier and heavier.

"Happy birthday, Poppy."

I heard Wyatt say the words, but I didn't notice when he left. Didn't hear my front door open or close, but right where he was standing now sat one single car key and a ticket for the first show of the *Lady Luck Salvation Tour.*

With shaking hands, I pulled the letter out of the envelope and started to read.

# 39

# April 5th

Penny,

Today is your sixteenth birthday and that blows my mind. How did you grow up so fast?

I thought a lot about today, and how I could make it a day you would remember forever because I know how important turning sixteen is.

You're not a kid anymore. That's wild. My baby sister isn't a baby anymore.

I know that it hasn't always been easy, with it just being the two of us.

I know sometimes you have questions that I can't really answer. I hadn't really thought that far ahead and I'll admit there have been times I've wished we could go back to a time where the hardest thing I was going to have to explain to you was that Santa Claus wasn't real. (...or is he?)

The first thing I want to tell you is; Ask your questions, Pen. Even if they're hard. Even if it hurts. Ask them. If they're for me then I'll always do my best to answer them, but if they're questions you ask of the world, don't be frightened.

You're probably wondering why I'm writing you this letter. I could have just said this stuff to you, but it felt important to write it down. I wanted you to have it just in case you ever needed to read these words back. In case one day when you set off and out into the world and we're miles apart that you might need to read them again. That you might miss your big, goofy brother and hear my voice while you read them.

Poppy, I'm so proud of you.
Sixteen is when you really start to grow up and I'm so proud of how you're growing up. I think a lot of the time people say that how kids grow up is really a reflection of the people who raise them, but they couldn't be more wrong.
This person you're becoming, it's all you. It's you who is teaching me, Pop.

Last week you told me you auditioned for the lead role in your school play. I remember the week before that when you were moping on the couch, down and out about how you didn't think you were good enough to get it. That you were scared.
When I got home today you told me you got the part. I wasn't even half way in the door and you were barreling into me.

I want you to remember that feeling, Poppy.
I hope you always run right towards the things that scare you.
I hope you remember how brave you are, how good and kind and generous you are. Because in the end those are the things that matter most and you have them in spades, Poppy Girl.

You can still be scared of things in life and want to grab onto them with both hands. That's sometimes the thing that makes it harder, wanting something so much and the knowledge that there will be times where it's just out of your reach.
I want you to ask yourself in those moments, whatever it is that scares you, do you want it with both hands? Is it worth that final jump?
If the answer is yes, then you do it. No question about it.

I thought to myself, 'how can I help her with that? To feel brave in running towards the things that scare her? How do I help her run towards them?' and then I thought of my car.

That car you always give me shit for was the first thing I bought for myself.
You were five and after everything…it was finally just me and you. It's the very thing that drove me right towards the things that scared me most.
Job interviews, your first day of school, your first school dance, the first call I got from your principal after you kicked that kid in the nuts for cutting your ponytail with scissors in class (still super proud of you for that).

So, now it's yours. (This is a good 16th birthday present, right?)

The world is scary, Penelope. There is no way to sugar coat that.
You will make mistakes. You will find yourself in situations that scare you. You'll find yourself in situations where you'll have to forgive people and sometimes, might even need to forgive yourself. I've found that last one to be the hardest of them all.
I know that all sounds scary, but I also know you can do it. You just do what you do best, you run hell for leather at everything life throws at you and grab it with both hands.
That's what your big brother would do, anyway!

I don't remember the day I was born, but I remember the day you were. It will forever be one of the best days of my life.

You're my whole world, kid. It hasn't always been easy but it's always been worth it.
I wouldn't change a thing about our story, Pop. It's my favorite one that's ever existed.

Happy Birthday.

Love Always. Your brother,
Cas

# 40

## April 5th

**Poppy**

I read the letter over and over.

I read it until I knew every word by heart. Until the curve of Casimir's gentle, clear scroll was embedded into my mind again. Tattooed anew with fresh ink.

By the time I snapped out of the trance I'd been in, the sun had set, and my feet couldn't move fast enough.

I had driven like a bat out of hell. The ticket Wyatt had left me clutched tightly in my hand, the rumble of the Taurus beneath me, eating up the miles that spanned between me and the arena. I was almost positive that I'd run a number of red lights, so much so, I probably gave Ina Minit a run for her money.

*Lady Luck* was meant to walk on stage at 9 PM, and I pulled the Taurus into what I was sure was an illegal park outside the main doors of the venue at 9:01.

My whole body was thrumming with a deranged sort of

panic. It was feral in the way it buzzed beneath my skin, clawed at my stomach and took over complete control of my body. It made my feet slap the pavement under my boots harder, *faster.*

I still wasn't moving fast enough.

The thunderous applause of a completely sold-out arena of a hundred and fifty thousand people cracked like a whip through the air around me. *Lady Luck*'s logo was all around the exterior of the stadium. The tour name just beneath looked like it had been written in red paint that was dripping down the building. All five members of the band were plastered there, watching me with unmoving gazes as I crashed into the glass doors that led inside.

I guess I thought I would have been able to just run straight in.

That was a very stupid thought to have had.

I was stopped no fewer than five different times going through different security points and body scanners. Wyatt had given me a VIP ticket, which gave me access to the mosh right at the front of the stage where there were no assigned seats, as well as access to the band after the show.

An older woman scanned my ticket no faster than a sloth might, completely oblivious to the fact that my heart was beating so fast that I was starting to see spots dance along the sides of my vision. She handed me back my ticket and a lanyard with a pass attached to it that I assumed gave me clearance of some kind and then I was off again with absolutely no idea where I was going.

The venue the band was playing at was one of the largest in the entire world. It was astonishingly impressive if I let myself think about the structure around me, but I didn't. I kept trying to look at my ticket, to find the right door to enter, but I couldn't focus on it long enough to actually understand what I was looking at. Not with the roaring of the crowd on the other side of the doors that I kept running past.

Running and running and *running*.

"Blazewood!" Wyatt's voice pierced through the booming screams and I couldn't help the sob that clawed its way up and out of my throat. I was *so close*.

"My name is Wyatt Smith!"

The screaming got even louder that I was tempted to cover my ears with my hands. "And it's my fucking pleasure to welcome you all to the first night of the *Salvation Tour.*"

Never say never, because the sound of the screaming sky rocketed and I had no choice but to cover my ears then. I wanted to stop, to ask someone for help because this entire building had been built way too big, but my legs wouldn't stop moving. It was like they literally just *couldn't stop.* There was only one destination they needed to get to, and until I was right before him they refused to let up.

The doors I ran by started to blur, my heart rate was picking up and I was breathing so hard I wondered if I was really getting any air in at all.

Aspen was *right there.*

"I'm a little lonely up here all on my own, I have to tell you," Wyatt said, his voice carrying so clearly it was like he was right next to me. I was certain they heard him across the entire city. "How about we get the boys out here?"

Another panicked sob started to make its way up my throat right when I smacked into someone. I half thought it was a wall and I wouldn't have been all that surprised considering that I'd run the perimeter of the stadium at least a couple times by this point and I was both exhausted and honestly a little dizzy. The shock of the collision landed me right on my ass, snapping me momentarily out of my frenzied panic.

"I'm so sorry," I stammered. Wiping at my eyes and scrambling back to my feet. "Are you alr–"

"Poppy?" Savannah was still sprawled on the ground in front of me looking for all the world like she'd just been slapped. I suppose it probably wasn't far off, considering I'd run into her traveling at what I assumed was a million fucking miles an hour.

"Savannah?" I was stunned for a second, just long enough for my head to clear and remember that Savannah was a bigwig at this exact venue and likely knew the layout like the back of her hand.

"Are you okay?" She got to her feet quickly, already reaching for me like we hadn't just met once. Like we were the sort of friends that spanned far beyond a single encounter. "Hey, what—are you here with the guys?"

I just shook my head, but changed half way through to nodding and then stopped completely. I didn't actually have an answer to her question.

"Come on," she said, taking my hand and starting to lead me back the way she'd just come. "We can wait in the green room until they're done."

*No.* My feet refused to move another step in her direction. I couldn't wait until after. *This* couldn't wait.

"No, I need to get in now." It was my first full sentence to her and it wasn't particularly kind or gracious. Usually I'd follow that right up with an apology but there was no room to be sorry for anything right now, all I needed was to get in there to *see–*

"I want to hear how loud you can *scream* for me, Blaze-wood!" Wyatt's voice cut me off again, my heart beating a frantic rhythm, the organ making its finest effort in trying to escape from my chest.

"Let me hear you scream for the one, the only, Rip Reynolds!" Wyatt yelled and you could tell the moment Rip walked onto the stage because the actual ground beneath our feet *shook*.

"Savannah, I need to get in there now." I repeated, handing her my ticket. She didn't miss the way my hand shook as I held it out to her. Her eyes flicked to the ticket in my hand then back to my face before a little smirk curved her bright red painted lips. She grabbed my ticket from me and stepped forward, reaching around to slide it into the back pocket of my jeans.

Grabbing me by my shoulders she looked at me, her eyes scanning me from head to toe. Savannah swiped her thumbs under my eyes and reached up to run her fingers through my hair, no doubt fixing any pieces that had gone haywire in my frantic attempts to get into the concert.

"Let's see if we can do better than that, shall we? I know just how loud you can be, Blazewood." Wyatt's voice pulsed around us again. The noise from the audience started to change, instead of clapping it turned into the rumbling stomps of a hundred and fifty thousand pairs of legs. There was only one member of *Lady Luck* that got that sort of reaction from the crowd and Savannah's eyes sparkled knowingly.

"Make some fucking noise for the bass guitarist of *Lady Luck*," Wyatt screamed. "*Angus Dravin!*"

I couldn't even hear myself think, but Savannah's grip on

my shoulders kept me right there with her. She turned me to my left to face a huge set of black double doors with a sign above it that read *'Floor Entrance K-1'*. Walking right over to grab the handle of the door, she looked at me before pulling it open.

"Go get your man, girl." With a wink in my direction Savannah opened the door, letting the euphoric sounds of the fans of *Lady Luck* pour out and over us.

I didn't even give her a second look as I walked straight into the arena, my legs taking me straight towards the stage.

# 41

## April 5th

**Poppy**

There were so many people.

*So many people.*

Packed together and screaming and sweaty and desperate to be noticed by the band on the stage.

I kept moving, just one foot in front of the other, step after step. It was like being stuck in quicksand; the more I tried to squeeze my way through, the less I seemed to move.

I was half way through to the front of the stage when Wyatt spoke up again.

Now that he was joined by both Rip and Angus on stage, all three of them had begun to play their instruments, filling the air around us with the addictive lilt of their guitars. There were people around me screaming like they were dying. Crying like nothing in their lives would ever beat this moment.

The song they were playing wasn't one I'd ever heard before

but the mere notion of them creating music right in front of their eyes was sending everyone into a frenzy.

It wasn't Wyatt's voice that crackled through the air next, but rather Luke's.

"Blazewood," he sang the name of the city tauntingly and the lights swapped from white to red. Rip changed what he was playing to the haunting introduction to a song I knew was from their last album called 'The World is Ugly'.

Wyatt stopped playing his guitar as the song shifted and started to clap above his head. The loss of whatever he was playing didn't last long before it was picked up by Luke. I watched him walk on stage just as the guy next to me started to scream, "*Oh my fucking God!*"

"I believe you all know Lucas Blake, rhythm guitarist for *Lady Luck!*" Wyatt said into the microphone and Luke walked over and planted a kiss right on his cheek. The screaming increased and I started to move again. I was still too far from the stage.

I was *too fucking far.*

No one was moving, if anything people were pushing me back and the frustration of it all made my nose start to string. I wanted to scream, because no one was fucking *moving.* A sob shook out of me, exhaustion starting to settle in from the press of bodies around me.

It was right then that I looked back up at the stage and locked eyes with the front man of *Lady Luck.*

Wyatt was staring right at me, his hands frozen above his head and nothing but shocked elation on his face, slashing into existence in the form of the most genuine smile I'd ever seen.

I kept on fighting against the people around me to get to

the front of the stage. Pushing and pulling against the bodies of fans that were desperately trying to claw their way closer to the stage too.

The kick of a bass drum permeated the space around me and my whole body just froze.

*Thump, thump, thump, thump, thump, thump, thump, thump.*

Wyatt grabbed the mic off the stand and walked along the stage, right over to the far left and held the microphone up to the people on that side of the stadium. "Do you know who's next?" He asked the crowd. The response was thunderous.

"Well…if you *do* know who's next, I want you to yell his name on the count of three. One…two…*three.*"

"*Aspen-Fucking-Smith!*" The fifty thousand people on the left side of the arena screamed his name so loud I could feel every syllable vibrate through my body.

"Hmm," Wyatt said, pushing his jet black hair back off his face and walking all the way to the right side of the stage. "I didn't catch that. Did you guys catch that at all?"

"Who?" Rip said into his mic.

"Nope!" Angus said.

"Not even a little" Luke said before jumping up onto an amp at the front of the stage.

"Let me try over here," Wyatt said to the right side of the arena. "Do *you* know who's missing?"

He held his mic out to them and I was still frozen where I stood, looking from Wyatt to the other guys in the band, across the whole stage to find the source of that drum beat.

"*Aspen-Fucking-Smith!*" They screamed and screamed and *screamed.*

Wyatt walked to the front of the stage and looked right at me as he announced the last member of the band. "There's no *Lady Luck* without him."

The drums started to pick up even more and I was positive someone to my left had just passed out but I refused to take my eyes off the stage.

"He's actually been here the whole time." Wyatt grinned at the crowd before his eyes fell back to me, like he didn't want to lose where I was standing. "Blazewood…let me hear you lose your goddamn minds for Aspen *fucking* Smith!"

The lights on the back of the stage ignited, casting the previously shadowed space into blinding light. Aspen sat behind the most impressive drum kit I'd ever seen, raised on a podium set above the stage. He had a black singlet on with his hat on backwards and the drum beat he'd been playing kept constant even as he stood up, twirling a drumstick in one hand and pointing the other out at the crowd.

I couldn't take my eyes off him and the fact he was *right there* made me start to move again with a desperation that I didn't have before. I had to get to him. He had to *know.*

Even if he'd changed his mind, even if I'd already lost him for good, he had to know.

My eyes hadn't been on the stage, instead they had been focused in front of me. Focused on the people around me, on how I could get through them, so I didn't see Wyatt move from his spot at the front of the stage, and walk towards his brother. Didn't see how he took the mic and stopped right in front of Aspen until I heard the words projected across the stadium.

"Ap," Wyatt's voice echoed. "Poppy's here."

The drum beat just stopped. It just cut out completely.

"What?" Aspen's voice was picked up by the mic his brother held and I finally pulled my eyes up from the people in front of me towards the stage.

"Aspen," his name tumbled from my mouth, getting lost in the chants of everyone around me even though their confusion was clear and the noise of the stadium had started to drop.

"Where?" Aspen hopped off the platform his drums were on and walked around to his brother. I watched on as Wyatt turned to the crowd and pointed right at me. I locked eyes with Aspen at the same time that roughly a hundred and fifty thousand people turned their attention on me.

"Aspen!" I called out his name again, louder this time, determined to get to him. He was stunned in place for maybe five seconds and then he started to move. Aspen walked to the edge of the stage, stopping at the very front to find me in the crowd again before he jumped down.

The stadium let out a collective gasp as Aspen walked to the guard rail at the front of the mosh and stood on it. Security swarmed him, the hands of huge, burly men reached up to hold onto him as the frantic hands of fans reached for him.

*"That's Poppy."* I heard someone say from beside me, but I refused to pull my eyes from his.

*"Hey, look! There she is."*

*"Help her through."* Someone else said.

*"Move aside, let her through!"* And slowly, people started to move. They finally started to *move.*

I kept my eyes on Aspen, clung to my name that I could see on his lips even though I couldn't hear him and I fought my way towards him until he was right there. Until he was so close all I needed to do was reach out my hand.

The feeling of his palm sliding into mine tore a sob from my throat so brutal I felt my legs finally give out. Finally, they stopped after fighting to get me where I needed to be.

Aspen hauled me up and into him, my arms wrapped around him, my face buried into his neck. The roar of the stadium seemed so inconsequential to the feeling of the strong band of his arms wrap around me, holding onto me so tight it hurt to breathe.

I didn't care, not as I kept repeating in my head that this was him, it was *him.*

I hardly registered it as he hauled me up and over the barricade. He just kept holding onto me fiercely as he walked us back towards the stage, clinging to me like if he didn't I might just disappear all over again.

The stadium erupted like a fucking volcano and I couldn't even hear the words in my own head.

"Guys!" Wyatt called out, trying to get the crowd under control and little by little they started to quiet.

"Poppy," Aspen's lips were at my ear, his hand on the back of my head. "You're here. I can't believe you're *here.*"

He set me down and the stadium continued to settle, every single pair of eyes on us, including the rest of the band on stage.

"I feel like I've interrupted something important here," I said against his neck and felt the rumble of his laughter against every part of my body that was pressed against his.

"It's okay," he laughed, pulling back to look at me. Aspen set me down and I realized that it wasn't just that I'd blocked out the screams of the stadium, but that every single person in the arena had gone quiet. I looked away from Aspen for the first time to see the view he usually had, to see hundreds of thousands of people with their phone lights up in the air.

I looked back at Aspen who hadn't taken his eyes or hands

off me for even a second. There were far more than twenty pairs of eyes on me now, but I couldn't find it in myself to care even the tiniest bit. Not a single person mattered more than the man in front of me.

"I probably should have waited, but I couldn't. This couldn't wait." I reached for his shirt and gripped it tightly. There was so much I wanted to tell him, so much I wanted to explain, but in the end, there was only one thing that really seemed to matter.

"You once told me that when you pictured going home, you didn't think of your apartment. Do you remember what you said?" I thought I heard my own voice echo around me.

"Yes," he said, nodding his head like it was still a fundamental, crucial truth. There was no mistaking it that time; Aspen's voice reverberated around us.

"Tell me again?" I asked, knowing full well the entire world was listening to every word we were saying. I didn't care, I wanted them to know. I wanted every single person alive to *know.*

"I said, I pictured you." His eyes were glassy as he looked at me, his grip on me tightening even more. I reached up to wipe away a silent tear that had fallen down his beautiful face.

I nodded my head, letting myself say the words I'd wanted to tell him for the moment I saw him standing in my living room. "I picture you too."

I knew in the very soul of me that nothing could have ever felt as right or true or perfect as those words. Aspen crushed his mouth to mine before the last word left my mouth. The moment he did I wrapped my arms around his neck, pulling him into me, keeping him close, all while the entire stadium went fucking *wild.* There wasn't a corner of the world that wouldn't have heard the screaming chants of the people around us.

I felt the sound through the soles of my shoes. In the tips of my fingers.

I laughed against his lips that had curved into one of his most beautiful smiles as he kissed me, vowing never to take for granted the way his skin felt beneath the palms of my hands again. The warmth of it, the roughness. Like a song I could go years without hearing but I'd never forget a single word.

"I love you," he said, and I couldn't hear it, but I *felt* it. I felt every word he said against my lips, felt the truth of them.

An undeniable and unwavering fact. Not something fragile and made of glass but of stone and steel. They would never break. They would *always* last. Again and again he said it against my eyelids, my cheeks, the base of my throat.

I pulled back to look at him, reaching up to hold his face between my hands. "To your *bones*, Aspen," I raised my voice so I could be sure he heard it over the crowd. Even as it shook, I shared the words I had thought I would have to carry on my own forever. Not because I was scared, but from the unbelievable *joy* of letting myself say them to him.

My tears made him blurry but not blurry enough for me to miss the look on his face. A look that I didn't think I'd ever forget as long as I lived. I only needed a glance at the small furrow of his brow, the widening of his eyes, the way his lips parted slightly to know that no one in my whole life had ever looked at me like he was looking at me right then, like he couldn't live without me either.

I wiped his cheeks with the sleeves of my sweater and pressed my forehead to his, "I love you to your very bones."

"He got the *fucking girl, Blazewood!*" Wyatt screamed into the microphone just as Rip howled at the audience in the way he always did and Aspen started to laugh again, his face pressed to the curve of my neck. I tried to pull away but he refused to let me go. Instead, he jumped back on the stage and reached down to haul me up after him. I thought he would just lead me off to the side but instead he reached for his brother's microphone and I watched him yell right out to the sold-out stadium, to the whole world, *"I got the fucking girl!"*

Aspen reached for me, pulling me in for another kiss that was not at all appropriate to be doing on stage before finally leading me off to the side and away from the applause of his fans. He handed me a set of noise canceling headphones and with a final kiss he turned to head back on stage. He took two steps before stopped abruptly and walked back to me so we were toe to toe.

"Stay, Poppy." His eyes were pleading and I knew he was asking from more than just right now.

I nodded, meaning it with every single piece of me. With every piece that was broken and the bits that were not starting to heal. Knowing that even if I'd gotten into that moving truck, I would have only ever ended up here, with him. Since the moment I saw him, there was never going to be anywhere else for me to go.

"Always."

# 42

# Epilogue

**1 Year 6 Months Later**

**Poppy**

Aspen was on the couch when I'd gotten home, forearms settled onto his knees and head in his hands. The visual lasted only a second before he bolted up straight to his feet and yelled right across the penthouse a very high pitched, "I've done something!"

He'd cleared his throat and tried again but I was already in a fit of laughter.

"Poppy, I've done something," he said for the third time once I arrived in front of him, dropped my bag to the floor and melted right into him.

Aspen's hands came up and around me, warming me immediately despite the balmy day outside. It was like now that I was home, after the sun had mostly finished it's shining for the day, *my* day was only just beginning. My sun was only now coming into view.

He reached up to tuck a strand of hair behind my ear and I caught his hand before he could wrap his arm back around me, placing a kiss to the little fish tattoo on the inside of his wrist. The twin to my own.

The day I had run towards him, when I battled my way through a crowd of thousands to reach him, the day I'd decided to finally stay still, we'd gone back to my empty house after that first show of the *Salvation Tour* to collect Natalie only to find her floating on the surface of the water.

Her little fins still, her little heart silent.

Aspen had sat with me as I held her tank in my lap until the sun had risen. Our backs pressed against an empty wall of my empty house. My head on his shoulder and one of my hands clutched tightly in both of his. It had taken some time for the shock to wear off, but by the time we had gotten back to his apartment all that was left was this feeling of complete and total peace.

Like she finally moved on because I had too.

It was later that day Aspen had come home to the penthouse and shown me his wrist. "It's not a spider web or fuzzy dice, but I still think it's pretty badass," he said, taking my hand and kissing the middle of my palm.

When I told him I wanted one too, we went back to the tattoo parlor that very hour and Nat had been with us both ever since.

"That sounds precarious," I mumbled against his warm, worn cotton shirt, shifting to peer up at him. That's when I noticed that he was biting the inside of his cheek and that his brows were pinched.

Aspen was nervous.

I knew he'd essentially been a 'yes man' with his friends for the last fourteen years but it baffled me how none of them had picked up any of his tells. Well, except for Allie, she'd been onto him right from the get go. Of course Dax had known but that had been different. Allie had seen him when the others hadn't. Always doing her best to support him when she could, to soften any exchange that she thought might have sent Ap spiraling. Aspen and I had been dating for a while when I'd realized the extent of her silent guarding of the man I loved and when I took her to the side and wrapped my arms around her with a whispered 'Thank you', all she did was hug me back. We'd pulled back to find one another with watery eyes which of course made us both laugh, then made us both cry.

"You're nervous," I said to him, resting my chin right on his chest.

He didn't say anything, just took me by the hand and led me into the small recording room that resided in our penthouse. It turned out that Aspen hadn't just been partial to the drums, he was a wonderful piano player, something Allie had taught him.

He pulled me down to sit on the piano bench right next to him, and with a final look at me, he started to play. I could *feel* my mouth hanging open wide, my eyes completely unable to look away from his hands. The way they moved; strong and sure.

Every single note he played pushed its way into me and stayed there. I was completely unable to let it go. The way he played was gentle, every note that came into existence rose and fell to meet one another in crescendos and decrescendos and it became clear to me why he'd written this song. He played and played until it came to a beautiful end, his fingers staying on the notes until the sound rang out.

The silence that pressed in on us was one of our usual kind. The kind we loved to sit in together when I could hear his quiet breathing and he could hear mine, when the world beyond the space around us didn't matter half as much as the one we'd built together.

"The first time you laughed it made me think of a small melody. Your actual laugh, it sounded like four notes strung together." He played those notes now, the same ones that started the song. "I used all the best notes," he went on, eyes still on the keys in front of him, "that's how you sound to me."

Those exact four notes played into the space around me as I watched Aspen turn around from his spot at the end of the aisle. His suit was all black, of course, and his hair was pushed off his forehead, looking for all the world like he woke up just like that. Like he'd maybe never even gone to bed but rather stood right there though the hours of the evening, waiting for me.

The song Ap had composed built in the air around us, this beautiful, soul grabbing melody.

I stood at the start of the aisle alone. I hadn't wanted to be walked down by anyone, even though every single one of Aspen's friends had offered, including his older brother who stood next to him with shining eyes, not as he looked at me, but as he looked at the man I was about to marry.

I hadn't wanted anyone to walk me down because even though I couldn't see him, I felt Casimir in the space beside me. I felt the ghost of his arm looping through mine. How he would look down at me, tears in his eyes the same way Wyatt had and he'd bump my chin with his rough and worn knuckles. His grease and tobacco smell lingering even though he'd have cleaned up nicely in his suit.

He'd say, 'we can still leave, I can hold them off so you can get a head start'. He'd be joking and serious all at once and I'd laugh and cry at the same time while I stared back at him. He'd keep me steady as I placed one foot in front of the other until he shook Aspen's hand before placing mine in it.

I opened my eyes, coming back into the present knowing that maybe in another version of this life my brother would have been beside me, but knowing for certain that no matter what, in every version of life that ever existed, I would marry Aspen Killian Smith.

In every single one.

So, I did what I'd been doing every day since I was eighteen; I picked up the front of my dress and ran.

Right down the aisle, straight towards the only thing I'd ever wanted.

I ran to Aspen.

I ran home.

# Acknowledgments

Writing this story was not something I'd ever planned on doing. When I wrote *Music to my Ears,* I'd been content with the story starting and ending with Dax and Allie. The other characters, of course, all had stories of their own, but I'd never intended on writing them down.

Then there was you, **the reader**.

It still baffles me that there were so many people who read *Music to my Ears* and messaged me asking when Aspen's story would be coming out.

At first, I thought, 'what? Aspen's story?!' And then I thought... '*Yes!* Aspen's story!'

I'd always known about Aspen and Poppy, and I've loved them both and their journeys for a really long time - my only hope is that it was all you'd all hoped for too.

So, thank you to those who loved *MTME*. Thank you for reading the stories that live in my head, thank you for loving these characters that sit with me every day - know they love you as much as I do because without you, their stories would never be shared.

**Joeli**, my very favorite person, a real-life superhero. This book wouldn't exist without you either because without you, there would have never been a *Music to my Ears*.

I think you were actually the first person to say, 'What about Aspen?'

Thank you. *weird hand grab wave thing we did at the Jonas Brothers concert*

**My husband**, who will always enthusiastically listen to random excerpts of the books that I write without any context and every time (daily) tell me how amazing it was. Marrying you was the best decision I ever made.

**My parents.**

There's no one I am more excited to share my books with than you both. Thank you for never wavering in matching your excitement and enthusiasm to mine in moments like this when my dreams come true.

And last, but certainly not least, **my brothers.**

My inspiration for the bonds between Aspen and Dax and Poppy and Casimir.

Anyone who's ever met me will have inevitably heard about my two older brothers. Sharing your existence with people is one of my favorite things to do.

"Yes," I say, "I have two older brothers. I'm the youngest of three!"

I'm so insanely proud to be your sister.

You've both provided me not only with the best sort of humans to look up to, but simply by being the exact people you are you've made *me* braver.

You make me wiser, more confident, you allow me to exist
and know that I will never be alone, no matter what.
Thank you.

# About the Author

Celine L. A. Simpson is an Australian romance and fantasy author, a dog mum, Punk Rock enthusiast, and owns at least 6 dungarees that she consistently pairs with Converse.

Most commonly known for her Romance publication Just My Luck (2023) and Music to my Ears (2021), she was raised on the Mid-North Coast of Australia and graduated from La Trobe University with a Bachelors Degree in Creative Arts, majoring in Creative and Professional Writing. Growing up with a passion for reading, she began writing at an early age, moving into content creation as a career path before writing and publishing her own novels.

# Also by Celine L.A. Simpson

**Just My Luck**

An 'enemies-to-lovers' romance by Celine L.A. Simpson. Dark, dirty, witty and steaming hot. Perfect for fans of *Ana Huang, Emily Henry, Tessa Bailey and Emily McIntire.*

*"The tension, the story, THE TENSION!"*
- Emma (Goodreads review)

*"Fantastic plot, brilliant story, characters you will fall in love with"* - BooksWithBanter (Goodreads Review)

**Lucky.**

Cole Thompson used to wish for my downfall.

He took every opportunity to break me, to best me. But this man? This was not the Cole I remember from my youth. Not the kind kid that played with me in my backyard, and certainly not the infuriating boy who had eventually realised that he had only been born with one to challenge me in every aspect of my life.

This man was self-made, dripping with the proof of how he climbed that ladder of success. And he was beautiful. *Too* beautiful.

It was really too bad he was still hell bent on breaking me. He thinks he can, now that I'm the lucky girl without her luck, now that I'm at the bottom while he looks on from above.

What he doesn't know is that, luck or no, I'll break him first.

**Cole.**

It was clear and clean before, what I'd wanted from Lucky Peters. I'd wanted her to suffer. I wanted her to see me standing at the top of the world she had insisted on taking from me time and time again, and I wanted her to *beg* me for mercy. I wanted to hold every single part of her in my hands. Her happiness, her freedoms, her career, her life. I wanted her to look at me and *know* what it was like to be powerless.

That was all I had wanted.

But that was then.

This is now.

## Convincing Florence
**Florence wasn't a people person.**

Flossy learnt right from the get-go that to expect anything from anyone (apart from her grandmother) would only ever lead to disappointment. That all the minutes and seconds of her life constantly intersected with the hard and tough minutes of everyone else's, right from the moment she entered this world and let loose a wail of arrival.

It was the friends who couldn't be bothered to return the friendship, the dates that were only ever interested in one thing, and the general strangers who were never interested in returning her smile.

Florence loved two things. Her job at the library and her grandmother, Dot.

Apart from them?

**People sucked.**


**Nathaniel Connors loved a challenge.**

Tall, dark, and handsome; Nathaniel Connors sailed through life on a dimpled smile and buckets of charm. But when Florence finds him in the library, breaking more than one rule, she might have been the first person who didn't give him the time of day.

If there's one thing that Nathaniel needed to do now, it was to convince Florence that he was worth her time, and that there were people who were worth her while.


She was sure he'd fail.

He knew he wouldn't.

Challenge Accepted.

**Music To My Ears**
**He had one of those side, half smiles that you read about...I always thought that was absolute nonsense - no single smile could make you want to cry out for mercy, but there you have it.**

I did manage to, however, maintain enough of my dignity to cry on the inside.

Allie could sum up her entire life in two whole minutes. She lived walking distance to everything; work, her best friend's place and perhaps most importantly, the 24-hour corner store that was only a 1-minute walk away. Allie frequently sought comfort from the bottom of premixed brownie boxes at all times of the evening when she perused the baking aisle alone, until one night...

Wyatt Smith was the front man of the most popular modern rock band to date. Lady Luck travelled the world, their look and their music was recognised by everyone, everywhere. That was until he found himself the midnight errand boy for a runaway baking ingredient where he met Allie. And she had absolutely no idea who he was...

It's true that when someone catches your eye you start to see them everywhere.

But what happens when you do see them again?

Sometimes it's easier to put feelings in boxes, and sometimes it's easier to run away when the going gets tough. But sometimes you find someone to help you unpack, someone who will stand beside you, feel the fear, and take that leap of faith with you.

## Terraleise (The Lost Child of the Crown #1)

Terraleise turns 18, only to discover she is now gifted with the elemental power of Earth. The thing about elemental gifts is that only those with royal blood possess them.

Terraleise is thrown into a life she never dreamed to be a part of, discovering all of the secrets entwined with her past, and her future. The heir to a kingdom overthrown by a corrupt branch of her own bloodline, Terra will see what it means to have courage and be brave, learning that the fate of the four kingdoms of Vaashaa rests on her shoulders.

Finding a life to fight for only to be faced with sacrificing it all, Terraleise will have to risk her love and her life to keep the world from falling into darkness. Will the Lost Child of the Crown find her rightful place?

**Heir of Vaashaa (The Lost Child of the Crown #2)**

The land is dying and the promise of war is thick in the air. With Terraleise still held captive by the enemy, Silas is forced out of his grief to move forward, to march on and ensure Terra's sacrifice, her life for his, doesn't go to waste.

The threat to the World of Vaashaa is more horrific than anyone could have ever anticipated. A long-forgotten darkness has crept back into the hands of the wrong person and time is running out to stop it. The Kingdoms of Vaashaa will have to come together to save their world from the bleak future it is heading towards, all while hoping for aid to come from the truths laced within myths and legends.

There is only one who stands to be a force between the darkness and the light, only one who can save them all. Will the Heir of Vaashaa rise from the ashes?